wandering city blues
volume one of the *fogworld* series

a science fiction novel
by jonny lupsha

A CARRIER OF FIRE

http://www.acarrieroffire.com
http://www.facebook.com/acarrieroffire
http://www.twitter.com/acarrieroffire

a carrier of fire. sterling, va. first edition. 2016.

isbn-10: 0692779329
isbn-13: 978-0692779323

thank you

kevin bednarz
matt carroll
mansa herndon
rob kaylin
matthew thomas
ben taylor
maggie wester
brian whitmire
nick whitmire

and as always, my conspicuously patient family.

praise for jonny lupsha's books

disasterland: centralia

"great read on the real life version of silent hill."
konami europe

the broken paragon

"awesome! this essay makes an interesting read."
laura perusco, telltale games, on the essay
"innovations in choice-based gaming."

"good stuff! great piece."
mel kirk, zen studios, on the essay "pinball
dichotomy: reality vs. fantasy."

penny cavalier

"[lupsha's] journey delving into this community is
fascinating, insightful and bittersweet. bottom line: read
penny cavalier."
defective geeks.

wandering city blues

timeshare

a murder on the theriopolis

additional content

100 words about walter atherton

His elbows resting atop the balustrade, Walter Atherton took one final bite of the apple and casually tossed it over the edge. When he was a boy he'd watch the apples fall, bouncing repeatedly against the steep, nearly vertical walls, but by now he'd lost interest. He could imagine it falling as he walked away though, down the hide of the great beast atop which they'd built their city. Eventually it would slip into the red-orange haze that covered the surfaces of the Earth and come to rest on her barren soil. *We should be somewhere near Chicago,* he thought.

Timeshare

moscow in the summer

Sean awoke in lurches from a deep sleep, a sleep brought on by his share of alcohol – and then some. He was in his cot. The daylight loomed bright outside, but the bright orange tent that he'd called home these last few weeks on Proteus was so thick that it was much darker inside. A sliver of blinding light tore a paper cut gash down the tent flap. The potted plant hanging from one of the tent poles swayed gently with each of Proteus's footsteps below him. At its stillest, the plant rested at a slight angle to the left from where Sean lay. His head dumbly ached as though the head of a spoon were rubbing somewhere against the middle of his brain. His mouth was dry and his tongue a bit swollen; his skin felt sensitive and thin. Gentle pangs of nausea probed at his abdomen and he was warm to the point of discomfort and slight dizziness.

He had to regroup, to take stock of what he knew in the moment. Sean knew this feeling well enough to know he should've stopped drinking before he did last night. He also knew that if he got up and left his tent, the man who lived next to this rented space would let Sean help himself to as much water as he could carry from the man's home supply.

What was his name again? John something? Something Johnson? For the life of him he couldn't remember the man's name, although they'd become acquainted since Sean's arrival, since Sean had a silver tongue – he was skilled at making friendly conversation with people and making them like him. Finally, he knew he needed more time before dressing himself and making his way to his temporary neighbor's house to quench his thirst.

Last night he'd gone out for drinks with some locals, including the mayor, to celebrate picking up the tourists today. Proteus would shamble into Moscow late in the morning, close to midday, to make his customary visit to the Moscow International Business Center. Once there, he'd stop for exactly one hour and admire the skyscrapers, which were some of the only man-made structures tall enough to still be visible over the fog.

Shit, the homecoming, Sean thought. He scrambled out of his cot and leaned his head out of the unzipped tent flap, looking to his right to check the time. The sunlight in the east blinded him for a moment and he remembered his hangover just as the throbbing came to his temples. After a moment, his irises adjusted and he saw that the sun was low enough in the sky that he wasn't late, but high enough that he should get moving.

His anxiety vanished. The relief he felt rippled throughout his body, affecting his hangover in various ways. The tremendous cessation of pressure in his body gave his skin a nice chill but caused his shoulders to ache, joining his head in their throbbing. Sean crawled back inside and collapsed onto his cot for one more moment. He laughed a bit despite himself.

After dressing, Sean checked his face in the shard of mirror hanging from the wall of his tent. He was a little worse for wear but his dirty blonde hair and thin face were still admirable. He had a few days' worth of stubble on his cheeks and under his nose and chin, but his high cheekbones, slender nose and pale blue eyes offset the more ragged elements of his appearance. He'd turned 30 the day he arrived on Proteus.

Sean talked his neighbor – whose name was Jeffrey Johns, as it turned out – into feeding him before he went to the reception. Sean figured it was enough of a price to pay to act sober and decent to his unwaveringly pleasant neighbor. Perhaps he had an easy time of it because Sean and Jeffrey were cut from the same cloth in regards to their amiability. Jeffrey wasn't much to look at – a plump, middle-aged man with a wide nose and round chin and skin that shined from a hint of oiliness – but even when he interrupted someone or if he spoke while eating, Sean found himself looking forward to hearing what the man had to say. Sean, meanwhile, had always fascinated people with his anecdotes and jovial nature. He was the type of person you just wanted to be around.

Sean's headache had returned with a vengeance from the seemingly Herculean efforts of dressing himself and walking to Johns's house, but now with some vegetables and clean water in his belly, he was starting to crawl out from under the rock of dehydration. He was better able to take in his surroundings now than when he had first entered. Johns's house was the same quaint size and offered the practicality of all the houses he'd seen on the titans. There was a small kitchen and eating area on the right when you entered, and past those there was a bedroom on the left and a living room on the right. The kitchen was open to the living room and, all in all, the house was less than 1,000 square feet. The walls were white and the carpet in the living room had seen better days.

While they ate, Sean spoke matter-of-factly about his uneventful journey to Proteus – leaving his assistant the responsibility of dropping the tourists off at OKO South Tower several weeks ago while Sean himself migrated from one walking city to the other to receive them on Proteus today. The mention of Proteus sparked a thought in Jeffrey's mind.

"Are your ankles killing you yet?"

"How's that?"

"The slope!" The gears in Sean's brain were still getting up to speed; it took him a moment to realize what Jeffrey was talking about despite Jeffrey using his knife to gesture a diagonal line several times. Sean watched the knife flick back and forth with bits of food stuck to it, then it clicked – he was asking Sean if he'd acclimated to the peculiar angle at which the city sat on Proteus's back. Proteus wasn't quite as tall as Triton, on whom Sean's hometown was built, but his front two legs were much longer than the back two. He walked on all fours, so his back sloped downward from his head to his hindquarters. When The Founders built the city on Proteus nearly 85 years prior, they constructed low stilts on which the houses would sit in order to compensate for the slant. To anyone unaccustomed to life on Proteus, walking up and down steep hills all day was murder on the ankles. This disorientation was furthered by some of the dwellings that were built since mankind moved onto these beasts. Either laziness or some sense of pride had overcome the residents and they put together much of the newer living space flat across Proteus's back without correctional foundations. Some of the newer buildings were constructed respective to Proteus's sloping back instead of to gravity like the older ones. This led to a hodgepodge of a city in which some new buildings – Sean's tent included – sat with one side higher than the other, their roofs pointing perpendicular to Proteus's hide. Whenever someone poured a drink in a new building like this, the liquid tilted towards one edge of the glass more than the other. Plants hung at angles that weren't quite 90 degrees to the floor. Towards Proteus's head, the problem got so severe that homeowners had gone to such measures as sawing off half the length of two table legs and installing belt buckles in their beds so as not to fall out.

"Oh! Yes, that was an adjustment. Truth be told, no offense to your fair city but I'll be much more comfortable getting back home to life on a flat plane. I don't know that I ever got my 'sea legs' out here."

Sean finished his food and set his fork down on his plate. Johns swallowed a bite of his own breakfast and pointed his fork at Sean, wagging it up and down. "You know that reminds me of a story Granddad used to tell."

"Oh yeah?"

"Yeah. About The Founders."

Sean tried to hide his excitement. He never missed an opportunity to hear about life in the old days, nor about the events surrounding mankind leaving the surface.

"If you need to leave, though, I don't mean to keep you."

Sean snuck a quick peek outside. It still looked like mid-morning; he had probably an hour before he had to be at the docks. "I've got time."

Jeffrey continued to eat as he spoke. "I'm sure you've heard about how crazy things were when people first moved up here. Nobody knew what to do with themselves. How would we maintain a global government if we had no idea when we'd meet? Why bother upholding our unique cultural identities when we only stood over our native homelands for a few hours at a time, and so rarely during the year? Sure, back on the surface immigrants from all over the world had brought their own cultures with them to new lands, but back then there were whole neighborhoods where one nationality lived. Some American cities had several square blocks that were called 'China Town' and 'Little Italy.' Since we moved up to the theriopolises, we've all been kinda one on top of the other. Anyway, soon enough, these 'discussions' about culture and law and order turned into quarrels."

Sean nodded impatiently. He'd heard all this before from his own parents and was starting to worry there wouldn't be anything new in this tale. But he let Jeffrey continue.

"Now, even besides the grade of the hill, do you know why it feels funny walking down our streets compared to yours?"

Sean didn't. He shook his head no, only realizing then that he'd been meaning to ask someone about getting his sea legs while he was here. It was something besides the slope, as

Johns had just said. He wished he'd thought of something to say about it before admitting his ignorance.

"It's because your body is used to the rhythm of your own leviathan, Triton, walking in his own way. With those big wide tortoise legs of his, the motion of your city is different from ours." Jeffrey made a spider-like shape with his hands by putting his wrists together and crooking his fingers out like claws. He then rocked his fingers back and forth, side to side, mimicking how Triton walked. "Like this, yeah? Here, Proteus's large forelegs also make him walk more on a two-leg rhythm instead of four." Jeffrey abandoned his Triton imitation and instead put his first two fingertips on the table and made them walk like a human. "See? It's a very different pattern than what you're used to. His hind legs don't affect his back movement as squarely as Triton's since they're shorter and smaller than his forelegs.

"So keep in mind that back down there, the surface is completely motionless. The ground is always flat, and immobile, like when Proteus stops to look at a skyscraper. And they were used to that being the norm. When we ascended, it took some of The Founders weeks before they got used to the ground under their feet moving. So granddad tells me they had a town meeting once, at the beginning, and these two officials were arguing with each other over this or that. Those boys kept on raising their voices and shouting, and so help me they were clinging onto tables and benches for dear life while they're screaming at each other!" Both men chuckled.

"And what makes it worse," Johns continued, "eventually this fight came to blows. These two old-timers

14

were trying to duke it out, both suffering vertigo and seasickness, and they're leaning on furniture to fight!" Jeffrey laughed harder and harder as he continued. "Finally one of them put his weight into it, cocked his fist back and leaned into this punch with everything he has."

"So did he knock the other guy out?"

"He missed him by more than a foot! He lost his balance and fell on the ground. He ended up throwing up all night. See, your inner ear has a bit of fluid in it that's sensitive to any movement. Since you were in your mama's belly, your brain's gotten used to the swaying of Triton's step. So when you set foot in our city, your inner ear lost its rhythm."

"No shit."

"No shit." Jeffrey batted his eyebrows up and down once to emphasize his point and took a sip of his water. Sean kept those men in his mind, hiding their unease with loud words and bravado even as they held onto support. It sounded like it would've looked very dramatic. He finally snapped back to his conversation and realized he had to go. He excused himself, thanked his host for breakfast, shook his hand and made his way to the docks.

Sean stopped just once while he walked to the docks. All along Proteus's back, there were small man-made outcroppings with balustrades on either side of the city and he made his way to one of them. He looked out over the horizon and saw a comfortably familiar sight. It was the same view he'd seen every day of his life: the horizon split into halves, with the blue daylight offset by the reddish earth. It was partly cloudy today, but the clouds were spread out enough that the sun shined brightly despite them. Below the sky, the rust-colored red orange fog sat mostly still. 82 years prior, that poisonous fog had driven mankind from living on the surface to living on the backs of the 13 colossi that emerged along with it from the depths of the sea. In his youth, Sean had heard hushed stories about what happened to the humans who didn't live in a theriopolis like he did. There were plenty of urban legends about whole tribes of people living on the dirt. They were child warriors with a life expectancy of less than 30 years, living in villages inside skyscrapers just below the 1,000-foot fog ceiling. His older relatives also talked about other people who lived in underground fallout shelters, and others still who had tried to develop floating sky cities. There were as many rumors as there were relatives, it seemed. Since there was no way to separate the truth from the fiction, these stories were often as frustrating as they were fascinating. And although Sean always denied believing in such fairy tales, whenever he found himself enjoying the view near a city he'd always lean forward a bit and squint, keeping an eye out along the top of the haze for feral adolescents carrying babies of their own. He'd never admit it, but the old stories stuck in his mind. *I'm just looking because I know I* won't *see any people like the ones in the stories,* he thought. *It's so stupid.* Sometimes he almost believed himself.

Sean rejoined the bustling life of Proteus. He passed the septic manager, who stopped at every house on the way to Proteus's tail end asking people to add their waste to his wheelbarrow. When it filled, Sean knew the man would drive the barrow to the back of the city and heave it over, then start again from where he'd left off. *You couldn't pay me enough to be the shit bucket guy*, he thought. Walking further towards

Proteus's head, he heard the humming of the people who had already gathered at the harbor. Some of Proteus's clever residents had moved their shops there for the day and were already haggling with customers over trade prices. A weathered old woman missing several teeth shouted in Thai over the din, attempting to barter away a piece of curved glass to an Australian man with a backpack in exchange for some plant seeds.

"ทีจะเริมต้นไฟ!" she said. "ทีจะเริมต้นไฟ!"

"Yes, yes, I got it! Thī ca reìm tn fị! Missy, I know what the bloody glass is for; these here are the only goddamn Rockingham cucumber seeds you're bound to see in this lifetime – or any other, for that matter. You understand? The last seeds above the surface! If you want them, I'll need three from you." He held up three of his fingers. "See? Three."

"ห้า?"

"Yes. Sām. Three."

She held up two fingers.

"No, no, not two," the Aussie said. "Three. Sām."

She paused, cursed in Thai and handed over the pieces of glass. He in turn gave her the small plastic baggie of seeds and pulled out a pre-rolled cigarette from his backpack. He stowed two of the curved glass pieces and held the third up as if inspecting it. The Australian man then looked back at the cigarette he held in his hand and gently turned the glass until it shined on one end of the cigarette. Immediately, the refracted glint of light from the glass began to burn the paper. The man took a drag from the cigarette before stuffing the third glass into his pocket. He walked away smoking and the Thai woman shook her head.

"Cheap son of a bitch."

Other merchants with an eclectic range of goods lined the street. One family had wooden toys and doll furniture with a sign out front that said "REAL WOOD BROUGHT FROM SURFACE, HUNG FIVE YEARS TO DRY OUT FOG." An entirely uninteresting-looking man had water filtration systems available. Teens sold pouches of custom-blended herb cigarettes. Two middle-aged women had fresh vegetables and pornographic magazines. Those with customers bartered shrewdly. Those without eyed passersby hungrily. Sean moved past all of them and rounded the dusty corner where he finally arrived at the docks.

It looked like half the city was at the pier, waiting anxiously to welcome back the two dozen or so wealthy vacationers. Sean Bellamy pushed his way through the crowd, trying not to draw attention to himself while looking for Proteus's mayor, Bill Pulaski. Finally they spotted each other. Sean made his way to the far back corner of the crowd where Pulaski stood on a small makeshift stage with his wife. The couple proudly beckoned Sean up to them. Now, standing on a stage with the mayor, receiving more attention and applause than he'd hoped for, Sean Bellamy remembered what it took to get to where he was.

Self-sufficiency had been a central part of titan society since before Sean was born. Most people didn't mind thinning their own soup once in a while to help their neighbor if his crops didn't come in, but too much dependence on others was taboo as soon as word got out – and with most people living 80 years in communities with a population as little as 1,000, word always got out. Like every other boy and girl growing up, Sean was raised learning to farm crops from hanging indoor gardens. He could salvage compost and soil substitute from his family's garbage and he could run the simple water filtration system that caught rain from the rooftop and drained to the barrel on the side of their house. Beyond that, however, most children showed talents in some trade and worked towards apprenticeship. Sean didn't. His natural charm let him slide by for some time, but eventually it wore out its welcome with his neighbors back on Triton. His father's disappointment in him weighed on Sean more heavily as the years passed. Sean's mother always said "Something will come along," but the confidence in her voice started to fade. Sean took odd jobs to bring in food and supplies, but his father's words were never far from his mind: "You go out and make something of yourself. Become the best at something – make yourself indispensable. Not this petty bullshit you been doing." He decided the best way to earn a name for himself would be to solve a problem the community faced and he wanted to be known as the one who solved it. If it were a big enough problem, god willing he could use it as the foundation for his career.

Every few years, in at least one theriopolis, people started to get bored and restless living in such a confined space. Sean had read of something similar once: the Hawaiians called it "Island Fever." Up on these towns they took to calling it the Wandering City Blues. People could walk around town and visit friends, but eventually it became so much of the same damn thing that people got fed up. On the theriopolis, it led to unrest. The crime rate spiked. There were even suicides, which were shocking – the culture of the value

19

of human life had shifted dramatically since Ascension. When Sean was a child, his father's father told him that there were once *billions* of people roaming the surface. Of course, when Sean questioned his mother, she gently reminded him how prone to exaggeration his grandfather was. Now with the human species down to five digits, every death weighed solemnly.

However, despite how important each life seemed – and no matter how much of the world people saw as their titans roamed its surface – so much of the Earth was swallowed up under the cover of fog that it often looked the same, mirroring their lives. Like Alexander of Macedonia, the human race seemed horrified that there were no more lands to conquer. So there were sometimes self-induced fatalities. The fog was so uniform that many people would visit their local cartographer just to ask where they were. The cartographer's office was a schizophrenic's dream, full of maps and globes and colored pushpins detailing the routes of the titans – or, at least, the titans who *had* steady migration paths. When people got too restless and the city officials noticed, they would try to arrange a party, event or cultural festival to spice up the quiet lives of those living on the beast-cities. It's why they'd started the street hockey league and the exchange student programs for the kids and the boxing tournaments for the adults. Then one day a year ago, Sean had an epiphany.

If people want off of the leviathan so damn badly, why not let them?

He spent plenty of time in the cartographer's office that spring, working with the old man and his maps. Triton walked 48,057 miles on his unending circuit around the planet,

20

stopping at 50 of the world's surface cities that had the highest populations pre-ascension. It took Triton over four months to circle the Earth.

"So if we keep a steady course, we'll pass Moscow once on March 2nd of next year, then again on July…15th. Is that right?"

The old man licked his lips. "Sure, but why Moscow?"

"Proteus stops in Moscow. That knuckle-walker loves skyscrapers and there's that huge cluster of them downtown at the uh, what's it called, Moscow Business Complex?"

"Moscow International Business Center, sonny."

"Right! And if you're really as good as you say you are at keeping track of the leviathans – "

"Hey, now; don't doubt *my* work for a second, smartass…"

"…Then Proteus will stop in Moscow a few weeks behind us. In fact, Proteus will get to Moscow on…" Numbers flew through Sean's head as he calculated Proteus's schedule. *Proteus gets home to Dubai on March 31st, plus 68 days around the world and another 57 to Russia makes* "August 3rd of next year!"

They double-checked their math, then triple-checked it. Dusting off his childhood sales skills, Sean drew up a three-week vacation plan and approached the city with it in the ominous town hall. "It would be like a…" Sean checked his notes and his next two words came out awkwardly, despite echoing throughout the room. "…'cruise ship.' Have you ever heard of one of those? Surface-dwellers would get bored of their own towns and book passage on a boat that would take them around the oceans just to get away from it all. Only instead of a motionless city and a trip around the ocean, we'd have an immobile getaway from a moving city." He knew Triton's mayor had a copy of his notes in front of him – in fact he'd had his nose buried in them since Sean entered city hall. Sean had learned from school that people tend to embed information in their brains better if they're reading and hearing at the same time, so he maintained his calm and consciously took his time presenting the idea so as not to skip ahead of the mayor's busy eyes.

Triton's deputy mayor piped up. "'Just to get away from it all?' It does have a nice ring to it."

The mayor, Will Staps, nodded in agreement. "We could really sell this 'getaway' idea. People are always excited about new things, and if it works right we could start booking them regularly. Travel would be a bitch but I think our citizens would pay for the chance.

"At the same time, we don't want to lose any of our population permanently. What with the missing colossi and those lawless lunatics on Sao, we can't even put an accurate figure on how many human beings are left on the theriopolises. 10,000? 20,000? I can promise you it's not more than that and we'd hate for Triton to suffer 10 or 20 family bloodlines Mr. Bellamy."

At the mention of his name, Sean perked up. "That's not a problem sir; they wouldn't be able to carry enough resources to develop long-term settlements atop the skyscraper."

Mayor Staps thought. "Bellamy, have you worked out all the kinks in this? Since it's your name – and your cut of the profits – at stake here, I'm assuming you have."

Sean hadn't, but this was his only chance. "Absolutely. I just need to take one final quick look at OKO South Tower next time we stop in Moscow."

Silence hung in the air. It was deafening. Staps finally looked up from Sean's papers.

"Okay. Let's give it a try. We have them sign liability waivers in case of any injuries and we book a vacation."

Word escaped Triton's city hall and buzz generated quickly. In a few months, half of the theriopolises and all their posh socialites had heard of the idea and were throwing riches at Triton and Proteus for the chance to be the first vacationers since the ascension. Amazingly, the faint-hearted gentlemen and dainty young ladies who won the bids for the trip underwent all the travel without a hitch. Over the next several months, these travelers spent considerable time working their way from the other leviathans – including Proteus, Galatea and Naiad – to Triton, where Sean had hired an assistant to provide them with their packs. Each pack held three weeks' food, several gallons of water and a sleeping bag scavenged from the surface years before.

And today was the big day – August 3rd. Sean Bellamy waited shoulder-to-shoulder with Mayor Pulaski of Proteus to welcome the first post-ascension vacationers back from their trip. Sean figured there was more glory waiting for him in the pickup than the drop-off, so he trusted his assistant, a young Triton resident by the name of Alan Vaughn, to get the vacationers onto Moscow's skyscraper by himself while Sean left for Proteus well in advance. Now, waiting at the docks for Proteus to lumber up to the Moscow International Business Center just 20 days after the tourists landed, Sean was brimming with excitement and pride in his work. He'd had a brilliant idea that not only helped save the theriopolises from another bout of Island Fever but could incorporate a whole new branch of peoples' lifestyles.

From the lookout tower behind them, they heard a young boy shout "Moscow dead ahead!" The excitement grew to a fever pitch. Musicians banged on drums that sounded throughout the late morning sky. Children chased each other in games of Tag through the crowd. The cigarette vendors announced they were offering free pouches of herbs to the travelers upon their return. Mayor Pulaski laughed and patted Sean on the shoulder. It was a veritable quarter-mile-high parade, a celebration of mankind once again overcoming adversity.

My God I'm going to be rich, Sean thought.

The dock workers readied a 15-foot ballista to fire to the tower. They'd done it a hundred times before. Two workers cranked the handle near the seat at the back of the ballista, bringing the string back until the limb itself bowed backwards and clicked into its set position at the latch. A third man, already seated and waiting, was handed a long, arrow-shaped grappling hook trailing nearly a quarter-mile of rope behind it. He placed it under and between his legs, into the flight groove on top of the long barrel. The poorly-named "string" that ran from one end of the limb to the other – and would project the hook on its path to OKO South – was more of a thick belt of rope than it was a string, but the name had always stuck. All that remained, as they knew from experience, was to await the order. When the hook fired and caught on the tower, they simply reeled it in on the spool and let the travelers strap onto the ropeway and climb back across.

As they neared the cluster of towers, OKO South came closer and closer. A minute before the harbormaster was ready to give the order to fire the ballista, something in the crowd changed. The onlookers at the front, who had surrounded and cramped the dock workers eagerly, got quieter. Their raised hands lowered and their faces fell. Each row of people stopped jumping, stopped shouting, stopped cheering one after another. The drummers stopped their music, stood and stared at the tower. Sean and Mayor Pulaski were the last to realize something was wrong. One drummer dropped his fat drumstick and it rolled noisily downhill, clanging and clattering towards the stage. An eerie silence enveloped the crowd, but eerier still was the sight that awaited their approach atop OKO South Tower.

Birds cawed and crowed. *Why are there so many birds?* Sean thought. The mayor charged up through the crowd, pushing people aside until he reached the balcony, its low railing chipped with dozens of marks from previous grappling hook attachments. He borrowed a pair of binoculars from a nearby gawker and glassed the rooftop.

27 bodies lay on the roof. They were slathered in a grotesque soup of blood, vomit and bird feces. Many of them were being eaten by the birds. The birds had been working on some of them for a while, picking through their fancy clothes and moving their jewelry aside to get at the carrion beneath.

"They're all dead." Pulaski didn't mean to let the words escape his lips, but they did, and though he spoke quietly, everyone heard it. He lowered the binoculars from his eyes and pushed them against someone else's chest. He thought it was their owner but he couldn't be sure. But he had no more use for them; he'd seen enough.

As he sauntered back to Sean Bellamy, his knees weak with the horror of the corpses he'd seen, the crowd's eyes followed. Sean could barely see the rooftop from where he stood but he knew something horrible had happened. The roof was a macabre light grey with trickles of red dripping down its sides and an abnormally large flock of birds perched on (or circling) it. There were no birds on any of the other skyscrapers nearby. The pieces of the puzzle started falling into place just as Sean looked down and saw Proteus's mayor within 10 feet of him, shambling slowly.

"What did I do?" Sean asked earnestly. His mouth was dry and the words barely croaked out of his throat. His thoughts slowly turned away from whatever happened to his tourists and towards the unfathomable amount of shit he'd gotten himself into. He cleared his throat and asked the mayor again – in a monotone voice, with tears welling up in his eyes – for the news. In a sense he was asking for the fate of the rest of his life.

"What did I do."

* * *

The harbormaster called to fire the shot as soon as Proteus stopped to look at the skyscraper, just like clockwork; the dock worker in the gunner seat didn't hesitate. The hook reached the top of the building and splashed in a puddle of fecal matter and blood. The other dock workers reeled the line

26

in, leaving a bit of slack to ease their journey. Then they fastened their climbing harnesses onto the ropeway and zip lined over to the rooftop on OKO South to retrieve the first body. Without the distant sound of Proteus's footsteps pounding against the earth, the hushed crowd seemed even quieter. When they got to the nearest corpse, one of the dock workers reeled and found himself retching over the edge of the building. This sent a wave of gasps and murmurs through the crowd. The few family members of the deceased who were in attendance were shocked back to coherence for the first time since seeing their relatives blanketed by excrement and entrails. They began to sob.

Pulaski's mood had turned from horror to anger. In his rage he knew the only proper course of action was to keep a cool head for the sake of the city, the dead and their families. Even still, he could only partly mask his tone and when he spoke it was through gritted teeth.

"Get the doctor."

It took the deputy mayor a minute for the words to reach his ears. He dumbly looked at Mayor Pulaski, who returned his gaze with a fire in his eyes. The deputy mayor blinked several times and ran to retrieve the town physician while the dock workers resumed their unsavory task.

They wiped the body off as best they could and batted two Eurasian Sparrowhawks off the corpse with the backs of their hands. The birds cawed with displeasure but flew off to peck at another body. The dock workers unfurled a tarp, which they usually carried for transporting supplies between colossi, and folded it into a makeshift body bag and put the body on it. They tied up either end of the tarp so it resembled a canoe, then they each fastened one end to their own climbing harnesses, near the men's spines, and began the long climb to transport it back to Proteus. The men talked while they worked their way back across the rope, the foot ascenders which were strapped to their boots preventing them from sliding back to the building.

"Is she slipping?"

"No. She's staying up on my end so far."

"What the Hell happened here?"

"Like I know? Just don't say anything unless someone asks you for info."

"Copy that."

"Of course you could've seen more if you hadn't blown chunks over the side there…"

"Man, fuck you. Those birds were picking her damn *guts* – "

"Okay, just shut up right there. Stop it. We're getting close to the docks and if her family is there and they heard you goin' on like that?"

"Alright, alright. Jesus. Let's just get there. How far we got?"

"I'd say another 200 feet."

"How are we gonna make 25 more trips?"

"26."

"My point is we've got less than an hour and we probably took close to 10 minutes getting to this one and bringing her home."

"Like I said, keep your head down and follow orders. Let the boss and Mayor Pulaski figure out this nightmare."

"Fine."

28

"And try to keep your breakfast *down* next time."

They arrived in silence, unhooked their cargo and set it down gently. Mayor Pulaski had returned to the front of the area with a reluctant Sean Bellamy. Pulaski offered his handkerchief to the dock worker who'd thrown up, shooting him a dirty look. "Clean yourself up for Christ's sake; some of the people on that tower were your neighbors and friends."

Just as the dock worker sought to defend himself, the deputy mayor arrived at the harbor with the doctor, who carried his medical bag. The doctor scurried up to the body and untied the tarp. With a full and close-up view of the deceased, the crowd backed away several steps in a hurry. A young man howled in agony and shoved through the crowd, kneeling in front of the dead woman and gently stroking her sullied hair. He wasn't too proud to cry for his loss.

Her boyfriend, Bellamy thought. For a half a moment he was proud of himself for his simple deduction but the overpowering odor emanating from the victim brought his attention back to the scene at hand. Reality sank in again and Sean Bellamy realized that for his negligence he'd likely be thrown off Proteus, every bone in his body breaking on impact with the barren surface after a quarter-mile fall from the city, liability waivers be damned. The only thing he had to wonder was if he'd die of a heart attack on the way down before he hit the ground.

ghettobelly

Proteus became a circus. Even before the public
pointed fingers and asked questions and demanded answers,
the decision was made not to retrieve any more of the bodies
until medical experts could convene and agree on a cause of
death. This infuriated the victims' families, who went so far as
to attempt to bribe every harbormaster on every reachable
titan to bring the bodies home for a proper burial. They
understood the logic: had the vacationers caught some fatal
illness, bringing them home could spread the disease and kill
an entire city. But the thought of the birds picking at their
relatives was too much to bear. Wild accusations were made
about one tourist or another losing their minds and killing
everyone on the vacation. Communication from one colossus
to another limited to mail boxes. These had been constructed
on as many structures as possible that rose above the fog and
were passed closely by several colossi. It took months for any
order to come at all.

In the meantime, several doctors and two police
detectives (along with the detectives' apprentices) met on
Proteus to examine the body the dock workers had retrieved.
It was first determined that no malicious intent had been

involved – there was no mass murderer among them. In fact any wounds to the exterior of the body seemed to have happened post-mortem, likely from the sparrowhawks. After some crude blood tests and an autopsy of the vital organs, the team of doctors noted the majority of damage had been in the lungs. There was some panic for a brief moment that Red Lung, the fatal disease that was inhaled on the surface through the fog, had crept up to the clean air atop the colossi. However, Galatea's general practitioner, a Dr. Iweala, finally cracked it. From a couch in the medical office he spoke up.

"Gentlemen, gentlemen!" he cried out, his African accent calling even more attention to him than his long frame. "This woman did not die of Red Lung. None of you have considered the role our flying friends have played in this tragedy."

Iweala scratched his well-trimmed salt-and-pepper beard, eyeing the dried clothes that the victim had been wearing, which had since been cast aside in a corner of the room. He rose from his seat and walked slowly towards the clothes, continuing to speak as he pointed one finger at the victim's dress.

"What has happened to the birds since we came to live on these creatures? We see that the avian world survives despite its dependence on materials from the surface. But who can tell me why?"

The room fell silent.

"It is because the parents sacrifice. Yes. They dive down, knowing the danger inherent in the mist, and retrieve what they need in order to provide for their nest. This shortens their lifespans grievously, and why?"

A young detective spoke up. "Does someone want to speed the wildlife lesson up and tell us what the Hell killed these folks?" He was met with sharp glances and short words. Dr. Iweala chuckled and addressed the apprentice, little more than a boy.

"Young sir, an ounce of patience saves a pound of grief. Please, wait.

"The birds die young because they expose their lungs to the mist. Miners in the old world would bring small birds – canaries – into caves with them, in cages. If the air in the mines were toxic, the bird would die and the miners would flee before they too fell victim. The birds atop the towers in Moscow sacrificed much of their lifespan for their babies, becoming quickly infected with the so-called 'Red Lung' upon their first foraging for food or supplies."

Another doctor spoke.

"Dr. Iweala, you told us these people didn't catch Red Lung from the birds."

"I maintain that they did not. The fecal matter of the birds still living throughout the world carries up to 80 diseases in it, does it not?"

There was a murmur of agreement in the room.

"Three of those diseases are potentially fatal to humans in the long-term, yes? In fact this woman's autopsy has shown that her symptoms align closely to one form of histoplasmosis, regularly found in the birds' feces. Further inspection will determine which kind, I am sure of it."

"But doctor, even acute cases of histoplasmosis didn't kill within three weeks on the surface. They don't even show *symptoms* that quickly."

Another doctor spoke up. "But the fog is known to accelerate illnesses and their effects, as we were told happened on the surface with untreatable forms of cancer."

Dr. Iweala pointed at the new speaker. "Exactly! How rapidly did the terminally ill back on the ground meet their demise following exposure to that Hellish mist? The epidemic of Red Lung combined with the sudden rapid fatality of other illnesses was too much to analyze in such a short time. In the rush to escape the surface, our predecessors never absolutely determined whether it was always a compromised body that simply couldn't bear exposure or if the other way around also occurred – that sometimes, the fog could affect the disease itself instead of the body, catalyzing fatality from whichever disease a person already suffered.

"I ask you, my colleagues," Dr. Iweala continued, "to consider these birds as carriers of not only the histoplasmosis that killed these poor souls but also small doses of the damned red-orange killer that wiped the surface of the planet clean. Birds are so porous; the creeping fog would have little trouble invading the rest of their bodies. Eventually, before their deaths, these birds could void their bowels with a new killer inside their waste: a rapidly fatal mutation of histoplasmosis."

With that, Dr. Iweala sat back in his chair. "Disseminated histoplasmosis, specifically, would be my guess."

The assembly of medical practitioners exploded into shouts and arguments, but in the end they arrived at his conclusion.

The rest of the story was put together by the detectives in attendance. Politicians focused on damage control. They had copies of the liability waivers, but 27 people were dead and *somebody* had to pay for it. The general consensus was to place the blame on whoever the party in question had heard the idea from. Law enforcement traced their line of questioning back one interview at a time.

"My darling Beatrice only went because she heard from Mayor Pulaski it was totally safe."

"I was assured by my colleagues that this abominable idea was foolproof. Ask them."

"If you want to know about all matters of inter-titan travel, talk to the harbormasters at the points of departure and arrival."

"Hey, I just get the people from Point A to Point B. My orders came from Mayor Staps here on Triton. He got this lunacy off the ground; you'd have to ask him."

Finally, a pair of detectives – including the boy who'd spoken up at Dr. Iweala while the doctors determined the cause of death – arrived at Sean Bellamy's rented tent. He heard them coming and gave himself up with no resistance. He had barely eaten and his neighbor, Jeffrey Johns, had turned him a cold shoulder. He offered his wrists for the cuffs and silently walked with them to jail. The blank expression on his face had been there since shortly after the discovery of the bodies in Moscow; the waivers the tourists had signed seemed written on air by now. In his naiveté he thought for a while that the city officials who had supported the vacation would stand by him and take some of the blame. After all, he had promised Triton's city council that he'd thought of everything, but wasn't it their responsibility to take safety precautions against such an atrocity?

Sean was extradited back to Triton to stand trial. Here, his city councilmen abandoned him. Mayor Staps and Triton's deputy mayor, Greg Davis, were conspicuously quiet; the detectives' and doctors' testimonies shaped Sean into an ice-hearted monster who was only too happy to throw lives away to feed himself. The worst came at the end. It was a cold bastard of a night in an even colder city hall. The sky was a dark purple and rain spattered on Triton in sheets when the senior detective on the case – who doubled as the prosecution in Sean's trial – reconstructed the events of July 15th to August 3rd on OKO South Tower.

"27 innocent souls gathered at Triton Port Costal Harbor, excitedly awaiting…what did you call it, Bellamy? Oh yes, 'some time away from it all.' They rode the line from Triton onto OKO South Tower in Moscow – where so many of them still remain, I might add – carrying only the supplies which *you yourself* had prepared for them before handing them off to your assistant, a Mr. Vaughn."

Sean wasn't angry with Alan. When word reached him that the young Vaughn had opted not to testify on his behalf, he understood it was a matter of looking out for his family's reputation. Life on the theriopolis was like that. The meaning of the family name had seen resurgence like it hadn't for centuries prior.

"These 27 people then unhooked the ropeway from the tower, tossing it back to be reeled in by the mid-day shift of the Triton Port Costal crew, according to the testimony here signed and seconded by said crew.

"Shortly after that, these folks must have tucked into their first meal. Ryan Fields and Josie Daly and Mr. and Mrs.

Akira Takahashi and all the rest of your 'vacationers' got hungry and sat down to eat. And when they did, that food attracted some guests."

Sean never thought the birds would be a problem. He figured everyone would just shoo them away and they'd get the hint. He was starting to dislike the detective and his grandstanding. Everyone knew Sean was going away; there was no use kicking him while he was down. He looked up to the bench for support, but the officials – including Mayor Staps, with whom he'd designed the vacation program – wouldn't meet his eyes. Sean realized they wouldn't step in, lest they appear to the public like they were protecting him.

"These avian guests, however, didn't want to leave. They saw an opportunity to feed themselves and their families for *weeks*. Who'd give up free fruits and veggies delivered straight to their doorstep for free? I'm sure all 27 of your tourists fought hard to keep those birds at bay, Mr. Bellamy, and that ruckus attracted other birds who wanted a piece of the buffet. It became a problem for your tourists, fighting to keep their every meal, but over the next week or so the real dilemma – the one that ultimately cost them their lives – was the shit.

"Birds shit everywhere. Flying a wide radius around the city, they could've plopped them down anywhere they wanted and our colossi would've just stepped on them on their way – they've probably been doing it since we moved up here. But you give those birds one small spot on which to focus, in which to live, to find plentiful amounts of food, and they are gonna crap all over that little area. And this summer, sir, that area was OKO South Tower. Several months ago, a convention of doctors was able to determine that birds carry 80 diseases in their feces. One of those diseases is called..." the detective checked his notes. "...histoplasmosis, which was likely accelerated by Red Lung residue in the droppings of these birds. Do you know what the symptoms of histoplasmosis are, Mr. Bellamy?"

Sean stared daggers at the detective. "You know that I don't."

"Well if you did, maybe you wouldn't have shipped over two dozen people to their graves last summer. Histoplasmosis, according to a medical text provided to me by a Dr. Iweala of Galatea, first causes fever and coughing, followed by chest pains, mouth sores and skin lesions...eventually leading to coughing up blood and a risk of death. It's especially dangerous to infants and the elderly. Mr. Bellamy, so we can assume that the widower and grandfather of seven, Rupert Singh, was one of the first to go."

In his head, Sean pictured the kindly old Indian man with the soft hands who he'd met the previous spring before leaving Triton. He then imagined him keeling over on the rooftop. Sean looked at the floor in shame. Nobody spoke up for him. He was starting to believe he didn't deserve for them to. The detective continued showboating for anyone who would listen.

"One after another, they dropped like leaves off a tree. Our dock workers say they found the body of Sheila Woodbine still clutching her infant son, Mr. Bellamy. A baby boy dies in his mother's arms and, later, she dies holding him, coughing up blood onto his cold body while the birds fight over scraps, raining pestilent filth on them both.

37

"And finally, their tears ran dry and their lives were snuffed out, all these men and women from nearly every city we have left. But that wasn't a cruel enough twist of fate, because some of the birds attracted to OKO South Tower – that is, after the initial squabble over the tourists' crumbs – those new birds were carnivores. Did you know that Eurasian Sparrowhawks eat dead animals, Mr. Bellamy?"

Sean was unable to lift his head. He softly shook his head "no."

"Did you know that Eurasian Sparrowhawks are native to Moscow, sir?"

Sean shook his head again.

"Did you know that upon seeing the aftermath of your little trip, one dock worker – a Mr. Meyers of Proteus – was so unable to reconcile the gore before him with human life that he himself vomited over the edge of the tower?"

"Yes."

"I beg your pardon?"

"Yes, I was there."

"Oh, that's right, Mr. Bellamy; you were there. Standing next to Mayor Pulaski of Proteus, you were there to receive your tourists and claim your fame and fortune. Riding high and mighty towards a skyscraper topped with bloodied corpses and bird effluence, a...a macabre ice cream sundae topped with whipped cream and cherries, you were there waiting.

"My hero...Topper."

* * *

Sean awaited sentencing in a quiet cell. The rain abated and he had just one visitor: Triton's mayor, Will Staps, had come to check on him.

"They hit you pretty hard in there, kid. They even gave you a nickname."

Sean raised his head and locked eyes with Mayor Staps. The mayor fought back chills; the man who sat before him now was but a shell of the ambitious salesman he'd contracted 18 months ago to sell a vacation in Moscow to the tourists whose deaths now bloodied his hands. Sean had always been thin but now he seemed positively gaunt. The bags under his eyes said he hadn't slept. His cheeks were sunken in and hollow, contrasting sharply with his high, protruding cheekbones. His eyes were the worst. They were glazed over, reddened from crying and unfocused. Sean was utterly lost, like a leaf blowing in the wind. Staps knew he had to choose his words carefully.

"Listen, Sean…"

"Save it."

"What happened in that tower – "

"I said save it!"

Mayor Staps took a breath and tried a different approach.

"What do you think you're looking at tomorrow? In sentencing?"

"Death."

Staps chuckled a little despite himself. "Nobody's gonna kill you, kid. I think we've seen enough death to last us all the rest of our lives."

"But…I *deserve* it."

"It's not always our job to give you what you deserve. Sometimes it's our job to make our people feel better. And this ain't the dark ages, kid; you're not swinging from a noose or being shut in the stocks in town square with people throwing cabbage at you.

"But they do want to make an example of you. 27 people paid the highest price there is. Shit, just in terms of the remaining number of humans on Earth that's a considerable number, waivers or not. 27 is probably 10% of the goddamn population flying around on Psamanthe right now, wherever she's perched."

Sean thought of Psamanthe, the 500-foot raven-like leviathan, flying and nesting and taking care of the humans who strapped themselves onto her back. He got choked up again.

"Aw Hell; I'm sorry kid. It was a bad choice of words. Look, I still haven't told you why I'm here. None of us could throw ourselves in front of the firing squad for you in trial. I think you know why. If people thought the leaders of their cities were so in…" The word "incompetent" caught in Staps's throat and he did his best to backpedal before insulting the broken man sitting in the cell. "…If they thought we could make this kind of mistake, there'd be chaos! And though they'd be so unforgiving, you and I know it was just a mistake. As do the other bigwigs in charge of keeping the human race going, and they're not going to forget that.

"Sean, sometimes making a mistake means you forget your anniversary. Sometimes making a mistake means forgetting to read up on local wildlife. Unfortunately, the first one means you sleep on the couch tonight and the second means you stand trial for negligent mass homicide.

"What the public will remember is that some guy did time for a colossal fuck-up. Justice served, everything goes back to normal. What the mayors of Triton, Proteus, Naiad and the others will remember is…our guy Sean fell on his sword for the greater good. And having friends in our offices can buy you a lot – starting tomorrow."

Sean took a moment to process what Mayor Staps was saying. His mind was an angry sea, wrestling with guilt, fear, anger, denial and extremes of wanting or avoiding punishment. He looked up to ask Staps a question but the mayor was already gone. At length, he fell into a restless sleep.

* * *

Due to Triton's height, his belly cleared the fog with room to spare. Decades ago, one of Triton's more outlandish mayors developed a housing project for the poor and a prison system for the incarcerated that people flocked to see from all over the world. The low-income housing project was a small shantytown resting on a raft-like platform of materials salvaged from the surface over a number of years. The platform itself was 40,000 square feet of ramshackle wood, plastic and sheet metal. The whole thing was suspended by industrial chain lengths harnessed to Triton's body. Since Triton's legs went out from his body before they went straight down – like a crab – there was room to spare under his belly without it being kicked by his enormous legs. They lowered the poverty-stricken and the homeless onto the platform after constructing crude shacks for them and told them to fend for themselves. There was virtually no contact between the upper city and the one that swung under Triton so precariously close to the fog, save for water deliveries. The prisoners didn't have it so easy.

Gibbets – solitary confinement prison cages in medieval times – inspired Triton's prison system. Prisoners remained alone in their cages 24 hours a day. A guard watched over the prisoners from a 100-square-foot platform above them, carefully lowering food to them. Gravity was their toilet. Prison sentences were doled out in lengths of chain, not years. The more severe a crime, the longer the prisoner's chain dangled from Triton's carapace. The more severe the crime, the closer to the fog they swung. Prisoners had two options to finish their interment: First, they could wait out the time. For every full year of imprisonment they served, a guard raised the gibbet by 10 feet. When the chain became short enough to meet the winch from which it hung, the prisoner went free. The second option was to reduce one's sentence by going fishing.

When a prisoner called for a fishing trip, the guard raised him up to the guard's platform and escorted him from his cell back up to the city. The mayor, the harbormaster and anyone who wanted to watch gathered at the pier where the prisoner was fitted with rappelling gear over a radiation suit as well as a duffel bag and several carabiners. When the prisoner was ready he rappelled down the side of Triton as quickly as he could via a large spool leading his rope. He disappeared down through the fog to the surface. He then had mere moments to grab whatever supplies he could (or lock them onto his rope via his carabiners) before Triton walked past him and began dragging him along the streets. When the prisoner was ready, he climbed several feet off the ground and tugged the rope thrice. The dock workers at either Triton Port Costal or Triton Starboard Costal – depending on which side the prisoner fished from – would reel him back in. Since both the prisoner and his supplies would have remnants of the fog clinging to them, they were then kept under quarantine until they were determined to be safe to the public, at which time the mayor would sift through the treasures and determine their worth. The more valuable the haul, the more time was taken from the prisoner's sentence, so prisoners would often try to estimate the time it took to set up a fishing trip and call for one that far away from an approaching city skyline. Smash-and-grabs in major metropolitan areas offered a higher likelihood of success and higher-priced goods.

  The risks were high. For one, the radiation suit only provided limited protection from the fog and ex-convicts often died of Red Lung years before their life expectancy anyway. Fishing trips also happened so rarely, nobody really knew what to expect from the surface. Buildings could have become unstable or fires could have recently started. Once, a convict who still had 200 feet left on his sentence smuggled a kitchen knife down with him on his fishing trip. He reached the surface and cut the rope from his waist. By the time the harbormaster and the mayor realized something was wrong and reeled the rope in, it came up so easily they feared what was waiting on the other end. When it came up, it was just the duffel bag secured to the line with the radiation suit inside.

"At least he was nice enough to give us back the suit," the old mayor had remarked sarcastically. The crowd roared with laughter. There was no turning back; the titans waited for no one. At some point the con must've succumbed to the haze. The old mayor leaned over the edge of the docks and cupped his hand next to his mouth. "Hope you enjoy dying from Red Lung, ya fuckin' scumbag!"

Sean Bellamy knew of all this when they called him in for sentencing.

"Sean Bellamy, you've been found guilty of 27 counts of criminal negligence resulting in homicide. Before carrying out your sentence, do you have anything to say in your defense?"

He cast a glance at Mayor Staps, the boy detective and the lead detective before looking back down at his own feet. "What happened to those men and women I carry on my shoulders every day unto my grave. Nothing can bring them back, but perhaps they and their loved ones can find peace in my punishment. I'm ready."

He was ready for death. He got just 150 feet. 15 years if he didn't fish. His eyes shot straight to Mayor Staps, who he swore gave him a quick wink before they took Sean away. He didn't know whether to feel relieved that he could one day walk the streets of his hometown again or cheated out of paying for the tourists' lives with his own.

Inevitably, some cried foul. A couple people even arrived at the very conclusion the mayor tried to hide – that 150 feet for "Topper" was a slap on the wrist in exchange for taking the fall of the worst tragedy in recent memory to befall the last humans on Earth. Publicly, however, it was made known that Sean Bellamy's record had been clean prior to the Moscow Tower incident, as it came to be known, and the waivers the vacationers signed cleared anyone involved with it from virtually all legal recourse. They all but said Sean was a scapegoat and a patsy but the public was lucky they got what they did out of him.

And what the people of the cities hadn't counted on, that had proved itself time and time again since the draconian prison system was enacted all those decades past, was something Mayor Staps, Mayor Pulaski and the other theriopolis officials had learned from their time in office: Out of sight was truly out of mind. Staps had told Sean as much the night before his sentencing. Once Sean was led to his gibbet, everyone felt a sense of closure whose absence had plagued them for nearly a year. They'd taken their boogeyman, locked him up and thrown away the key. Life truly went back to normal.

Sean promised himself never to go fishing. He deserved the years he got and he'd serve them without exception. He had plenty of time, then, and spoke occasionally with the other prisoners in the gibbets who came and went during his 15 years under Triton. Just after the first shortening of Sean's chain, he met one. This convict, a slender middle-aged woman, had returned home early from work only to find her wife in bed with another woman. She grabbed her wife and flung her against the wall, knocking her out, and she beat the other woman to death with her bare hands. By the time the wife came to, there was little left of her lover but a pile of meat. At least that's what the wife testified – the convict didn't remember a moment of it. "Temporary insanity," they called it. She'd broken her hands in five places tenderizing this other woman; she was still bandaged up when they put her in her cage.

Another man hanging from Triton, who was imprisoned near Sean for several years, was said to have had such a rift with his neighbor that he broke into the neighbor's house while the neighbor was at work and destroyed every crop in his hydroponic garden. The neighbor rationed what he'd already harvested to last an extra week or two, but had other townspeople not chipped in he would've starved to death before he could grow a new harvest. "Attempted murder my hairy ass," the convict said. "If I really wanted to kill the sumbitch I'd a thrown his ass *off*. Pewwwwwww *KER-SPLAT*." He spit outwards between the bars of his gibbet and watched his oblong ball of saliva fall down, lost in the fog.

"Ker-splat."

But mostly Sean was left to his own devices. He stared down at the red orange mist that had made barren all the Earth's surface. It was thick; Sean noticed whenever he passed near a skyscraper that he couldn't see more than two or three stories below the highest point that the fog touched the building. Sometimes he listened to the silent pauses between the distant booming noises of Triton's stride. He heard the wind blow and sometimes he could hear the sounds of city life going on without him hundreds of feet above. He got more and more used to the sight of a large roof over his head. He never got wet when it rained. Sometimes the other prisoners would try to harass the guards. They insulted them, cursed at them or teased them for hours on end, hoping to provoke a reaction. Some of the woolier cons even threw their food at the guards but that never made sense to Sean. *You're only going to go hungry,* he thought. Sean left the guards alone and they left him alone. They reeled his chain in another 10 feet every year and he said "Thank you" when they gave him his meals. The only personal items he had were a pair of nail clippers and a toothbrush. Whenever he reached the last sip of his drinking water, he dipped the brush in and ran it along his teeth as best he could. He trimmed his nails when he needed to do so and his gibbet was raised to the guards' office every six weeks or so for a shave and a haircut.

More years passed. Sean grew pale. He grieved for each of the 27 tourists who died on the tower because of him. He recalled their names and faces over and over again in his mind like a chant. As the years rolled by, however, his pain faded and he felt more and more ready to rejoin society. He put more effort into keeping himself hygienic and he used the bars in his gibbet to do pull-ups and sit-ups after meals. He didn't know what he'd do when his 15 years were up, but he knew Triton's belly was getting closer.

Finally the day came. Sean waited in the guards' office quietly, his belongings in a small sack in his lap. It was the winter of 97 P.A. and the deputy mayor rappelled down to finalize his release. Sean greeted him.

"Ah, but it's *Mayor* Davis now, Mr. Bellamy."

"What happened to Mayor Staps?"

"William Staps retired, I'm afraid," Greg Davis said. He couldn't be bothered to hide his excitement at bearing the news, either. "He's moved in with his son and daughter-in-law on Naiad, if memory serves."

Sean remained quiet as he was outfitted with his own climbing harness. Every man, woman and child on a theriopolis knew how to equip rope ascension gear and secure his or her lifeline to a ropeway. Using locking carabiners, foot ascenders and the rest of the gear was second nature to everyone on one of the colossi and Sean found that despite being 15 years out of practice, he could pick it right back up like it were yesterday. He joined Davis at the bottom of the main rope that ran from the prison guards' office up to the docks. Davis stopped him.

"Staps asked me to give you these."

A pair of tinted goggles was shoved against Sean's chest. He grabbed them, fumbling a bit as he put them on, and asked what he'd need them for. He realized the answer as soon as he asked the question, but before he could tell Davis not to bother, the mayor had already started ascending the rope and talking – and Greg Davis loved to hear his own voice.

"When's the last time you were exposed to direct sunlight, Mr. Bellamy? I'm sure some peeked in for a few minutes around sunrise and sunset as the sun squeaked past the fog to or from your roof here," he said while patting Triton's hide, "but judging by the tone of your skin I'd say you haven't seen a sunny day in…my God, has it been 15 years?"

"To the day," Sean replied flatly, following him up Triton's side. He was glad he'd been exercising; his arms were aching by the time he reached the docks and they shook forcefully as he heaved himself over the railway and back onto the surface of his city. He collapsed on the ground and caught his breath. He was dizzy and as he sat up he felt light-headed, but he'd never been happier to see the streets of Triton and its people going about their everyday lives, even as some of them stared at him and hurried along their way.

"Jesus wept."

* * *

Sean returned to his house. He expected the broken windows and the graffiti on the walls – enormous insults and profanities scrawled in capital letters – but he was surprised that they constituted the majority of the damage. Some of the junk thrown through the windows had broken his mirror and scratched the paintings that hung on his walls, and there was some water damage from years of storms passing overhead and raining on his broken windows, but his domicile was otherwise intact. Sean stepped back outside and picked up the large plastic garbage can that had collected and filtered his rainwater before the Moscow Tower incident. He walked to a lookout on the edge of the city and emptied the can's contents over the railing before returning with the empty garbage can to his house.

He carefully picked up the shards from the broken mirror and set them on his kitchen table – mirrors were hard enough to come by that he decided it best to reassemble the mirror later. He broke down the ruined paintings and their frames and he placed them in the garbage can. He added the junk thrown in by the vandals to the can. Sean dumped the load of trash over the edge again and returned home. He slept deeply on his bed that night, waking the next morning.

Sean needed new windows and something to mask the graffiti on his walls, but first he needed to eat and he obviously had no food growing yet. He stopped to see Allison Mackey, the city gardener. She tended to the tall building in town square built by The Founders to house hydroponic and aeroponic gardening systems and the city's supply of seeds for future use. Using those methods of farming and containers filled with soil substitutes made mostly of sand and compost, she was able to maintain dozens of hearty crops including quinoa, potatoes, onions, strawberries, tomatoes, cantaloupe, bananas, spinach, kale, lettuce and cucumbers. Virtually every home in the city had its own small garden inside or out, but Allison's remained the largest and most diverse, serving as auxiliary in case of some unforeseen food shortage (or population boom). The stock of seeds that shared space in the greenhouse was also sold to any family who wished to expand or change their own supply.

When she saw him she dropped her spray bottle. "By the Goddess...Sean? Sean Bellamy?"

He offered a meek smile. "Hi, Allison."

She wrapped her arms around him and cried tears of joy. She was a short woman with a medium build and straight brown hair. Her large brown eyes were always alight with wonder and a love for her work. She was close to his age – they were both in their mid-40s now – and they'd been friends before he put together the Moscow deal.

She regained her composure and they exchanged pleasantries. She boiled potatoes in a pot and mashed them with a fork, seasoning them with fresh oregano pulled from one of her crops. They caught up while they ate and at the end, she sent him on his way with a wide variety of seeds, a gallon of water, a jug of coconut milk and a signed order slip for rocks and sand – both coarse and fine – to bring to the pier. Sean was to keep these last supplies to rebuild his water filtration system.

Bit by bit, Sean's house became a living home again. He lined the bottom of the garbage can with paper made of pulp from coconut fibers and he poured the fine sand on top of it. He then added the coarse sand and several rocks on top, lining the rig up under the spout from his house's drainpipe. A hole in the bottom of the can fastened with a smaller drainage pipe dripped clean water into a second, small container. He scrubbed the graffiti from his walls – it seemed to be a simple ink of vinegar and berries and came off slowly but surely. He boarded up some of his broken windows and nailed clear hard plastic over the others. Eventually the house was a reflection of the owner – not quite its former self, broken and reassembled in some places, but still standing. When Sean looked at it, he couldn't help but think of the jilted spouse in prison, her broken hands growing mostly back together. She'd lose some functionality in them, and she would develop arthritis, but she could still open and close a fist.

* * *

It was almost alright. It was almost enough. It was almost a full life. Mayor Staps's promise that the city governments would remember Sean's sacrifice proved to be little more than empty words. Mayor Davis turned him away and his letters to the other officials were never answered. Sean's surprise and anger on this matter faded to complacence and acceptance.

Sean worked several part-time jobs to maintain him in Triton's barter economy, much as he had in his youth. He kept his head down, still fearing his own ambitions. Nobody asked him much about his past, and he became friends with some of the younger people from his work who were too young to remember Moscow. Some of the older residents of his neighborhood nudged each other and nodded their heads towards Sean when he passed, but he pretended not to notice. As long as they kept it to themselves and let him move on, they could think what they wanted. He borrowed books from the library to keep himself occupied. A year after rejoining society, he was even asked to come out to eat with the boys after work. They sat around a small fire in the marketplace eating their dinners and drinking the fermented cider from the apples grown in a container in a co-worker's backyard. Sean had a pleasant buzz going and the group shared plenty of good laughs about their boss, local girls, one another's tolerance levels of the fermented fruit ciders concocted on Triton and so on. Suddenly a voice pierced their personal space.

"Holy shit."

Sean and his co-workers turned to see the voice's source. A man with his arm around a young woman's waist had stopped in his tracks and was staring directly at Sean.

"I spend 18 months off-Triton for business and I get back and I've got to see *this* son of a bitch walking the streets again?"

Sean's expression darkened. His colleagues stood up and began to defend him, but he knew what was coming.

"Watch what you say about Sean, asshole; he's our friend."

The man laughed in disbelief. "This man is your friend? Sure he is, until he decides he's all too happy to take your money and leave you for dead in the wasteland."

The young men looked to one another and to Sean with uncertainty. Sean stared into the fire, his eyes glazing over in the same way they had in the courtroom 16 years before.

"What the Hell are you talking about?"

"Shit boys; don't you know who this is? Ain't you never heard of the Moscow Tower incident back in 82? Why the Hell you think everyone gets so goddamn quiet every time we pass that cluster of buildings in downtown Moscow?" His eyes fixed on Sean for the rest of his speech, slowly walking towards him and leaving his girlfriend where she was. "Some 30-odd people paid up for a vacation – three weeks relaxing in the Russian summer breeze on the roof of OKO South Tower – and when Triton dropped them off, them Russian birds fought 'em for their food. Ended up shittin' some killer disease all over these folks who died coughing up blood all over each other. The damn vultures were picking 'em clean by the time Proteus came back around to pick 'em up, all because the fella who came up with the plan didn't bother to look into the local wildlife!"

One of Sean's co-workers, Freddie Jarvis, who hadn't said a word all this time, knit his brow. "I…I remember hearing about that. My old man said they locked somebody up under the city for that and he'd been hanging there ever since."

The man concluded. "And who do you think it was sold them 30 people their deaths? Who was it who piled a skyscraper with bird shit and half-eaten corpses so they called him the 'Topper'?"

Freddie turned to Sean. "Topper? Mr. Bellamy, he's got you mixed up with someone else doesn't he?"

Sean stood slowly. He tossed the rest of his meal in the fire and took one long look at each of his co-workers, knowing this was the last time they'd see him as a friend. Silence hung in the air like a dead man swinging from a rope; the fire crackled to remind the boys it was still there. Finally Sean locked eyes with his accuser. "They were 27, not 30." The atmosphere around the fire shifted dramatically. Topper continued. "And there are no vultures in Moscow. They were sparrowhawks. And I...I served my time."

"They should've thrown your ass off this city, Topper," the man taunted. A long moment passed before his girlfriend pulled him away and they continued walking. The boys stared at the ex-con, whose eyes drifted to the floor.

"How...could you do that?"

"Jesus Christ; I thought you were my friend, man."

"Wasn't one of them a baby or something? What the Hell kind of man could..."

Topper turned away from them and walked home as their voices stiffened and grew angrier. He found his front door by muscle memory alone; his vision was clouded with tears. For the first time in over a decade, he felt a weight press down on his shoulders that led to a restless sleep.

His co-workers told everyone, as the young are prone to do. Memories resurfaced, wounds were re-opened and Topper became a pariah. He fumed, but to keep himself fed he held his head up and took it all in stride – the name-calling, the threats, the garbage thrown at him. They taunted him with the nickname he'd hoped died off with his trial. Work was harder to come by, but he managed. Soon his anger subsided into something quieter and duller within him. The streets looked a little narrower and darker, but he started to seem resigned, almost indifferent. He visited Allison at the gardens a second time, and she consoled him as best she could.

"You paid what you owed, Sean," she said. It was nice just to hear his name; they both knew she was the only one he could count on for that. "15 years for those talking heads in city hall. But people are always looking for someone to hate. To them, it's not about what you do or don't deserve. They just want – "

Topper interrupted her. "To feel better. Yeah. Someone told me that once. Look, thanks Allison. I'm…I'm headed out now."

She mustered up the most optimistic face she could. "Take care now."

Some mornings Topper struggled to get out of bed. It seemed like the world outside was poised and ready just waiting for him to step out onto the street so it could start picking away at him one stranger at a time. He procrastinated and invented excuses to stay indoors. He knew he could go see Allison again but couldn't convince himself to make the trip, short as it was. When he woke up for the day he'd look out his window with dread or stare at his breakfast in a daze for an hour. Every day at work he looked at the floor, unable to look anyone in the eye. Some people threw their waste buckets at him. "How you like a taste of your own medicine, motherfucker?" He could feel everyone glaring at him and he did his best to wait it out and hope it would all die down again, or that he could get used to it.

In late July, 99 P.A., Topper walked to the gardens to visit Allison Mackey for the third time. He'd been living the last several months as though everything was fine, almost to the point of seeming sedated. To his acquaintances, it seemed he'd accepted their name-calling as a gentle ribbing, no matter how hatefully they addressed him. He didn't seem to notice when they spit on him as he walked, or flicked their still-flaming cigarette butts at him. Every day promised a regular schedule of ridicule and isolation.

Topper brought Allison a quinoa-based risotto he'd managed to put together at home as a token of appreciation for her advice. The gardens were a quaint, quiet place and in his increasing ambivalence towards himself, they started to look like sanctuary. He'd hoped they could sit and eat together. He knocked on the gardens' front door and Allison opened it with her usual smile.

"Hey, Top –" She clapped a hand over her mouth. "Oh Sean; I'm so sorry! I know how you hate that name…"

She was relieved that he was so nonchalant about it. "It's okay," he said, only wincing a little. "I've gotten pretty used to it."

"Well would you like to come in?"

"Oh, no thank you," he said. "I was just…I was just dropping off this dinner I made for you. When I first came back you helped me out so much and cooked for me; I just wanted to return the favor."

Allison recovered quickly, pouring extra sugar on her voice. "Well thank you so much! You know you didn't have to do that for me!"

"It's alright; it's not a problem at all."

"Wouldn't you like to come in and eat with me?"

"No thanks; I just ate," he lied. "I appreciate the offer though."

"Are you sure?"

"Yeah. Yeah; I'm fine."

She relented, afraid of pushing him too hard even as he politely backed off her porch. "Well okay. Thank you so much for the dinner; if you come by tomorrow I'll make us something Italian. Sound good?"

"It's a date," he said with a smile. She watched him leave. He seemed fine. She was looking forward to their dinner together the next evening. Allison felt bad for Topper; she'd seen how the people in the neighborhood treated him and she tried to convince them to stop, to no avail.

Topper's smile faded as he walked down the street towards his house. He crossed paths with the septic manager, an elderly fellow named Gary Royce, carrying his wheelbarrow of human waste down to Triton's rear end. Topper remembered the luck he'd felt not to have that job back on Proteus. Here, he pitied the man. The septic manager nodded at Topper with a smile.

"Evening," he said.

"Good evening," Topper said.

After a brief conversation about the thankless nature of Royce's job, which Topper said he could relate to through his own labors, Topper offered to carry the barrow the rest of the way down Triton's back and drop its cargo while the old man headed up to his next stop and took a rest. Topper would then return the barrow to him further up the road. The man thanked him profusely, agreed, shook his hand and went on his way with a spring in his step. Topper proceeded slowly so as not to tip its foul contents.

The next morning, the septic manager reported to the authorities that he hadn't seen his wheelbarrow or Topper since that moment. He accompanied them to Topper's house, agreeing to stay on the scene for questioning in order to clear up the matter. Detective Leon Adler broke the front door in and entered the house. Even at the front door the odor was an angry wife's slap in the face. Adler entered slowly, carefully, finally searching the bathroom. He knelt by Topper's bathtub with a rag held up to his face. Adler's low, gravelly voice cursed the visage before him. "Dammit Bellamy," he said. "I thought you were going to be alright."

The septic manager spoke up over the clamor of the growing crowd outside. "Did you know this man?"

Adler nodded. "He was my first case. I was learning the business from my predecessor and we were assigned to the Moscow Tower incident. I was just a boy." Detective Adler remembered interrupting Dr. Iweala and the scolding he got afterwards. He remembered how shaken he was by his mentor's damning testimony against Sean Bellamy in court and the anticlimax of hearing Bellamy was imprisoned. Adler looked over the contents of the bathroom and pieced the scene back together.

Judging by the empty wheelbarrow on the floor next to the body, it looked as though Topper had returned to the house straight from meeting with Royce. He had pushed the wheelbarrow into his bathroom, rounding the corner carefully, where he left it and went to the kitchen. He took a paring knife – which now lay on the floor, caked with crusted bloodstains – from a drawer and returned to his bathroom.

After Topper had returned to his bathroom with the paring knife, he must have removed his clothing and sat in his empty bathtub, resting the knife on the sink within arm's reach, and leaned forward to grab the wheelbarrow. It would've been heavy, so with both arms he'd upended it into the tub, spilling its contents around him, filling the bathtub up to his waist.

The smell had made Topper gag; he dropped the barrow and it fell to the ground with a clang as he threw up onto the excrement and on himself. He held the paring knife in one hand, desperately, and let himself out through his veins. Topper joined the victims of the Moscow Tower incident in the same state as they left this world – covered in other creatures' defecation and his own blood and sick.

"Poor Topper," Royce said.

"The man is dead; you want to call him by his real name?"

"No," Royce replied. "Sean Bellamy died somewhere along the way between the OKO South Tower 17 years ago and the humiliation those people outside have been giving him since his release."

Adler knew he was right, but he'd never admit it. Sean Bellamy was long gone. All that was left in this body was Topper – and had been for some time. As the life drained from his eyes, he'd raised his wrist and rubbed a final marking of atonement on the wall in his blood. Adler looked at it and shook his head.

28.

A Murder on the Theriopolis

the body

"Damn."

Dawn had broken over an hour ago and for the second time in a week, Leon Adler stood over a dead body. He didn't like it. There were under five thousand people living on the theriopolis on Triton and every life was, generally speaking, considered of great value. There were rare exceptions of course. Most recently Sean Bellamy's peers ridiculed and bullied him to suicide. But when Sean let himself out through his wrists, Leon had hoped that it would be the last unnatural death he'd see for some time. This morning those hopes proved to be in vain.

Public fatalities – and in a town this small, they all became public – lowered morale. Everyone seemed to know everyone, so the grief that came from loss rippled throughout the community. People questioned their own mortality, and by extension, their own purpose. Just a few days ago, as word of Sean's suicide spread, his same tormentors and self-appointed judges who had pushed him over the edge spoke in solemn tones, walked more softly and hugged their kids more tightly when they left for work in the morning. The same people who had thrown their garbage at him were hit with the

61

ironic surprise and remorse a child feels after squashing a bug. With this second death following so quickly, Leon knew the city had a difficult end of the summer ahead. He worried that the Wandering City Blues would cast a dark shadow over the city.

Leon was 5′9″. His raven black hair was parted on the right and its color matched the stubble on the lower half of his face. He was tan, and lean, spending much of his day walking the streets. His eyes were hazel, and under them were bags. He'd slept decently, but he was 35, and given the average life expectancy topside, that meant he was now middle-aged.

He needed a smoke. He looked around for the nearest street lamp and told the patrolman on duty not to let anyone near the body. He crossed to the lamp, its flames licking upwards at the cable that suspended the small fire in the air, and pulled out his cigarette case. The case was his grandmother's but had originally come from the surface. It was silver with an intricate Victorian pattern on the front. Leon unfastened its clasp as he neared the street lamp and opened the case, removing one rolled cigarette and shutting it again. He dropped the case back into his pants pocket and leaned into the handful of fire, lighting one end of the smoke as he inhaled the other. When he was confident it was lit, the orange glow pointing out at the city, he made his way back to the crime scene.

Tobacco was a thing of the past. Leon had developed a habit of trying to imagine what it tasted like, how different it would feel in his lungs when he inhaled, but he knew it was a futile effort. The problem with growing tobacco was that it took so much from the soil and gave so little in return, farmers had to rotate their crops and grow it in different places every year. Back on the surface there was plenty of land to cycle tobacco in and out, but there was so very little on each colossus it became an immediate impossibility. Grudgingly, the first generation gave it up in favor of herbs that grew more easily in the hydroponic and aeroponic gardens which adorned every house on nearly every titan above the fog. It led to lucrative small businesses around the globe – kids offering a variety of blends and flavors, trading with one another wholesale. Leon's brand was a mixture of damiana, originally brought up from Mexico; kanna, from South Africa; and a pinch of wild lettuce, which left him with a pleasant buzz for a short period after he smoked. Pouches of herbs sold inexpensively, but rolled cigarettes held considerably more value. They were bound in a homemade paper made of plant fibers that had been ground and molded into a pulp via a deckle. The deckle had been fished decades ago by a prisoner looking to reduce his sentence. The city allotted Leon free paper for his files and reports, but it was scarce enough that even had he possessed the skill to roll his own cigarettes, Mayor Davis would notice the uptick in his material requests. So he frequented the vendors. Sometimes Leon looked the other way on the local smoke shop's unregistered trades, sometimes he bartered like everyone else.

Leon squatted by the body despite the warmth of the morning. It was Allison Mackey, the municipal gardener and horticulturist. She had been murdered less than 100 feet from the public garden and seed shop where she worked. She lay on her stomach, her head turned to her right. The vacant stare in her open eyes was the kind reserved for the gaze of a being with no more thoughts, no more wonder, no more life. A substantial amount of blood had pooled and dried on the pavement around Allison's head and neck. There were also minor injuries around her body including a series of oblong, dark red marks – likely from manual strangulation – around her throat and a bloodstain on her right arm where the arm met the shoulder. Her clothes were dirty and slightly torn. A shadow grew over Leon's shoulder and overtook him and the body in the early morning sun.

"What are we looking at, Detective?"

It was Anthony Nash, the same young patrolman who had found the body and protected it from tampering when Leon had walked off a moment ago. Volunteer patrolmen were the only around-the-clock law enforcement the city had, but they prided themselves on adhering to the code of conduct and ethics upheld by the best police and military in Europe and the Americas, Pre-Ascension. Leon pointed at Allison's head with two fingers, his cigarette held between them.

"Cause of death looks like some kind of trauma to her head," Leon replied, "although that roughness on the neck looks like strangulation." He began to think out loud. "There isn't enough blood loss anywhere else on her body besides what's pooled around her left temple there. The scuffs and cuts on her forearms and knees suggest a struggle. It was probably on the ground – see how this scrape on her elbow has a pebble and some dirt embedded in one end? She must've skinned her arm, and maybe crawled a bit before she picked up her harp and halo."

Nash bristled. He didn't consider himself overly squeamish, generally speaking. Even still, the thought of a foreign object – no matter how small – being stuck in a wound gave him the willies. He sought to change the subject.

"Allison was the only person close to Topper since he –"

Leon turned and looked sharply at Nash. "Sean, son. He paid what he owed. You call him Sean Bellamy."

"Sorry sir. Allison was the only one who seemed to care for…Sean…during his final days. She was pretty vocal about people giving him such Hell. You think this has anything to do with that? Maybe she pissed off the wrong guy, or somebody figured 'guilt by association' or something?"

Leon turned back to the body and looked it over again while he smoked. "Hm."

Leon had no reason to believe Mackey's death had anything to do with Sean's, but it was a coincidence he didn't want to rule out – and he didn't want to discourage Mr. Nash from noting and analyzing crime scene details. The last thing Triton's law enforcement needed was another thoughtless soldier, and Nash was a clever cop, if a bit naïve. In the last couple years, the two men had developed a good working relationship and Leon thought of him as a sort of protégé.

A long silence followed while Leon studied the body.

"Nash."

"Yes sir?"

"If you were going to bump off Allison Mackey…besides the company she kept, as you suggested…what would be your reason?"

Nash thought for a long moment while the gathered crowd spoke in whispers and excited gossip behind him.

Finally he resigned. "I can't think of a single reason. None whatsoever."

Leon stood and faced him. "And that's the kicker. Now, why would you *not* want to kill Allison Mackey?"

"Well Hell, common decency for one."

"Besides that, Anthony. Think a bit more selfishly, go on."

Nash took off his cap and ran his hand through his hair. "Well, this city needs Allison. I don't imagine anyone could run the public gardens as well as she can, keeping all them plants and seed supplies and whatnot in check."

"Exactly. So what happens if she dies?"

"I suppose we *could* figure the gardens out, with that apprentice of hers, Christina Flint? But we'll at least lose some crops this year. That'll make it a little harder on everyone to get through the winter."

"It would. So who the Hell would put their own meal ticket at risk?"

Neither man had an answer for that. It didn't make sense, but Nash spoke first.

"Maybe someone who didn't know who she was?"

"Do you know a single soul who hasn't ankled it to that building and gotten a bit of something, some extra food or goods over the years? What man, woman or child in the city doesn't know Allison Mackey?"

They fell silent again. The doctor's intern, Breanne Dibble, rounded the corner from the nearest building and approached the men quickly. Ordinarily at this time she'd be at the clinic three blocks over; Leon and Nash realized simultaneously when they saw the stretcher under her arm that she must've heard about Allison and had come to move the body to the clinic for an examination. Breanne set the stretcher down and gave Allison a precursory glance.

"Cause of death?"

Leon didn't speak. He let Nash take the lead.

"Either this trauma to the head that caused the blood loss killed her or she was strangled with something." Breanne knelt down next to Allison and spread her fingers in line with the four marks on Allison's neck, laying them over them but being careful not to actually touch the victim.

"Yeah. Four oblong ligature marks; I'd be surprised if this strangulation came from anything but our killer's hand. And it's a large hand, by the looks of it. You need anything else from her, Detective?"

"No. She's all yours."

Breanne directed Nash and the two of them gently rolled Allison over onto her back. Nash took one look at her face and ran to the nearest bushes. His breakfast fought for air – and won. Leon and Breanne grimaced at the body but didn't look away.

Little more evidence came from their quick observation of Allison. The trauma on her face appeared to be caused by several direct blows to her left temple from the concrete. It was the source of the blood loss at least. The silver lining to this cloud, if there were one, was that the actual confrontation between Allison and her assailant had been hurried. Rushed crimes meant sloppiness. Sloppiness meant mistakes. Mistakes meant evidence. Evidence led to arrests.

Nash sauntered back to the crime scene. He was more embarrassed than disturbed. Leon offered him his handkerchief. When he had recovered, he and Breanne moved to load the body onto the stretcher. Leon interrupted them.

"Nash."

"Detective?"

"What did we learn about our innocent dead today?"

Nash lowered his eyes. "They're paid up with The House – I mean, His House."

"That's right. Give Allison Mackey's body the courtesy you forgot to give Sean Bellamy's name, you hear me?"

"Okay."

"Breanne?"

"I know. Top priority. I'll do the autopsy and let you know what I find."

"You don't want Doc Frazier to take a slant at it?"

"Sheila Gibbons just went into labor; he'll be tied up with her for the day."

"Alright. Send him my best if he stops by for anything and give my congratulations to the new mother. I'll check in with you to follow up around midday."

"Make it late afternoon; I've got other appointments to see to if Doc Frazier's out of commission."

"Can't they wait? I've got a murder here."

Breanne raised an eyebrow. "There are other human beings living on this leviathan besides you and your criminals, Detective. Late afternoon, and you're lucky it's not tomorrow."

Leon put his hands out in surrender, apologized and let it go. It seemed to be getting warmer by the minute. If it continued, by lunch it would be hotter than Hell's office on the sun. He didn't envy Nash and Breanne carrying a body halfway across town.

Breanne and Nash finally loaded Allison onto the stretcher and bore her away to the clinic. As they were leaving, Leon became frustrated with the crowd of gawkers and he loudly – maybe a bit too loudly – ordered them to move along. They dispersed, though not without looking back over their shoulders at what was left of the grisly scene or walking slowly by the stretcher. It gave Leon an idea he should've had 10 minutes earlier, an idea that hit him like a ton of bricks. He called back towards the stretcher.

"Nash?"

"Yes sir?"

"Who actually found the body?"

* * *

Christina Flint's thin face was the kind of red you only saw on drunks and at funerals. Her eyes were bloodshot and her blond hair, pulled back in a ponytail, stuck out like a sore thumb in contrast to her ruddy complexion. She was a young woman of 20 and lived with her parents while she apprenticed at the gardens. Her mother sat with her, her hand on Christina's back, rubbing softly. Leon and her father leaned on walls at opposite ends of the room – Leon in front of Christina and her mother, the father behind them. Judging by her despondent, empty mood, Leon guessed she'd just gotten over a fit of tears that had lasted a good portion of the morning. He knew he had to choose his words carefully.

"Now listen, Christina; I know you've been through a lot this morning and I hate to trouble you further. But if I'm gonna catch the mug who did this I need every bit of information I can get my hands on – for Allison's sake, you see."

"Honey, you don't have to do this right now," Mrs. Flint said.

"It's okay mom," Christina replied. "I owe it to Allison if nothing else. She was a real friend to me, ever since I was a little girl. She told me just a few weeks ago that I wasn't too far from taking over the gardens."

She turned to Leon but he knew she was speaking just as much to her parents as she was to him. Maybe to feel safer. "Allison has been my mentor for almost five years. I got to speaking with her one day after school when dad asked me to go to the gardens for some extra coconut, since some of ours came in so poorly. Suddenly it was almost dark out and I knew I was in for it." She laughed a bit. "I found myself spending more time with her than I did most girls my own age and I'd help out with simple tasks around the building – refilling the spray bottles, counting inventory. In a few months I fell in love with the job and everyone noticed but me. Finally my parents and I went to the gardens and asked Allison to interview me to see if I was right for the job. And Allison said – "

Christina got choked up. Her nostrils flared a bit and she fought back a new wave of tears. Again her mother protested.

"Baby…"

"Allison looked at me with a smile and asked why she'd have to interview someone who'd already accumulated over 100 hours of training.

"And that was that. We went to City Hall and filed the paperwork the next day. She's been one of my best friends ever since. I started full-time when I finished school. That was three years ago."

Leon waited patiently. He'd been at this long enough to know witnesses started with relationship histories, remembering the best times to prepare themselves to get into the worst. On cue, Christina's face darkened. Her eyes glazed a bit and she looked off to the side.

"Dawn woke me this morning, the sunlight in my face like always. I washed myself and dressed and walked to the gardens like I have most days the last five years. And when I got there she was dead. She was just…dead. Just gone."

"Christina, did you see anything or anybody peculiar on your way to work or at the scene of the crime?"

Christina seemed a bit flustered, trying to no avail to jog her memory. "I…I don't think so…"

"Did you try to move her?"

Silence.

"Christina, if you moved Ms. Mackey, it's okay. You're not in trouble, now. I just need to know so I can take it into account when Breanne and I – "

"Breanne Dibble? The doctor's apprentice?" Christina asked.

"Yeah."

Christina nodded. "She's a good person. She'll take good care of Allison; I know it."

Leon and Christina's father exchanged glances. The father raised one hand, palm out at the detective, but Leon continued despite him.

"That's right. Breanne and I have a long history working together. Now there's nobody I'd trust more than her to take care of your friend, and I'll tell the world. She'll be gentle as a mother with a newborn babe helping lay her to rest."

"No."

"No?"

"I didn't move her. When I saw her, I screamed and ran and found Anthony – I mean Mr. Nash. I wanted to see her face but I couldn't…I couldn't bring myself to…oh God, what if I could've saved her somehow?"

Everything after that happened at extraordinary speed. Even as Leon assured her there was nothing she could have done for her friend and employer, Christina broke down into hysterics and her mother comforted her. Her father came around to Leon. "This interview is over, goddammit!" he shouted. More obscenities came as he ushered Leon out the door, but Leon resisted long enough to yell to Christina to contact him if she remembered seeing anything strange, that it was the best possible way to stop Allison's killer. He barely had the words out of his mouth before the door slammed in his face. Through the front door he saw her father join the women on their couch comforting his daughter.

Leon cursed himself – he hated upsetting witnesses and potentially leaving information on the table. At the same time, he hadn't learned everything about the job from his own predecessor. Christina Flint reminded him of himself several years ago. His own mentor was a showboat and a drunk. One night in the middle of a bender fueled by free drinks, he stumbled off the edge of Triton while relieving himself over the side of a lookout point near the bar. Half-trained and still a teenager, Leon Adler found himself the lead law enforcement in the city. He was no prodigy, either – that much responsibility thrust upon him at once crippled him for several years as he learned through trial and error how to enforce the law independently. Over the years and with the help of the older patrolmen and his mentor's colleagues, he figured it out. He didn't envy the bumpy road ahead of Christina. Nash was right when he said they could lose crops on a large scale.

Without any leads to follow, Leon wasted the morning fruitlessly chasing down potential witnesses until lunchtime and then made his way to the city square. He ate half a baked potato and some mushroom caps stuffed with artichoke and when he was done he kept beating the street. As he walked through the city he thought about the case. The only conclusion he could draw was that Allison had seen something she wasn't supposed to see. But with no other crimes reported – not a theft or a burglary or an assault – there was nowhere to go with it. He became frustrated and embarrassed that he'd made no progress all day. The intense heat bothered him; he was sure the residents he passed knew he hadn't made any progress. He even felt a warm tickling on his ears and the back of his neck. Part of it was guilt. He hated it any time they had to roll the dice on an autopsy in hopes of getting a lead. It wasn't fair to Doc Frazier and Breanne to have so much riding on them. Another part was feeling the citizens of Triton looking at him, watching him as he pointlessly patrolled the town for clues. Or was someone else watching him? Maybe the killer himself? Had Leon passed Allison's murderer in the streets today? If so, how many times? He tried to shake it off. He knew no good came from this particular kind of conjecture. As much as he disliked it, Leon knew he had to wait for the autopsy. He looked at the roof of the clinic, eyeing its solar paneling with a hint of jealousy.

The afternoon crawled by. Leon passed the medical clinic a half dozen times. The regular thud of Triton's feet so far below him was like a clock ticking out every moment. It fed his impatience. *After almost 100 years up here, how much do we really know about these creatures?* he thought. *We scrambled on up and built homes on them to escape the fog but what can we really say for certain?*

Thud.

There are 13 of them – or at least there were at Ascension. Two dead, we've seen, another two AWOL for years. They came from the sea along with the fog. They don't seem to age, eat, drink, sleep or knock boots.

Thud.

They just beat the street on these same damn routes they developed independently – like routines formed by their habits. They won't deviate from those migration patterns either, even though they seem to like one another. Whatever blood flows through those mammoth veins of theirs glows and pulsates a pale blue whenever they cross paths. On the other hand, they don't seem to care much about us one way or the other. Except Psamanthe.

He was still at least an hour early for Breanne's autopsy results but he couldn't bring himself to wait any longer. He sat in a chair in the waiting room and impatiently, but quietly, tapped both his feet on the floor. He took off his hat and set it on a side table next to him. The crisp breeze of the air conditioning soothed his discomfort and he found himself swimming in memories of his childhood.

As a boy, he ran outside and played with the other kids until nearly suffering from heat exhaustion. He returned home, nearly collapsing onto the sofa next to his mother while his father prepared dinner.

"Mama, why's it so hot in here?"

"Because it's hot outside, sweetie."

"Oh. But why can't it be cold like at Doctor Frazier's?" Leon continued catching his breath, the sweat cooling his forehead.

"Well sweetie, a long time ago before you were born, there used to be a way to catch the sunlight and use it to power machines that played music and turned lights on inside the house and –"

"-and kept the air cold?"

"Yes, baby, some machines kept the air cold when it was hot outside. Then, one night when I was still growing in Grandma's tummy, some bad men had come to Triton and many of the other giants that people live on, and they waited until everyone was asleep and they broke all the solar panels that –"

"What's a solar panel?"

"It looked like a flat board or door and it was the device that caught the sun's energy and made all the machines work. So now the air won't be cold when we want it to."

"They should not have done that; it was mean."

Leon's mother stroked his hair and blew gently onto his face, the redness in his cheeks fading. "Yes it was, honey."

"So they missed the sun catcher at Doctor Frazier's?"

"Well, no; he got a new one just like the doctor's offices in the other towns."

"How?"

Leon's mother chose her words carefully. He was too young to understand reduced prison sentences and fishing and Red Lung, regardless of what rumors or off-handed comments he'd heard from his friends or their parents, respectively.

"There was just one time when you were a tiny baby, when someone was able to get some more solar panels from down on the ground. They had to try a lot of times but they found several boxes of them."

"Will they find more so we can make the air cold again?"

"I don't think so, Leon. Now why don't you get washed up for dinner? The water will feel nice and help you cool down – you're old enough to fetch it from outside now."

"But Mommy, why did the bad men break all the sun catchers?"

His mother and father exchanged glances. His mother took a deep breath and began speaking but Leon's father interrupted her.

"Because they were crazy people."

"Why were they crazy, daddy?"

"They're crazy because they're from Sao, and everyone from Sao is crazy."

"Why?"

His father paused. "Your mother told you to wash up. Go do it."

The sound of a door opening jolted Leon back to the present. Eventually Breanne exited the adjacent check-up room, preceded by a teenage patient nursing what looked like a sprained wrist.

"You rest that hand, Billy, and you'll be off the bench in no time."

The boy thanked her and left. She gestured towards the door he'd just closed.

"Street hockey. Come on back, Detective. I've undressed her and put her into cold storage; let me brief you on her clothing before we fully perform the external examination."

Leon obediently followed Breanne through the check-up room to the door on the other side as the last of his childhood memory played out. That night he told his mother he wanted to stop bad men from taking things when he grew up. He heard much later about the immediate release of the prisoner who fished for the solar panels and the uproar when the city councils all decided to distribute the panels to the clinics or hospitals on every colossus. Power was restored to the medical facilities on the titans and mankind got back a glimpse of modern life before Ascension.

Breanne and Leon entered the morgue, which wasn't much larger than the living room of the houses on Triton. The white walls were offset by the cold, impersonal steel cabinet of drawers and doors that made up the morgue's freezers. Breanne opened the small door to one of the cold chambers and frozen air billowed out, a quick fog escaping around the corpse's feet. She pulled the drawer out and together they lifted the body, now wearing nothing besides a sheet, onto the examination table. Leon knew that Sean Bellamy was still in another of the cold storage drawers, awaiting a funeral.

Breanne took her notepad – one of the few in town, also fished from the surface – and brought Leon up to speed. He knew from experience she spoke in long sentences and flipped from personal phrases like "her" and "she" to impersonal ones like "the body." It was Breanne's way of wrestling with the definitive end of life and what remained here after the fact as well as the struggle of staying clinical and detached versus personable and caring when it came to her patients.

"Patient is Allison Mackey, date of birth January 14th, 50 P.A., time of death approximated by rigor mortis after midnight, July 28th, 99 P.A. Items found on the body include one necklace of hemp rope fastened to a moonstone gem, likely revering the goddess Hecate, and one ring of keys, presumably Allison's own, in the left front pocket of the pants. Damage on the clothes includes scuff marks and some tearing on the knees of her pants as well as dirt and minor scuffing on the shins, suggesting she was crawling at some point pre-mortem. This theory *appears* to be corroborated by similar disturbance to the palms of the victim's hands, though of course no formal external examination has been performed yet."

"I know. I'm sorry I'm early."

"It's fine. One more thing before we confirm cause of death and perform an external examination: do you remember the odd presence of blood on the right shoulder area of her shirt?"

"Yeah. It looked like she'd fallen and injured it during the attack, maybe?"

"I don't think so," Breanne replied. "I've never seen a fall do *this* to someone."

Breanne pulled the sheet down to Allison's waist and Leon instinctively looked at her shoulder.

"Oh my God," he muttered.

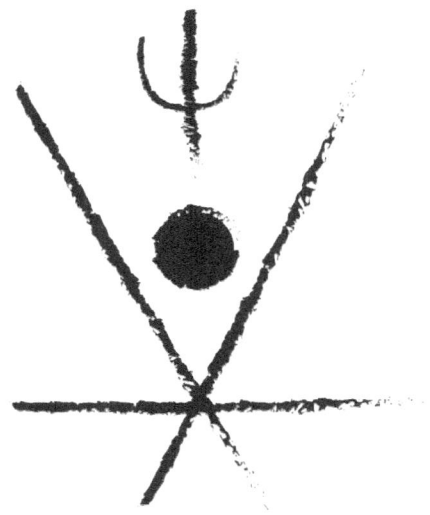

The symbol was eight inches from top to bottom, reaching from the top of Allison's shoulder nearly to her elbow. It was simple, tribal in nature – hardly more than three stick shapes and two basic characters. At its base, it resembled a simple horizontal line crossed at its center by a large X. However, above the intersection, the X's top stretched further than its bottom. A carved-out circle seemed to be cradled by the top of the crude asterisk-like shape. Finally, crowning the disturbing visage was a character that seemed to resemble the sharp end of a pitchfork – a U-like shape, halved by a vertical line that extended slightly downward past the U itself.

It was clear. Deliberate. Methodical. And oddly enough, it was hard to stop looking at – almost hypnotizing. Despite how grisly it was, Leon had to consciously make himself turn away from it so he could continue his work alongside Breanne's investigation. Even as she performed the remainder of the autopsy, he found himself looking again and again at the symbol on Allison's right arm.

An hour later, Leon and Breanne compared notes to determine a definitive cause of death, alternating between looking at their own notepads, each other's notepads, each other and back. During their quick altercation, the killer had strangled Allison, believing her dead, but she was merely unconscious. She came to, and he finished the job by repeatedly slamming her head into the pavement. Little more than that made sense.

"Do you think we're looking at a serial killer?" Breanne asked.

"Why do you ask?" Leon replied.

"The carving on the victim's arm and the lack of a clear motive are consistent with –"

"That's true, but historically, serial killers bring a murder weapon with them."

80

Breanne wasn't ready to let the idea go so flippantly.

"What about a serial strangler?"

Leon looked at Allison's neck and weighed the possibility in his head. He offered a small sound from his throat, a one-note hum. "I don't think so."

Breanne rolled her eyes.

"This marking on her arm," Leon said, "is there a way to tell if it was made before or after she bought the farm?"

Now it was Breanne's turn to lead. She walked around the examination table and looked more closely at the wound. She was curious to see where Leon's head was at, though.

"What's *your* theory?" she asked.

"Maybe he strangled her and went to work on her shoulder, thinking her dead, and that woke her up."

Breanne felt no guilt in the enjoyment she had shooting down Leon's theory.

"No," she said. "That's not a possibility."

"Why not?"

"Look more closely at the individual cuts themselves," she said, moving aside so he could move up to the area of interest.

"I see 'em. So what?"

"No inflammation," she said. "While you're still alive, cuts and scrapes put you at risk of infection. Your body responds by flooding the area with white blood cells to defend against illness – hence the swelling near a regular cut."

"And?"

"No inflammation means no surge of white blood cells. No surge of white blood cells means no signal from the brain to send them there. No signal from the brain means no brain activity whatsoever. These cuts were made post-mortem."

Leon and Breanne stood.

"This is a warning," Leon said.

"Or a dare."

There was a distant knock on a door. A young woman's voiced called from the waiting area.

"Hello?"

The detective and the doctor's intern quickly covered the body back up with the sheet, lest exaggerated details of its state – or private evidence – make its way around the gossip circles of the colossus.

"Hello? Detective Adler?"

They awkwardly made their way to the front of the clinic, making sure to close each door behind them as they passed through. Leon even set his notes on the bed in the check-up room to avoid anyone seeing them; Breanne had left hers in the morgue. Christina Flint arched her neck around the corner in the waiting area towards another adjacent room full of file cabinets, checking to see if Leon or Breanne were looking at any patients' medical records for the case. She heard them approach and looked around to meet their gaze.

"Christina?"

"Hi Detective. I'm sorry about earlier, when I…"

"Don't worry about it," he replied. "You were probably still in shock. How'd you know I was here, though?"

"I was looking for you and I ran into Patrolman Nash and he said you'd probably be…examining Allison."

Breanne stepped forward. "Ms. Flint, I don't think it's a good idea for you to –"

Christina realized what she was about to say and interrupted her. "Oh no! No; I'm not here to watch that. I couldn't bear it. I actually snuck out of the house to tell you that I remembered something, Detective Adler."

Leon's face perked up. "You did? Wait, first – you 'snuck out?'"

Christina wavered. "Well, yeah...Daddy would be furious if he knew I was getting involved in this, but I feel like it's important to help out. For Allison."

"Okay," Leon replied. At the mention of her father, Leon remembered how this morning's interview had gone. He tried to keep it light, so as not to upset her again. "We won't tell if you won't." He smiled. "So what did you remember?"

"Well, I didn't think anything of it at the time, but when I left the house this morning for work at the gardens, there was like...*something* stuck in our front door."

"What was it?"

"It was a piece of paper with some kind of weird picture or something drawn on it?"

Dread blanketed the room. Leon's and Breanne's faces fell. They thought the same thing at the same time. Breanne walked briskly to the morgue for her notebook and pen.

"Do you think you could draw it for us?" Leon asked.

Christina was unsure of herself but she wanted so much to help. "I...can try."

Breanne returned. They stared at Christina while she drew. They knew what was coming and her every penstroke confirmed their suspicions by degrees.

She finished and held up the paper. Her drawing was a perfect match for the symbol carved into Allison's arm.

Leon rushed to gather his things, rapidly telling Breanne to put the body back into cold storage.

"Leon, where are you going?"

He was already halfway back from the check-up room with his pad and pen.

"Nash – and anyone else he can gather by sundown. We need at least two coppers to protect the Flints until I say otherwise. Christina – have Ms. Dibble escort you back home to your parents; the three of you are staying at Sean Bellamy's vacant house. You'll be safer there than at your own house." He grabbed his hat and put it on.

"But Detective, my parents will *kill me* if I'm involved in this and –"

He stopped and held her shoulders. "No, kid, they won't, but someone else is sure as Hell going to try to if you can't talk your parents into leaving. I'll send Nash and catch up with you soon. Did you talk to anyone else on the way here about that note on your door?"

"No, I…I didn't tell anyone."

"Are you sure? Not an old classmate, or your fella or any other lawman besides me?"

"I'm sure."

"Good. Good job kid. Aside from your parents, don't tell anybody about any of this." He flung the door open and started outside. Christina called out to him.

"Not even the other detective?"

Leon stopped in his tracks and spun around.

"*What* other detective?"

the illusion of levitation

Shadows grew long; time grew short. A gentle breeze blew in from the open window in the mayor's office and the rustling curtains were dancing ghosts, taunting Leon for his impatience. Triton's mayor, Greg Davis, was reading over Leon's case notes. Leon felt like a schoolboy sent to the principal's office. The mayor was furious that Leon had already found and identified a murder victim, handled the crime scene, interviewed a witness, conducted the autopsy and arranged a sting operation without keeping him in the loop. Mayor Davis didn't even know there had been a murder until someone approached him at a late lunch with questions, which he was in no position to answer. While Leon was debriefing his small posse of officers for tonight's lookout at the Flint place, the mayor burst into his office, practically knocking the door off its hinges in a fit of anger, and started reprimanding him. Davis said that Leon was to prepare a report to bring him up to speed in 30 minutes, heeding no protests from the detective that he needed to be on the scene with his men by nightfall. Leon hurriedly began to cough up all the info he had so he could skip the meeting but Davis was hell-bent on sitting with him one-on-one.

Leon wanted nothing more than to get up and walk out – he had no idea how long Mayor Davis would keep him, but Leon knew he should be the extra pair of eyes watching the streets for anything unusual tonight. He had a knack for it, which is how people ended up pursuing a lifelong career on the theriopolises. Express a genuine interest in something, show an affinity to it and there's your next 40 years. He'd seen it his whole life and it didn't end with him. Christina Flint had told him that very morning that she just sort of fell into working at the gardens. Nobody forced the kids into doing one thing or another, but playing to one's strengths was encouraged and eventually, everyone had to do *something* – another carryover from life on the surface. He supposed it was an attitude that reflected early 20th century conservative views – pull yourself up by your bootstraps, find a trade, take pride in your mastery of it, make a name for yourself and take care of your family. And it worked. Of course, it was as much a matter of necessity as it was personal pride, similar to The Great Depression in the United States so long ago. If someone failed to pull his or her own weight, there was the real possibility of starvation. Sadly, it kept families small on the beast-cities, and the limitations of surgical possibilities on the colossi cut life expectancies down to as short as they'd been in the early 1900s. However, this sense of immediacy and survival also brought everyone closer. Life was different, and harder, but neither unbearable nor pointless. This closeness meant every death had an impact on the community, which is what made the horticulturist's murder not only seem personal, but bizarrely counter-intuitive to the whole town.

Leon remembered he'd had the same thoughts this morning outside the gardens after they discovered the body. He had to stop thinking in circles or he'd never get any work done, but it was all he could do while the mayor read. Leon dared not interrupt the fuming city official. He dreaded the moment at which the conversation would turn to motive. It was clearly the least developed part of the case and he knew it wouldn't go unnoticed. They had cause of death, they knew there was no other murder weapon and they'd established opportunity and one signature piece of evidence – the insignia that made two appearances today – but no motive.

Leon carefully cast his glance around the room while he waited. The mayor's office was beautiful. A volume of books along the office's rear wall had stood the test of time over the last 100 years, as had much of the wood on the walls and furniture – save for two of the legs of the mayor's desk. These had succumbed to the weight of the desk's inventory over the years and snapped, now replaced by crudely-fashioned metal counterparts. The flag of the Alliance of Skyward Republics hung lifeless from a six-foot pole in the corner. The flag was of a grandiose design adorned with 13 uniform stars, each one a vibrant yellow, each one symbolizing a leviathan on which humanity now lived. They were connected via straight lines and formed a triskaidecagon. The background was blood orange on the bottom half and a pale blue on the top. All in all, it bore similarities to the flags of Lichtenstein and Micronesia. Like the mayor's desk, the flagpole itself had also taken plenty of wear over the years, though from exposure to the elements like the salty sea air. As far as Leon could tell, it would have to be replaced by the time Davis turned over his office to his successor.

Quiet as the room was, the mayor's voice almost startled Leon.

"Tell me about the crime itself."

"Mr. Mayor, Allison Mackey appears to have been murdered sometime after midnight last night. Judging by the external examination performed by Ms. Dibble, we've concluded that she was strangled and assumed dead. What the killer didn't plan on was that she woke back up, made a go of crawling away and was forced back down to the ground only to be...well, to have her nut cracked on the concrete. Blunt force trauma."

Davis sighed in disgust at the image, allowing himself a brief look outside at the reddening sky before returning to the business at hand. The sky changed in hue, slow as melting snow. It would soon match the fog, and for one terrifying minute that came almost every evening – a moment that had haunted Greg Davis since his childhood – the view would suggest that Triton was floating in an endless, motionless globe of orange. *It wouldn't be so bad if it weren't so goddamn quiet,* he thought. This singular moment of every early evening had been, and would always be, a source of incredible anxiety for the mayor. It was forever associated with his grandmother, a broken-down old drunk who told the children that the whole lot of Triton had died and were rotting in Hell but were too stupid to know it. He'd spent his life convincing himself otherwise, unable to reconcile his years of communal interaction with her vile assessment of the human race. *But this type of chaos always lends the old bitch credence, doesn't it?* He looked back at Leon and tried to forget about Purgatory.

"What does it mean, this carving? It doesn't look like one man's calling card."

Leon hesitated. "Mr. Mayor, it's still pretty early to say –"

"You don't know what it is, do you?"

"…No sir."

"Okay. And this case is related to this, what, this spy operation you have set up tonight?"

"Yes sir. Patrolmen Nash, Chopra, Eriksson and I are casing the Flint residence at a safe distance to see what turns up. We also have some extra muscle around the block from the immigration officers. We're not due for our next stop for another couple days; they're all happy to get away from pushing paper at the harbor tonight."

"Why so many men?"

"We're not taking any chances. Usually the button man returns to the scene of the crime, but being as it is in a public space and all, we're sitting on the only other lead we've got – the symbol on the victim's arm, which was also placed at the Flints' place on paper. Now, we think he could have left it just to brag. This mope thinks he's clever enough that he can give us a clue and make a clean sneak of a separate killing without us clapping bracelets on him. He'll learn different tonight."

"Is any of this public knowledge?"

"Very little, sir. Several people saw the body, but other than that…Only Breanne Dibble and myself saw the actual carving on the body. Christina Flint received the insignia on a note in her door but she's in the dark about it and she and her family have been in protective custody since she mentioned it to me."

"And you don't have any security leaks? Breanne, Nash, any of the other patrolmen, maybe some loose lips somewhere?"

"No sir."

"And you're sure about that?"

"Yes sir…why?"

Davis ignored him. "Why was this woman killed?"

"Sir, Allison Mackey wasn't just a pillar of the community, but the best bet for a hungry family to get a second chance at their house's crops…or a hot meal. Any way you slice it, killing her would jeopardize the entire town's food supply –"

Davis's tone of voice darkened from disregard to bordering on anger. *"Why, Detective?"*

Leon wanted out of this topic fast so he chose the shortest answers he could, with the lowest risks of Mayor Davis blowing up. "There are three options that hold water. First, could be someone caught the Wandering City Blues and just wants us all to suffer. Second, she was witness to another crime in progress, though that's unlikely since no other crimes have been reported today. Third, this was a deliberate act of anarchy to hurt our agriculture for the coming winter. We've seen similar crimes to terrorize the public before, when those loonies from Sao took out the solar panels. Home gardens are just harder to bang up, being inside the house."

"But without any further leads, right now you still don't have a motive."

Leon cleared his throat and shifted in his seat. "No sir."

"Well, not an hour ago I spoke with someone who you may just want to meet. Iris?"

Leon's gaze turned to the door through which he'd entered. It opened and a thin woman stepped through the doorway. Leon had never seen her before. She had stringy black hair that reached her chest, hiding some of her face. Her skin was fair. Her eyes were completely devoid of color, an icy gray. Her nose and mouth were small. Despite the heat, she wore long sleeves and gloves and a pair of ripped cargo pants. She was clad entirely in grey and black. Held in some kind of holster on her back were two crossed nightsticks, sandwiched between her back and a backpack she wore. He rose to greet her, extending his hand and shaking it with as much courtesy as he could muster.

"Detective Leon Adler, this is Iris."

"Iris…?"

"Just Iris," the woman responded. Mayor Davis picked the conversation back up.

"Iris heard about the murder this morning and has kindly volunteered to help with the investigation."

The other detective, Leon thought. *No wonder Christina had clammed up after telling me another gumshoe was working the case. This gal looks a little off.*

"I'm sorry; how is she going to help exactly?"

Mayor Davis stood up for her. "Iris has some information that could be pertinent to your murder."

"A few weeks ago, someone I've never seen started poking around my street. He set up camp on a nearby rooftop and something about him seemed strange – like he was always high, but really solemn. He stuck out like a sore thumb; I've been keeping an eye on him. Anyway, last week I looked out my window and saw him changing shirts. He had this weird tattoo on his right shoulder. Then yesterday he just disappeared. Left everything behind, haven't seen him since. It's even weirder because the guy's been there nonstop until then."

"What's so strange about this tattoo?"

"Well, he kept staring at it, for starters. It really seemed to be bothering him. And the image was some freaky design. I approached the mayor with all the info I had once I'd heard about the murder. I drew the tattoo up for him…" Iris fumbled in her pockets for a piece of paper but Leon knew what was coming.

"…And he said I should talk to you."

She handed him the paper and he looked at it. "Thank you for your information, miss, but we're already proceeding with an investigation and have a good idea of where to catch this mug."

"Great," she said. "I'll go with you; I can point him out to you."

"I don't think that's –"

"Detective," the mayor said, "if this woman can positively ID your suspect, you could save a lot of trouble with her eyes on the scene."

"Mr. Mayor, this is highly irregular."

"Adler, you had a chance to do this by the book and in the end I got blindsided with the whole goddamn incident. Now you have the only person who can *possibly* identify

Allison's killer and you think you're going to turn her away? As of right now, she's on the case with you."

Iris gave Leon a satisfied smile. "Where to?"

* * *

Almost a full 24 hours had passed since the murder and Leon Adler's only lead was the weird marking that appeared on Allison's body and her assistant's property. He was annoyed with allowing a civilian to tag along, but he grudgingly agreed and Iris accompanied him to the scene. It was a punishment, he figured, for embarrassing the mayor. Babysitting duty on a so-called witness by whom he wasn't fully convinced. Even Mayor Davis knew something was up. As they left, he pulled Leon close to him and softly said, "She can help us. But I get the feeling she knows more than she's letting on. Keep an eye on her, Detective."

Night had fallen some time ago. Leon and Nash sat in the living room of the Baker family, who lived directly across the street from the Flints; Iris stood behind them. The Bakers had agreed to let the law enforcement team use their home for the stakeout so long as one officer remained on-site during any excitement that could occur. Leon and Nash stared, virtually unblinking, looking for anything out of the ordinary.

Since Sean Bellamy's death, volunteers had done a full sweep of the house and cleaned it. Once Doc Frazier and Breanne had removed the body, the volunteers opened every window and door in the home and carefully moved his bathtub to Triton's rear, emptying its foul contents over the edge, along with what was left of the septic manager's wheelbarrow. They took Sean's water supply from his filtration system and used it to rinse and wash out both the tub and the barrow. They gave the barrow back to the septic manager and returned the tub to the house, scrubbing it and the floor to presentable conditions. The Flint family had reluctantly agreed to stay at the Bellamy residence until things blew over. The smell just barely lingered when the Flints arrived, which, along with the suicide itself, caused much of the Flints' hesitation to relocate to that specific spot. But in the end, the cryptic note and its intent fueled their superstitions and fears until they agreed. Besides, if the killer knew Christina well enough to identify her as the only other horticulturist on Triton, Leon didn't want to take the chance that he might or might not know where the Flints' friends and families lived. The uninhabited Bellamy house was the safest bet – especially with another officer staying with the Flints tonight.

"Do you see anything of interest yet, Detective?"

"No," Leon said, "aside from that dish coming back from the cat house with Old Man Patel. I guess his wife's on Nereid again visiting her parents."

Nash laughed. Leon smirked.

"I swear, Nash, it must be going on four hours we've been sitting on our keisters waiting for this goon. If he doesn't show soon enough, I'm gonna start thinking this whole stakeout's a waste of a beautiful evening."

Without turning, he addressed Iris. "I need you to put together some more pieces for me on how you're involved in this. 'Concerned citizen' doesn't explain why you talked to my only witness."

She growled out a frustrated sigh. When she spoke, her tone almost made Leon wish he hadn't asked. "My reasons are my own. I saw your man here carrying a body away on a stretcher with some woman in a lab coat this morning. You two named the girl who found the body. I followed you and listened by the side of the Flint house and wasn't satisfied with what I heard, so I talked to her myself around midday after she'd calmed down. I told her I was a detective, but I didn't want to scare her so I didn't ask about the tattooed man or if she'd seen the symbol. I just asked her not to mention me."

Leon rubbed his palm on his eyes and forehead. "You probably scared the poor girl half to death – again – and you could've given up valuable information to her or her family. If it gets back to our killer, if anyone saw you poking around the crime scene or the Flints'…"

"You still haven't told me why you think he's coming here," she said. She had no regard for his sense of caution and he found it obnoxious. He spun around in his chair and stood.

"Fine. You want to be involved in my case, you want to play private eye; I'll fill you in."

"Sir –"

"No no, Nash," Leon said. "If Mayor Davis has so much faith in our new friend and how she can help us, we may as well tell her what we're up against."

Nash shut up.

"This morning we found Allison Mackey choked and beaten to death in the street by the agricultural building she tends, see? Carved into her right shoulder with a knife or something was this symbol – the same one you showed to the mayor that's tattooed on your mystery man. Next, Christina Flint – oh, you remember her, right? – comes telling us there was some note stuck in her door this morning with the same damned image on it. So this mug is likely coming back here to take her out. Only none of this adds up because Allison and Christina are our best hopes for our future of farming on Triton. Anyone here would have it in their best interests to let them tend to the gardens and –"

"Wait," Iris interrupted. "So your killer beats a woman to death in the streets for apparently no reason and vanishes without a trace, but he leaves you a clue to his next target? That really *doesn't* make any sense."

"That's what I'm telling you, doll, let alone that he'd kill our largest-scale farmers –"

"Don't call me 'doll,'" Iris said. "That tattoo on his shoulder, maybe he couldn't lay off it because it was new – hard to stop looking at, strange to get used to….?"

Leon shook his head. "No, no, the only inker in the city has been off-titan for the better part of the year, so he couldn't have gotten it recently."

"He couldn't have gotten it recently *here*," she said. "But if he emigrated here from somewhere else…"

"…He also wouldn't care about risking *our* food supply if he were just visiting," Leon thought out loud, "especially if his goal was to try to make us starve. But wait. If he doesn't care about the gardens, then why the Hell would he leave a clue to the Flints'?"

"That's my point!" Iris said.

The three of them thought for a long moment. Iris realized it first.

"How many officers do you have scouting this location?"

Leon sank. *Everyone I could get my hands on,* he remembered himself saying.

"He wants us all here," Nash said.

"So we're not where he is," Leon added.

"Guys, which regular posts did you pull these men off of tonight?"

"Nothing important," Leon said. "Aside from us, they're just paper pushers from immigration."

Nash was confused. "Even if he brought us all out here, there's nowhere he could travel to except –"

Leon grabbed his hat, not quite believing the implication she was making, but following her for reasons he couldn't fathom. She drew her weapons from their holster and put her backpack back on. They were out the door in a flash. Leon and Iris sprinted down the block and around the corner, passing Eriksson and ordering him to come along for backup. Eriksson barely spoke a word of English, but it was enough. They raced to the harbor. As the largest colossus, Triton had a larger and more secure border at its points of travel. The immigration office was a veritable library of filing cabinets with detailed travel histories. The office was adjacent to an antechamber with locked doors on either end. One end of the antechamber opened to the city; the other end led to the small bay with the ballistae where people arrived and departed between the titans when the time was right. Unlike the smaller colossi, here there was a high wall with thick windows separating the bay from the rest of the city. Even before they reached it they could see that the door to the office swung open, broken by their murderer no more than an hour ago. The trio burst through the hall into the bay but it was too late. The killer was long gone. Iris holstered her weapons and Leon pulled a cigarette from his pack and lit it on a streetlight in the bay.

They approached the edge of the harbor. William Eriksson ran a hand through his blond hair and looked down. 1,500 feet of nothing stretched out straight below. . "You think he…um…Tror du att han hoppade?" He pitched his fingers away from himself and down.

"Nej," Leon replied, already at work on his cigarette. "Han inte hoppa. He's still up here somewhere."

Eriksson scanned the horizon and checked the ballista to see if it had been fired. Leon looked along the balustrade for a climbing rope tied to it. Iris approached the mammoth cable that ran taut across Triton's entire back and down over his side. "You both know where this leads."

Leon looked over to her but he was still skeptical. "That's not possible. The mayor has the only climbing gear on Triton's back for traveling between here and there – the right grappling hook and the only rope long and thin enough to accommodate an ascension system from the harbor balustrade. And that cable's huge; you couldn't fasten a carabiner in there, let alone a foot ascender. Besides, you said he lived near you."

Iris reached into her bag and pulled out a flipline rope and a climbing harness. She climbed into the harness and buckled it, fastening one end of the flipline to the hook on the left side of her harness at the waist. "He does live near me," she said. "Where did you think I meant?"

Ghettobelly. The shantytown for prisoners and the forgotten poor. Rappelling down might work with a rope fastened just right, but without the proper climbing gear, the only way anyone could climb up to the city would be manually, hand-over-hand up the cable. It was so big it would be more like climbing up a 400-foot tree with no branches. Iris took a pair of climbing spurs from her bag and strapped them to her boots. She wrapped her legs around the cable, holding her flipline in one hand and squeezing the cable with both forearms. Eriksson and Leon were too shocked to do much.

"You're not secured in to anything! The cable's too tight up here; you can't weave your rope between it and Triton!"

Iris began to shimmy down the cable. "It won't be once I get down and around his flank. Our killer isn't up here anymore, Detective. I'll take a look around Ghettobelly for him now but he's probably already settled in somewhere for the night. I'll meet you at the anchor point for this cable in the morning. Do what you have to do here tonight and I'll see you then!"

She was gone, leaving the two men behind. Leon knew he'd have to acquisition the 500′ climbing rope from the mayor and get his own climbing gear from his office before he could go down to Ghettobelly. Iris must have inferred as much since she didn't ask them to follow immediately. Leon and Eriksson looked up from the cable beneath them to each other. Eriksson pointed at the last spot at which they'd seen Iris.

"I like her."

the woman from ghettobelly

Iris controlled her full-body grip on the cable to slide down Triton's flank. When she felt that the cable's pressure against Triton was beginning to ease, she slowed her descent. She'd fastened herself into her climbing harness up on the harbor and locked the flipline into the harness on her left side. She knew that the flipline was the same device that lumberjacks had once used to fasten themselves to large trees. This she held in her left hand and could feel it with her right fingertips. Iris breathed slowly and deliberately as she secured a firm grip on the rope with her right hand and got to work. With her face against the cold steel cable, she closed her eyes and brought it carefully to her right hip from memory, securing herself to the cable. Looping here and pulling there, she finished tying herself tightly to it.

It was done. She looked down and saw her feet out of the corner of her eye. The cable was so thick, she could thread her climbing spurs in between two strands of the cable without severing any of them. She did this and took a slow, deep breath. Gravity couldn't lower her down an inch without her permission. She looked down at the fog in the moonlight, imagining the hard surface over 1,000 feet below.

Not today, she thought. It was a bit primitive, but Iris walked down the cable backwards, adjusting the tightness on the flipline rope when she needed. Before long, her feet reached the anchor point on the corner of the floor of Ghettobelly.

She knelt and untied the flipline from the cable, then from her harness. She removed her harness and packed the whole system back into her bag where the rest of her climbing gear awaited it. Iris stretched her whole body, then rubbed her back and sat down and rotated her ankles before starting into town.

The moonlight barely illuminated any of Ghettobelly. Triton was so large that his undercarriage blocked the sun most of the day and the moonlight most of the night. As Iris thought of this, she cursed herself. She'd wanted to get a good minute-long look at the stars when she was up top but didn't want to risk raising suspicion. If she'd had her druthers she wouldn't have told them where she lived at all. Of course, in the rush to catch the tattooed man, she had completely forgotten about the stars – and with the revelation of her and the murderer's ease of passage topside, tightened security hereafter was inevitable. She looked out along the horizon at the usual belt of stars swinging low near the fog, but it wasn't the same. It could be months before she could sneak back up and enjoy the view from her own colossus. Even still, what she saw in town comforted her. The maze of shipping container homes and sheet metal shacks and tents, the usual winos gabbing around the fires, the gibbets gently swinging in the breeze and the prison guard office all brought a smile to her face.

It was good to be home. Iris walked among her
neighbors, enveloped as they were in their optimistic humility,
and greeted them in turn. She asked the few people whose
paths she crossed if they'd seen anyone walking through the
neighborhood, but luck was not on her side. She patrolled the
streets a bit, looking out for the tattooed man she'd seen,
working her way from her point of descent to her home – and
his. There was nowhere to run to, but by now he could be
hiding anywhere. Would he have already packed up and
covered his tracks, or was he so sure of his anonymity that
he'd still be camped near her house? What won out: his
stealth or his arrogance? She'd find out when she got there.
Small as Ghettobelly was, it seemed to take forever to search.
It was darker than she'd hoped; she could barely see 10 feet in
front of her face.

Eventually Iris had to give up. The direct and indirect
sunlight in the morning would make for much better
conditions than she had in the dead of night. She made her
way back to her residence, a 12′ x 8′ x 8′6″ shipping container
fished from the surface long ago. With help from friends, she
had rolled the whole pod over 90 degrees and fixed its
swinging doors together before removing the hinges
completely from the bottom door. When the weather suited
her, she propped the extra-large door up with two lengths of
pipe, providing a makeshift awning that let in light and
offered a welcoming atmosphere to the rest of the
neighborhood. She was standing under it when she first got
her unobstructed view of the stranger. From his elevated
position atop another storage pod nearby, her overhang kept

her hidden from him for the vital moment she needed to study him and commit him to memory.

She squinted in vain to see his campsite. *Too dangerous to go over there while I can't see,* she said. *If he's awake or nearby and I go in poking around, I could be caught off-guard.* With a small groan she let it go. Tonight, her door was closed, just as she'd left it after preparing for her trip to see Mayor Davis. She liked to be home at a reasonable hour of the evening so as not to disturb her neighbors when she heaved the container open, but it felt like it was after midnight by now. As much a matter of courtesy as maintaining her privacy, she approached her door and opened it as quietly as she could. Kneeling, she pried the bottom corner open and threw her bag in first, then came around outside and opened the door further with both hands. She took one final glance at her surroundings and slipped inside, softly lowering the door behind her.

Iris removed her boots and pants and, in the darkness, felt her way towards her cot. When she got to it, she sat on it and sighed. She took off her bra under her shirt and flung it to where she estimated her boots lay before laying down for the night. Her long gloves followed. Despite the warmth she pulled a blanket over herself. She worried about the implications of the tattooed man and his crime. Who would emigrate to a different titan just to kill a total stranger either as their endgame or as a means to an end? In all her travels over the years, she knew the list of potential villains was short. Short enough that one name on it, one name from her past, would justify her personal involvement. That name was worth her risking life and limb, climbing up and down Triton by a support cable, using this Detective Adler and his patrolmen to help her solve this mystery. Everything depended on her talking to the killer first. All she had to do was get him alone.

She slept.

Leon Adler and Nash were waiting for her when she got to the corner of town in the mid-morning. Leon gave his climbing rope a few tugs and a moment later it was careening down to him. He spooled it in along his arm and they exchanged greetings, but she could tell he was in a sour mood. "The mayor wants results on this," he grumbled. "Goddamn town's in an uproar, rumors are flying. We don't bring this goon in and we're looking at a world of hurt."

Nash looked around cautiously. It was his first time in Ghettobelly. "Who do we report to down here, Iris?"

"Report to?"

"Yeah; where are the local lawmen?"

She laughed in surprise. "Don't have any. We mostly just look out for one another."

He was embarrassed at his ignorance and shot back before thinking. "Except when a murderer comes to town?"

"Yeah, nobody would ever be found dead in the streets if we had some big strong policemen on the beat, right?" she responded.

Nash reddened, reminded of the Mackey murder. Leon shot him a glance that stopped him from pursuing the argument any further. Leon changed the subject.

"What did you find out?"

Iris turned to Leon. "I didn't see him again, but on my way here I saw he's still got his camp set up."

Leon's eyebrows raised. "Really? Did you search it?"

"No. I realized the less I do without you two around, the fewer questions I have to answer later."

There was an awkward silence as Iris led them to the killer's habitat. She knew they didn't trust her, and she wasn't concerned with making friends as long as they didn't make up a reason to lock her up along with their murderer. At the same time, in the last 24 hours, Iris had realized that law enforcement on Triton was still somewhat of a boys' club. Leon's pet names for her were a bearable nuisance, but she was concerned that the mayor only put her on this case to score points with her. It annoyed her, but she had to put up with it for now.

Together, and nonchalantly, they arrived at Iris's. She pointed out the killer's campsite and they deliberated on the best course of action. If he were intelligent and careful enough to leave no clues but distract the police while he made an escape, he would return to this scene to gather up his camp – even if just to toss the gear overboard to rid himself of the evidence rather than take it with him. However, he hadn't done so yet. This led to only two possible conclusions. First, perhaps he was arrogant enough to assume that nobody had caught onto his actions yet, and was saving the task for later – whether out of careful method or because he figured he had time before the police ran out of leads upstairs and came down to poke around when they had nothing else to go on. Second, much like the decoy of the Flint residence, he could be using his campsite as bait to see if anyone came poking around – and who they were.

In the end, they decided to send Nash to investigate the camp alone. If the camp was bait for the law, Nash was the bait for the chaos. If things went wrong, he could defend himself long enough that they could swarm the scene and subdue the criminal. Despite his brash tendencies, Nash was a skilled peace officer and could also report anything that he saw to Leon and Iris. They put their faith in him while they waited under Iris's overhang.

Things were quiet. A group of Muslims passed, their prayer mats tucked under their arms, and settled on a space for salah. As they passed, one of the men in the group smiled and nodded at Iris and Leon.

"As sala'amu alaikum," he said.

"Walaikum as sala'am," Iris replied. The man beamed and kept walking.

Leon raised an eyebrow at Iris. "Are you a Muslim?"

"Not that I'm aware. Why, are you?"

"Do you speak Arabic?"

"Just a few words. Aamir taught me that one," she said with a nod towards the man who had greeted her.

Leon waited for her to keep answering. Iris sighed. "It's really a beautiful greeting. Say it one time; it rolls off the tongue."

He hesitated.

"Oh come on, try it on. Give it a run."

"Ozz…Oss s-salamoo…"

Iris laughed. "As…sala'amu…"

He repeated the two words.

"Alaikum," she added.

"Alaikum. What does that mean?"

"That first phrase means 'Peace be with you.'"

106

"Peace be with you? What, did they grab that from John 20:21?"

"Don't fudge your frillies, Detective; all religions have borrowed from one another at some point."

"What's the other part?" he asked.

"Walaikum as sala'am."

"Walaikum as sala'am," he repeated.

"Very good! 'And unto you also, peace.'"

"You mean like 'And also with you.'"

"Sure."

Leon smiled a little to himself for having learned something new. They turned their eyes from the prayer group to the suspect's campsite and back.

One of the Muslims swept the ground and there was some brief discussion about where Mecca was in relation to Triton. Once they had agreed, they laid their mats down facing the proper direction and began performing wudu by washing their face, elbows and feet. They stood and began their rakat, quickly getting to the Surah Al-Fatiḥa.

"بِسْمِ اللَّهِ الرَّحْمَنِ الرَّحِيمِ
الْحَمْدُ لِلَّهِ رَبِّ الْعَالَمِينَ
الرَّحْمَنِ الرَّحِيمِ
مَالِكِ يَوْمِ الدِّينِ
إِيَّاكَ نَعْبُدُ وَإِيَّاكَ نَسْتَعِينُ
اهْدِنَا الصِّرَاطَ الْمُسْتَقِيمَ
صِرَاطَ الَّذِينَ أَنْعَمْتَ عَلَيْهِمْ غَيْرِ الْمَغْضُوبِ عَلَيْهِمْ
وَلَا الضَّالِّينَ"

Something about the group worshiping in peace warmed Iris, though she knew their prayer was not for her. She saw Nash arrive at the stranger's campsite out of the corner of her eye and redirected her focus to him. He approached the tent from behind, an unzipped corner of its flap rocking back and forth in the breeze. Instinctively, Leon unbuttoned the holster of his gun and rested his hand on its handle. Nash looked around one final time, nodded at the two of them, unzipped the tent and entered. After a tense moment, he emerged with a dissatisfied look on his face. The killer wasn't there. He fixed his gaze on Leon and Iris and shook his head.

They let their guard down and took a deep breath. Leon took his hand off his gun. From his position diagonally across the street from her, Nash looked at Iris's gloved forearms and nodded upwards at them. "So what's with the –"

The side of Nash's head exploded. The roar of a revolver put everyone in Ghettobelly into a state of shock, including Leon and Iris, and the sounds of the exit wound on the right side of his head were nauseating. Leon shouted Nash's name and they both ran to him without thinking. The Muslim group disbanded in the middle of their practices, grabbing their prayer mats and fleeing for home. Every resident of Ghettobelly who crossed their paths added precious fractions of seconds to the distance between the pair and the scene of the new crime. By the time Nash fell to the ground, he was dead but Leon and Iris finally laid eyes on his killer – and Allison Mackey's. He'd returned, backpack on, to clear out his campsite. This time, they'd gotten the drop on him. He must've assumed Nash was the only one looking for him – the tattooed man was still smirking, the smoking gun in his outstretched right hand, when he came into their view. When he had climbed up and shot Nash next to his tent, he had been obscured from their vision behind a tacked-on sheet metal shack that sat atop of a sturdier housing unit, but as they ran, he entered their field of vision.

When he saw Leon and Iris, he panicked for a brief moment. Then, as he was turning to leave, a macabre grin crossed his face. Finally he fled. Leon drew his gun and told him to freeze but he ignored them. They checked their momentum from running to Nash and redirected themselves towards the killer, Iris drawing her escrima sticks from their holster on her back. The chase was on. They didn't want to admit it, but they knew there was nothing to be done for the young patrolman.

Keep running, Leon told himself. *Don't think about him now. Grieve later. He'd want this son of a bitch in bracelets and you owe it to him.*

The killer was spry. He rounded corners and grabbed people and shoved them behind him to obstruct his pursuers. He led them on a winding path among the streets, changing direction at random in hopes of losing them. They followed him over bonfires and through houses.

Iris ran faster – faster than Leon, faster than she had been. She hadn't told the men that she had strong suspicions of who the killer was and why he was on Triton. She hadn't told them the real reason that she'd requested to be put on the case. She needed more eyes looking out for him so they could catch him before he killed again, and she was sure she could do what she had to do quickly and claim self-defense later. She had to catch him and ask him one question, just to be sure, and then not let him breathe a word. At all costs she absolutely had to stop this man running and grab him and get that one answer and then kill him before he opened his mouth again – before he told Leon that he knew her.

And from where he knew her.

He knocked down a small unattended child, who started wailing loudly. Iris had outpaced Leon and side-stepped the child; Leon tripped over it and went down hard. After the killer rounded two more corners with Iris hot on his tail, they were headed in a straight line towards the edge of town that faced the disconnected platform of the prison guard's office.

He's going for the jump, Iris thought. *He's either stupid enough to think he can make the guard's office or he's got a parachute in that bag and he's risking Red Lung by waiting on the surface for another ride. I can stop him but I'll only have 10 seconds or so alone with him before Leon catches up with us. I have to be fast.*

Her right hand came out and she threw one of her sticks, sidearm, at the killer's feet. It caught his legs and he tripped and fell against the ramshackle balustrade on the edge of town.

Nine.

In one fluid motion, Iris picked up the escrima stick from the ground and jumped down, sliding on her knees to club the killer in the temple with it as hard as she could.

Eight.

He howled in pain and rolled onto his stomach as she sheathed both her weapons. She tugged his left arm out and smacked his hand flat on the ground, palm down.

Seven.

She pinned his hand with her knee. Her right hand entered the bag on her back and returned with a pair of handheld pruning shears fished from the surface. She held his index finger with her left hand and opened the shears, placing the finger between the blades.

Six.

"Did he have you kill that woman because of me?"

Five.

He laughed. "Bitch Iris forsake re-destiny gone meat."

Hearing her local dialect again after so many years brought new rage up from within her. She squeezed the shears shut and wrenched her hand up and over his. He howled in pain and the digit came off the hand.

Four.

She grabbed his middle finger next.

"Answer me, god damnit!"

He seemed to be going into shock. "Suck dick."

Three.

The stump where the index had been squirted blood onto her hand and her shears, but not enough to stop her from repeating her interrogation method on the middle finger, which failed to completely sever.

Two.

"Answer me Jeremai!"

The sound of his name brought Jeremai back. His head on the ground, he looked up at her and grinned. His teeth

were long and jagged and browned. He had a severe
underbite to the point of a protruding jaw and his face looked
asymmetrical. He was a perfect image of all the worst
memories of her past. He was the only one who could ruin
her life here with a sentence, but to her, he wasn't saying a
word.

One.

Fuck this, she thought. She kicked him over onto his
back and raised the pruners in both hands. She straddled his
chest to keep him on the floor and focused on his face.

"Freeze!"

She looked at Leon. He was aiming his pistol straight
at her. He was still 20 feet away, but closing in on them
slowly.

"Put down the shears."

She tossed them next to her. They landed near his
severed index finger.

"Now get off him."

Jeremai began laughing as Iris slowly lifted herself off
him. She stood and moved behind Jeremai, on whom Leon
turned his gun.

"Now you – Chuckles. Stand *slowly* and stay where
you are."

"Leon, this man –"

"Zip it, sister; this ain't the time."

Jeremai struggled to his feet and put his hands up. His
index stump continued to bleed, as did his middle finger –
which hung down on the back of his hand by only a tendon.
His breath told Iris he was on the verge of hyperventilating
and passing out from the pain. No crowd had gathered.

112

Likely they'd heard the gunfire and the chase and were staying indoors until things settled.

Iris's worst fear came true. She hadn't killed Jeremai before he spoke. And now that he'd seen she was trying to live a new life on Triton and she'd cost him two of his fingers, he wanted to spill everything he knew about her.

"Hey meat man wit' shooter. You mess of years been stay Bitch fren?" he asked, taking a step towards Leon. Iris knew she was supposed to stay put but she was inching her way forward. Leon was taken aback by his voice and his language.

"I said stay where you are! I'm asking the questions here. You answer 'em right and maybe I have a talk with the city council and get you out of taking the long trip down to the surface."

Jeremai laughed, unafraid. "Man, seen secret Bitch fren? I gon' speak straight up: Iris turn meat, no eater."

Iris spoke again. "Shut *up* Jeremai…"

"Wait…how does he know your name?" Leon asked Iris. "How the Hell do you know *his* name?"

Jeremai took another small step forward. Leon had been in similar situations before, having drawn his gun on criminals in the past, but something about this was all wrong. Maybe it was the way Jeremai spoke, the likes of which Leon had never heard before. He realized he'd spent as much attention trying to make sense of the killer's speech as he was keeping control of the situation. He wanted to take it back from Jeremai, so without thinking, Leon began to walk forward to confront them both.

113

"How Iris keep Jeremai name?" Jeremai asked. "Got why; I gone speaked secret once time. Iris forsake re-destiny, gone meat seen 15 year."

"Leon, listen to me," Iris said. "We can't take him in alive, he'll –"

Jeremai turned his head halfway around to her and sharply raised his tone. "Close hole, cunt; eater Jeremai speakin' meat Leon." Leon inched his way forward. He was within 10 feet of them now and had no idea what to do when he got there.

"Both of you shut up."

Leon looked down for the briefest of moments to check his footing and Iris drew an escrima stick with her right hand and brought it around Jeremai's front, pulling him back to her and choking him with the weapon just enough to make him stop talking. She couldn't see Leon very well so she moved her head around Jeremai's, and Leon pointed the barrel of the pistol at her again.

"Iris, what the hell are you doing?! Drop it!"

"Leon, listen to me! This man isn't acting alone; he was specifically sent here by someone."

"I said drop it!"

"The man who sent him here *runs* one of the other giants," Iris said. "He will have Jeremai extradited off Triton and he will *never* see a day in jail let alone a death sentence."

"Bullshit," he said, trying to convince himself as much as her. "I'm taking him in."

"Iris speaked fact," Jeremai said, his voice barely croaking out past his pinched airway. "Jeremai fly home. Eater Jeremai come Triton do God's work. Jeremai gone killed meat woman, gone killed meat intruder, vanish erase woman link Jeremai. Triton law meat make Jeremai stay jail? Piss. I seen eater family again. All eater families treat I like king." Jeremai choked out a laugh.

Leon's blood was boiling. Nash was less than a half a mile away, dead for just minutes – the thought of it made Leon's eyes start to tear up – and his murderer was toying with him, bragging about some diplomatic immunity. No doubt it would've been easier for Jeremai had they not caught him, but he still didn't seem to care about any of it.

"Leon, he killed Nash. He killed Allison Mackey and he is going to *walk* unless we end it here and now."

"Dammit, Iris, stop talking!" Leon put Iris in his sights, then Jeremai, then Iris again.

"This is our only chance, Leon."

"Meat law man bring Jeremai to meat law boss Triton. Jeremai speak Bitch-meat Iris secret Triton law boss. Law boss stay I new bes' fren, forget Jeremai kill meat intruder just now. Triton law boss knee-walk, slobber I dick." Jeremai laughed again despite Iris tightening her hold on his throat, his despicable teeth like the gates of Hell. The sound of his voice brought Leon's gun back on him.

"Leon, just let me end this now and I swear I'll tell you what's going on," Iris said. Leon's gun was beginning to lower. Leon weighed his options. He took a solemn oath and upheld it most of his life until now, to serve justice and keep the peace. He'd never considered taking the law into his own hands, and there was due process. However, this could be his only chance to confront Allison Mackey's killer – Nash's killer. Were Iris and Jeremai telling the truth about him coming from a titan with extradition? If so, could Leon let his killer go free for the sake of foreign relations?

"Meat Leon kill Jeremai start war. Leon spill gallons blood many innocent Triton baby. Seen."

Leon's gun was heavy in his hand. It was time to decide. They all knew it.

"Leon," Iris said. "I brought you down here to him. You know I want this bastard to pay. But this is the only way. If you turn around and walk away, I'll avenge your partner – your hands stay clean. Just let me do this. For Nash, for Allison, let me finish this."

Leon looked at her again, through bleary eyes and confusion and fear and consequence, and he raised his gun back up.

"No," he said softly.

He fired.

One shot rang out into the air. It seemed to echo forever, out into the void. The shell bounced along the floor with a high, quiet metal ting and rolled like a thimble around in a wide circle, before everything was silent. The force of the impact brought his target back a couple steps. Leon lowered his gun and dropped it on the floor – it seemed so heavy now – and he saw all life, all light drain from the eyes as they lost their appearance of shock, a few drops of blood moving down between them. The departed tumbled backwards over the railing. Instinctively, Leon rushed towards the body to stop it, but he knew before he started he was too late. The corpse fell silently, head first, down towards the red-orange fog. Leon watched it plummet through the mist, making a small dent in its cloudy top, and he concluded his thought from before he'd pulled the trigger.

"I'll finish it myself."

Iris was frozen stiff. The bullet that laid Jeremai to rest passed within inches of her own brain. Her hands were at her waist and she still had an iron grip on her nightstick. She had to remind her legs to move so she could turn around. Leon gave her a vacant stare.

"You've never killed anyone with that thing, have you?"

"Life's too short for stray bullets."

Iris nodded silently and turned back around, away from the balustrade and the detective. *Easy, girl,* she thought. *He needs to convince himself he's got a handle on all this.* She barely moved, looking down at the floor instead and waiting for him to come back to the present. She saw Leon's pistol, one empty shell rocking back and forth with the sway of Ghettobelly, her pruners and Jeremai's index finger.

Leon's voice came weakly from behind her.

"He 'came here to do God's work?' Where did he come from?"

Iris turned and looked Leon in the eye, sheathing her sticks. Everything had gone wrong. She couldn't hide it anymore; if she refused to answer or if she lied to him in this state he might grab his gun and make her join Jeremai.

"Sao," she said. "The same as me."

rabbit boom

Iris, Leon and Mayor Davis were the only three in attendance at Sean Bellamy's funeral. As was customary, he was brought to Triton's back side on a stretcher and cast over the edge, his body's final resting place somewhere in Zambia. Breanne Dibble marked the approximate location for the city's archives, though with so few mourners it hardly seemed necessary. The tension in the air was as thick as the fog below – all present knew Allison Mackey's funeral would follow in a few days, as would Nash's, and neither Leon nor Iris had given the mayor a full statement about the incident in Ghettobelly yet. By the time Triton got back north to Europe, they knew the city would be three bodies lighter than it had been a week ago – four including the killer.

Leon didn't like how Jeremai had mentioned "erasing the link" between himself and Allison Mackey. On a hunch, the moment he returned topside with Nash's body he asked Patrolmen Chopra and Eriksson to do an inventory on the city gardens building and note what was missing. He told them to report their findings to him immediately and gave them his expected whereabouts the rest of the day. He was still thinking about this as he and Iris walked back to the mayor's office to debrief him on the day's events.

Iris's thoughts were occupied by everything else as they sat down to once again speak with Davis. Leon had learned where she was born and raised. Given Sao's relationship with the rest of the colossi, she was supposed to have mentioned it when she moved to Ghettobelly. Failing that, she should have told Mayor Davis when she met him, and failing *that* she should've told Leon when she first met *him*. On top of her birthplace, she'd tried to get answers from Jeremai the fast way – the gruesome way. Torture was illegal on Triton, she knew that. She could be kicked off at the next rooftop they saw above the fog. At the same time, she'd seen Leon murder a suspect in cold blood, his body landing on the outskirts of Johannesburg. The remaining evidence – Iris's pruners and Jeremai's index finger – Leon threw into a nearby trash barrel fire in Ghettobelly. It was all gone by the time anyone emerged from their houses. Nobody knew but Iris. Her ears perked up – as did her heartrate – when she heard Leon speak her name.

"Iris reached the suspect – Jeremai – first. I'd been caught up in the foot traffic of people trying to reach safety."

"You did?" the mayor asked, surprised.

"I tripped him up with an escrima stick –"

"A what now?"

Iris gestured to the weapons on her back. "My…nightstick, sir."

"Before Detective Adler caught up with you, did you learn anything from this 'Jeremai?'"

Iris cleared her throat. "No sir."

"I caught up with them in two shakes, Mayor Davis," Leon said. "Iris had just finished detaining the suspect.

They'd grappled for a moment but when I brought out my iron," he said, patting his pistol in its hip holster, "he went stiff – at least for the moment. Sung like a canary."

"All just because he saw the gun?"

Iris's heart leapt into her chest. Leon saw what made Jeremai start talking. And now it would come out. She could feel her heart pounding and hear it in her ears.

Leon looked at Iris. "Yes sir. Looking down the barrel of a gun is all it took."

The mayor paused. "So what did he tell you?"

Iris breathed a sigh of relief. In an attempt to remain in the conversation she took back over from Leon. "He mentioned being sent here by a partner. Someone off-titan."

"Who? Where?" the mayor asked.

"Sa-"

The door opened, interrupting Iris. An out-of-breath Patrolman Chopra entered just far enough to lean in and hand Leon a note and leave. Leon eyed it quickly.

"You were saying, Iris?"

Leon fixed his gaze on the mayor. "Psamanthe, sir. He last met his partner in Psamanthe."

Iris turned and looked at Leon again as he put the note in his pocket. This was the second time in the last minute he'd lied to the mayor's face, and neither time could she ascertain his reasoning.

Mayor Davis was as surprised as she was – though for different reasons. "Psamanthe? Who the hell on Psamanthe would want to kill Allison Mackey? The whole population's Indians and hippies, isn't it?"

Iris rolled her eyes at his ignorance. She was lucky nobody saw her.

"Well, we don't think they're from Psamanthe *originally,* but that was their final meeting spot," Leon said. "It's likely someone who's just hitching a ride on Psamanthe right now, Mr. Mayor. She flies east-to-west compared to Triton and Proteus moving west-to-east, so that could just be where he is for now – heading back to the Americas maybe."

"Jesus Christ," Davis said. He changed the subject. "Now how in the hell did our murderer wind up dead?"

The pressure off her, Iris now noticed Leon begin to struggle.

"Adler, I know you and Nash were close, but if you're about to tell me this was some kind of vigilante justice…"

"No sir," Leon said, his ears burning. "Uh…in fact –"

"Detective Adler acted in self-defense, Mr. Mayor," Iris said. "It was my fault.

"I thought I had Jeremai dead to rights – I was damn near strangling him – and in a flash, he headbutted me, knocked me off-balance and drew the same revolver he'd used to kill Nash on Leon. The only clean shot he had was at his head; I was behind the rest of him. Had the detective hesitated a quarter of a second, I wouldn't be here now. He saved us both."

Mayor Davis looked again at Leon. "Is this true, Detective?"

"Yes sir," he replied. "I won't pretend it wasn't a bit satisfying though."

"Satisfying?" The mayor paused for several seconds. Leon and Iris didn't know if he'd buy it.

"I'll bet it was," Davis finally said, with some resignation. He looked over the notes. "Okay. So I've got two murder victims on ice at the clinic. Their killer eluded us once but you followed him down under Triton and now he's flattened on the streets of South Africa with a hole in his head. Are we any closer to a motive?"

"When Jeremai mentioned his partner, he implied Allison was a loose end he was tying up," Leon said. "He was just the button man; the mastermind is still out there. I had a couple of my men examine the gardens but they turned up nothing – that's what Patrolman Chopra came in to say. Our killer's partner will have the rest of the story."

"And you're both inclined to see this through to the end?"

"Absolutely," Iris shot back. She had to know why Sao was sending assassins to her new home.

"I think people around here will sleep better knowing why this happened," Leon added. "This would be a Hell of a collar. It would really boost everyone's spirits seeing this crook get his comeuppance."

"Agreed," Mayor Davis said.

"With your permission, sir, when we get back up north to Europe in a couple weeks we'll disembark Triton at London – no, Paris would be better – and wait for Psamanthe to nest. We'll talk to her residents when they're camped in Paris and in London. Depending on how long it takes to shine a light on this caper, we'll be waiting for you somewhere in the United States with this con in bracelets – along with enough evidence in tow to buy him an express ticket to the surface."

The mayor gathered and closed the notes in a file, handing them to Leon. "Alright. And Leon?"

"Yes sir?" Leon asked, taking the notes.

"No more bullshit. I want a clean collar on this son of a bitch."

Leon nodded meekly and stood to leave. Iris followed suit but the mayor stopped her.

"Miss?" he said, reaching into a desk drawer.

"Yes Mister Mayor?" she replied.

"I'm sorry," he said.

"Sorry for what, sir?"

He pulled a shiny metal object from the drawer and handed it to her. It was a badge.

"Sorry you're stuck with this shlub as your partner."

They left. Iris's badge sat heavily in her pants pocket. Leon secured a tent for Iris for free after she turned down his offer to stay at either his house or his office. He wanted to press the issue but in the end he let it go. As an act of goodwill, he led her to the city square to have dinner with her. On the way he showed her the note Chopra had given him.

Minor discrepancies between records and physical inventory of tomato, kale, coconut. Total lack of stored inventory – unknown plant, nomenclature erased on paper and label torn off from drawer.

"Do you have any idea what he might've derricked?" he asked.

"No," she said. "Do you?"

"We'd better find out," he replied. "Gardening ain't usually in your average mook's M.O.."

"I know."

He stopped them both and changed the subject. "Listen…I need to thank you for not telling the mayor about Jeremai. I don't know if you know this, but it could've –"

"It could've gotten you fired," she said, "if not imprisoned."

"So why didn't you tell him?" Leon asked.

She shrugged. "You'd just covered my ass for disfiguring a defenseless suspect. Besides, he'd just killed your best friend – *and* you're going to have to live with what you did the rest of your life. I think what you're going to feel is punishment enough."

Ouch, Leon thought. *She ain't kidding.*

"So while we're asking," she said, "What made you lie for me?"

Leon didn't want to admit it, but he knew he couldn't have plead that he'd killed Jeremai in self-defense if Mayor Davis knew he'd already taken a beating from Iris and lost two fingers. He couldn't expose her without implicating himself in the process. Here he was supposed to be keeping tabs on this woman and in just a couple days he'd already started covering for her. Whatever awaited them in the future was likely going to be complicated – and messy. Thinking about it made him uneasy so he changed the subject.

"Why not just tell them you're Sao-born when you moved here?" he asked. "It's not illegal."

"It's honestly nobody's business," she replied.

Iris could tell that answer wouldn't hold him over. "I imagine for the same reason your friend Sean Bellamy didn't advertise his past when he was released from prison," she said.

Leon was confused. "But you didn't commit a crime. You even looked ready to axe Jeremai before he could tell me. Why hide it?"

"Because a woman's reputation is a fragile thing, Detective," Iris said. "It may be the most fragile of all things. She spends her life building it with her actions and her beliefs, and with one word from a man it can go up in flames. If an ex-boyfriend calls a girl a slut, suddenly every interested party treats her like they have a right to what's between her legs. Or if she stops a groping hand at a bar, she's a 'dyke' or a 'bitch.' And once that seed's planted in someone's mind, it's a bell that she can't un-ring. But the funny thing in her case is, like you said, the thing they're accusing her of isn't even a crime. Shit, if they treat your average woman like that, how do you think they'd respond to a woman from a city known for its cannibalism?"

He was embarrassed. "I never thought about all that before," he muttered.

"That's because you've never had to," she responded.

They resumed walking towards the city square. He was quiet.

"So, are you married?"

Leon laughed. "No, definitely not. You?"

Iris shook her head nonchalantly. "Mostly I keep to myself. You know how when you go on a first date with someone, you tend to ask where they're from and what they do?"

"Sure," he said.

"How long do you think I'd last in that conversation?"

Leon nodded. He saw no reason to press it further.

"But how about you? You seem like a pretty stable guy, honorable career, all that. You never got hitched?"

"Came close, once," Leon replied. "Girl on Proteus a few years back. We got along like gangbusters."

"So what was the problem?"

"She was too much like me," he said.

"Oh, God help her."

"Ha! I mean I worked long hours and she didn't mind; she worked long hours and I didn't mind. Eventually we were only seeing each other a night a week. That was that. The weird thing is how easy the transition out of it was. It was smooth, quiet and almost emotionless. I guess we both saw it coming."

"That's a shame. I'm sorry."

"It gets a bit lonely sometimes, but…I don't know. I don't really want to talk about this anymore," he said with a feigned chuckle. "Is that alright with you?"

"Sure, no problem," she said. The night air hung silent but lightly, like a wisp of cloud or the lingering trail of perfume a woman leaves in her wake after she walks past.

"Okay. So it's two mushrooms roasting over a fire," she said.

"Okay…"

"And one says, 'Whew, it sure is hot in here.' So the other one says, '*Holy shit it's a talking mushroom!*'"

He stared at her for a second before coughing out an involuntary laugh. "That's honestly the worst joke I've ever heard."

They had two weeks before Triton would reach Paris.

126

* * *

Iris studied the ceramic plate she held in her hand in front of the table loaded with buffet chafers. She rubbed her thumb along the plate's edge and listened to the sounds of the city around her as she and Leon edged their way up the short line. The square bustled with activity. The traders had closed up shop for the night but in the late hour, restauranteurs sold meals made from recipes passed down from great-grandparents - though adapted to compensate for ingredients unavailable on the colossi. Salads and French fries had survived, as had mashed potatoes, stuffed mushroom caps, corn on the cob and risotto. Meat dishes were uncommon, but not quite extinct. Leon knew the city like the back of his hand and they were waiting to be served at the only food stand on Triton that had any meat at all. He held a small bag of vegetables in his hand. Night had fallen and a cool breeze blew, causing her to look up at the stars. It was a clear summer's night and there seemed to be thousands of stars twinkling against the black sky. The scene was peaceful and lively. *I could live here the rest of my life,* she thought, closing her eyes for just a moment.

"Next!"

She snapped back to reality and spied the kiosk. A thin, weathered-looking woman was ladling a brownish stew onto one half of Leon's plate, then a scoop of quinoa onto the other. Next to her was a barrel of clear liquid. She dipped a mug into it and filled it and handed it to Leon. He gave her the bag of vegetables and nodded at Iris, then he moved aside and the woman reached her hand out for Iris's plate. Iris handed it to her and she began repeating the same process.

"Carol Lee, what's the special tonight?"

"It's Tuesday. Braised rabbit stew tonight, hun."

"Everything copacetic, angel?" Leon asked.

"Still tickin'," Carol said with a smirk. "Who's that with you?"

"This is Iris; she's working with me on the Mackey murder."

Carol smiled at Iris. "You got a last name darlin'?"

"Just Iris," she replied.

"Fair enough. Terrible thing what happened to Ms. Mackey; y'all close to catching the bastard that killed her?"

Iris and Leon traded a tense glance as Iris retrieved her full plate and drink from Carol Lee.

"We're working on it, Carol. May be traveling soon."

"That so? Well sugar, business's slowin' so I'll take a break in a minute and come by and jawflap with you and your lady friend here.

"Nice to meet you, Just Iris."

Iris gave her a small, courteous smile and they walked away.

Iris and Leon sat at a small table near Carol's food kiosk. Leon took off his fedora and set it next to his plate. He tucked into his dish immediately and noticed the odd way Iris inspected her dinner. She picked up a piece of the shredded rabbit like it was evidence and looked over its every angle. She smelled it twice before taking a cautious bite of it. Then her expression changed and she ate hungrily. Once she saw Leon mixing his meat and gravy into the quinoa, she did the same. The savory, salty meal was like none she'd ever eaten before, but it made her thirsty. She picked up her glass and raised it near her face.

"It's nice of her to give you a glass of water with your dinner."

Leon could've stopped her, but the devil in him didn't allow it. She opened her lips and let the drink pour in her mouth. Then he spoke.

"That's not water, doll; it's hooch."

It was too late. The strong alcohol caught in her throat and she coughed and sputtered. She forced some of it down, swallowing with difficulty. Several other drops spilled onto her lap and her plate. Leon laughed hard enough that several other of Triton's residents looked at the two of them. Iris recovered, breathing slowly to avoid another coughing fit. The drink was strong and the volume she swallowed went to her head. Her cheeks flushed from a mixture of embarrassment and moonshine.

"Wow."

"Not bad, is it?" He casually toasted her with his mug.

"I've had fermented cider before, but…Jesus, that could fuel a generator," Iris said. She sloshed the drink around in her mug and blinked several times.

"Yeah, but it'll keep your toes warm when that winter air comes nipping."

They continued eating. Despite the surprise of the drink and Leon's obnoxious prank, she decided to keep drinking – although in smaller sips. As she finished her food, Iris saw Carol Lee approaching their table with a rag slung over her shoulder.

"How are my favorite customers enjoying their dinner?"

"It's amazing. I've never had anything like it in my life."

"Well aren't you sweet?"

Before Leon could speak, Iris pointed back towards Carol's table.

"But I don't understand…if everyone farms vegetables, why do you need any from us?"

Leon took a deep breath and put his hat on, rising and taking their plates. He had heard the story of Carol's rabbit farm so many times he couldn't bear to sit through it again – and she loved to tell it.

"I'll excuse myself; you dames enjoy your conversation."

Iris started. "I'm sorry; if I said something wrong, I…"

She looked to Leon for help but he was already on his way to a trash can fishing a cigarette out of his case. He wouldn't be back for several minutes. Iris felt a bit worried, left alone with this stranger. Carol laughed deeply and slapped her hand on the table.

"Oh my goodness no. You're fine! You're fine." Before Carol started her explanation, she looked back at her station and saw her assistant struggling to move the barrel of moonshine away from the table.

"Oh Lord," Carol said, gently slapping Iris's hand. "Walk with me, baby, and I'll tell you all about it." She turned to her table and shouted "Never you mind, Jimmy; we're on our way!" As they stood, Carol noticed Iris's drink was empty. She snatched her mug away. "Looks like you need a refill, hun."

Iris worried again. "I don't have anything to give you for –"

"On the house," Carol said. "Maybe this mug's got a hole in the bottom." She winked.

Carol and Iris made their way to Carol's kiosk and the women retrieved a moving dolly and rolled it up next to the barrel. Jimmy meekly apologized for needing help and he cleaned Iris's mug while Carol told her tale.

"Iris, I don't farm."

"But I thought everyone –"

"– is supposed to, yes. You look around town and you see folks trading goods for crops, crops for goods: veggies in, hardware and day labor out. Now we've managed over the years to put together one Hell of a diverse cuisine based on what we can grow in these hanging gardens, but don't nobody want to stop eatin' critters if they can help it."

Jimmy handed the mug to Carol, who removed the lid off the barrel and dipped the mug in before refitting the lid to the container. Iris thanked her.

"Truth be told, none of my family were ever much for farming. We had a ranch in north Georgia but when those behemoths came out of the sea along with that damn mist, it seemed almost every business went belly up."

They lifted the heavy barrel just inches off the ground and Jimmy nudged the dolly under the bottom with his foot. They let it go and Carol started securing the barrel in with the straps that hung down the dolly's sides. Iris nursed her drink.

She didn't know what "north Georgia" was but figured it was somewhere back on the surface.

"My great-great-granddaddy caught the Red Lung early on – and I mean early. His wife, Marianne, buried him and didn't have the help she needed tending the ranch. Before she knew it, George Willis from the Savings & Loan came knockin' with papers in his hand, ready to close it down and put Marianne and the kids out on the streets."

Carol interrupted herself. "Jimmy! Take the 'shine back to the farm and don't waste no time getting back here. We ain't done by a damn sight."

With the barrel secure, they relaxed and Carol wiped her brow. Iris liked her; she tended to her store with an ease and natural air that seemed practiced and confident. A customer walked up while Carol caught her breath but she waved him away. "Oh Hell, Enrique; give us a minute. Can't you see I'm fit to burst a lung over here?"

"I don't want to be a bother to your work," Iris said, eyeing the man, who didn't seem to be leaving.

"So Great-Great-Grandma Marianne says to herself, 'Fine. If we're losing our land here anyways, we ought to move to *higher* ground.' So with my newborn great-grandma in one hand and mortgage papers in the other, Marianne got in her car and drove straight to the Georgia State Capitol building in Atlanta and she didn't leave until she had papers for all of us. She acted as helpless as she did tenacious about our farm. They agreed there wouldn't be room for cows to graze but a chicken coop or a pig pen would fit just fine. The Department of Agriculture – they enforced laws for plants and farms and whatnot – sent some quickly drawn-up

132

recommendations for animal habitats, but they were part of a bigger government and the states didn't pay them much mind anyway."

Carol interrupted herself again. "Iris, you care to get this hungry man a plate before he starts crying all over my nice clean counter?"

Iris awkwardly took Enrique's plate and did her best to replicate serving the rabbit stew and quinoa to him. She reached for a mug for his drink before remembering Jimmy was halfway back to Carol's house with the barrel of liquor. She leaned in towards Carol.

"There isn't anything for him to drink," Iris whispered.

Carol shrugged. "Ain't *your* fault."

Iris waited for more direction, but it wasn't coming. She handed Enrique his plate and took the ears of corn he handed her as payment.

"No drinks tonight, Carol?"

Silence fell. Iris broke it.

"Should've come earlier, Enrique."

She hid a smirk as Carol burst into laughter. The man took his plate and walked off.

"So how did she go from pigs and chickens to rabbits?"

"That's the best part," Carol said. "The day before Ascension – so March 22nd – Marianne loads the kids up and drives out to the field where they've got Triton sedated. Of course it's a madhouse with people fighting to get aboard; there were walls and armed guards and gunfire and all sorts of craziness. But all of her papers checked out so they ushered her on through, towing just one trailer behind her car, the car full of kids and packed high with clean clothes."

"One trailer?"

"Yes indeed. And Marianne drives right up next to this sleeping beast and the governor says 'Okay, Mrs. Lee, welcome aboard; you can leave your car over there and we can have someone load up the chickens you brought and we'll send them back for the rest.' But there's just one problem."

"What?" Iris asked.

"There wasn't no chickens.

"'Pigs, then?' the governor asked. 'No pigs,' she said. 'Well what have you got then? I've secured you a double lot of land on the new city for all your livestock…' So she takes him around to the back of the trailer and opens it up."

"Rabbits," Iris said. It was as much a guess as a deduction.

"Rabbits."

"Where'd her chickens and pigs go?"

"Never had any. Between the chaos in those days and the hands-off government that preceded it, nobody much looked in too closely on the Lee farm. Now keep in mind the breeding and ranching of bunny rabbits wasn't exactly within the boundaries of the law. But nevertheless, there's Marianne Lee on a cool spring afternoon with a car full of screaming kids and an army of half-crazed American citizens at her back who are about to be left behind on the last pilgrimage the human race will ever make, trading her family's way onto salvation with nothing but a hitched trailer full of illegally-farmed, long-eared, fluffy critters and a yarn of bullshit she's been spinning since they tried to take her land in the first place."

"Wait. Why did they give her the deal in the first place?" Iris asked. She couldn't help herself, but once the words escaped her lips she realized how it must've sounded. "No offense. I mean, she sounds like she nobody to mess with but that's a huge deal to strike."

"Well, when she stormed the capitol building that day, the state figured they had her over a barrel. A widowed mother, questionably educated, desperate to keep her family together would take any deal they made. They figured they could have her work for cheap, close to slave labor, and keep them supplied with hearty meals and never hear the end of her gratitude. 'Sure, you can have your land; we'll just talk terms when the dust settles and we're all living happy up in the sky,' they said."

"But what about the other ranchers? If there were so many people desperate to get onto the titans, didn't the politicians get other bids?"

"Of course they did," Carol said, "but cattle were too big to keep for the limited space so they were out of luck before they knew there *was* a need for ranchers. As for the folks who the state thought were her competition – the pig and chicken ranchers? Marianne played the damsel in distress so well that she had them working for *her*. 'Sorry,' they'd say. 'We already have a deal with another party.' She'd undercut any possible offer that could be made by any fat cat in the business – or so it seemed."

Leon returned to them but Iris still had questions and she wasn't leaving without answers.

"I'm amazed the governor didn't turn her away when he saw the rabbits," Iris muttered, finishing her drink.

"Think about it this way. Let's say you vouch for someone as a supplier of food for thousands of people. You promise your colleagues 'This is one of a handful of people who can either provide sustenance for thousands of people or teach them to grow their own.' You've solved a major problem. Now let's say she shows up with nothing but some mangy rabbits in tow, in all that chaos and death and urgency, under your promise of her worth. What image would you want to present? In front of a panel of maybe a dozen people finalizing the decision of which several thousand people were necessary to save and which *tens of millions* were allowed to die, would you want to appear a competent and noble leader whose life was worth bringing to this new world, or someone who underestimated one woman and never bothered to double-check, which could lead to the starvation of an entire people?

"I guaran-damn-tee you that's the thought that went through his head in that one single moment before one of the other pencil-pushers looked in Marianne Lee's trailer. Self-preservation, Miss Just Iris, turns honest men crooked and crooked men straight."

"So he started talking her way onto Triton for her?"

"If I'm lying I'm dying."

"And they all went for it."

"Turns out the governor was as good a salesperson as she was. 'Oh, rabbits multiply so fast and they reach adulthood so quickly, and they eat vegetables we can grow so they're practically self-sustaining' and blah blah blah."

136

Carol took Iris's mug and cleaned it. Jimmy had returned with the dolly and was loading the empty chafers and what little leftovers there were onto it.

"Once Triton woke up and we ascended on March 23rd, Marianne took to serving up kabobs, stews, curries, stir fry and more. She bartered away meat for new spices and seasonings to broaden her menu, and toys for the kids and cooking supplies to supplement their living situation while their crops grew.

"But she had a problem. The cities pressed everyone to sustain themselves and we've never been much for farming – besides critters of course. Marianne couldn't get her vegetables to come in, but if she only fed her kids off their own supply of rabbits they'd eat themselves out of business. She tore down all the hydroponics and gardening equipment in the house, removed all her grow containers and compost and used the space to breed more rabbits. She traded away all her gardening supplies for enough grown vegetables and grains to last the children until she had enough business to take food instead of trinkets from her customers."

"Didn't the city object to her defying their orders?" Iris asked. She turned to Leon. "Wouldn't they have stepped in?"

Leon flashed a sheepish grin and Carol folded her arms smugly.

"Go on, Detective; tell her."

"All the cops on the beat were Marianne's biggest clients," he said. "They looked the other way and *still* paid her in full for her food. It was partly due to the quality and the rest was how afraid they were to give up another piece of their normal lives. We'd already left solid ground for a lifelong ride on half-mile-high monsters; nobody wanted to give up meat too. The mayor's office couldn't have turned 'em if they'd tried, see, and they knew better than to try.

"I just can't make heads or tails of rabbits being so valuable," Leon added. "Your recipes are one in a million, Carol, but for folks to be trading away their only good pots and pans for them? It's like they were hooked on those rabbits like dope."

It was Iris's turn to surprise the rest of them. "It's like the Tulip Boom the Dutch went through in the 17th century."

Carol's eyes lit up. "Very good, missy," she said.

"Can someone explain this to me?" Leon asked.

Iris continued. "Tulips, the flowers, came to Holland from Constantinople in the late 1500s. They absolutely exploded and people started giving away furniture, beds, hundreds of pounds of food and more just to get their hands on some bulbs to plant tulips."

"No shit," Leon said.

"Vendors made enough money off them that they could buy…" Iris did some quick math in her head. "…a new house every three or four months."

"So what happened?"

Carol chimed in next. "Eventually the rapid growth of the business overwhelmed the entire country. One day someone didn't show up to buy their tulips, and someone said it was because they weren't worth anything anymore. The whole market died quicker than someone falling off Triton."

"I guess I missed that day in school," Leon said.

"I guess we didn't," Carol and Iris replied in unison. They shared a laugh.

138

"Anyway," Carol continued, "it turns out Marianne did have one thing in common with old George Willis from the bank," Carol said. "Like her, he couldn't farm vegetables worth a damn. Now I don't know how he talked his way onto Triton, but he did. And one day he shuffles up in line with an empty plate."

"No he didn't," Iris said. She believed Carol but she realized where the story was going.

"The hell he didn't," Carol replied. She couldn't contain her pride. "The Founders could never agree on a singular currency so everyone just started bartering for everything they needed. And with that, there was no use for loan officers. People wiped their asses with money or used it to roll cigarettes."

"Did she feed him?"

"Hell no; she told him to learn a real trade and come back with something she needed."

"Well, did he?"

"They say he scraped by somehow. Emptying the shit buckets or something I reckon. Grandma told me Marianne used to call him 'The Thinnest Fat Cat Alive' which she thought was hilarious.

"Listen, I gotta get back to the rabbits, y'all. Iris, it was a pleasure meeting you. Detective Adler can fill you in on the rest; Lord knows he's heard the story enough times now."

Leon said goodbye to Carol and Jimmy with the tip of his hat. Iris did the same. Her head buzzed pleasantly from the drinks and the story. Leon told her the rest of Marianne's story but Iris put the pieces together before he spoke. She never remarried, and the practice of apprenticeship became not only common but virtually expected. She taught her kids how to cook and farm; they married and did the same. Marianne's restaurant was now one of the only businesses in the city that was both handed down directly from generation to generation and that remained in the family of a Founder.

Marianne's culinary abilities may have found public value by bringing a piece of home up to the theriopolis, but as new generations were born who had never eaten steaks, ribs or chicken, the uniqueness of her wares earned Marianne and her children respect bordering on fame. Boys cleaned themselves up more than usual to earn favor with Marianne's daughters; grown men and women dropped the Lee name into conversations to impress friends. 99 years later, Carol was a fifth-generation public figure – a chef with a monopoly for carnivores.

"All this from a widow on a con job with a car full of rabbits," Leon said.

"All this from men who took advantage of a mother who had babies to keep safe," Iris replied. They walked back to their respective living quarters in silence, their heads full of rabbits and flowers and corn liquor. The task ahead of them seemed a distant cloud that only threatened their minds in dreams that night.

layover

On August 14th Leon and Iris waited after dinner for Triton to approach the Hermitage Towers in Paris. They stood at the port side harbor. Leon leaned his back against the wall of the immigration office; Iris sat cross-legged by the ballista the two would soon be using to disembark. They were as serious as they were quiet. The only sounds were the thud of Triton's feet and the quiet discussion between the nearby harbormaster and the dock worker who would soon fire the ballista, creating the ropeway they'd cross to the towers. Iris reflected on her last two weeks.

The city changed after Allison Mackey's funeral. Doubt hung in the air. Worry. Nash's only exacerbated things. Everyone had known about their deaths, but seeing with their own eyes that they had lost a member of law enforcement and their veteran food supplier was troublesome. Mayor Davis made more public appearances that week, hoping to keep the Wandering City Blues at bay, but many couldn't help but wonder if Triton was coming apart.

Nash's widow, Julie, was a small blonde woman. She cried hard at his funeral and bent over his covered body; her tears were vessels of loss rolling down the hills of her reddened cheeks and regrouping at her chin. Seeing their mother cry scared her children, but no one could bring themselves to chide her for her grief. When Leon and the other pallbearers finally pulled her away from her late husband so they could put him overboard, she fought to get one hand free and used it to slap Leon in the face. "My Anthony always looked up to you, you son of a bitch," she said. "He wanted to be just like you. And look where it got him." Iris almost stepped in to help but Leon put out a hand in protest. Nor would he meet Julie's gaze. He kept his eyes trained on the floor and let her take her anger out on him. *This is what you get*, he told himself.

Even still, Iris had had a fine time overall. Leon showed her around Triton and she met dozens of its citizens. Every night she looked up at the stars, a liberated woman gazing into infinity, taking charge of her destiny. Of course her personal stake in the case – her reputation, her past rearing its ugly head to interfere with her new life, the potential involvement of her family and old friends – had sobered her thinking as the day approached. Her dread also doubled when she returned home to Ghettobelly the day prior to retrieve more clothes and other utilities for her long trip abroad. But in that moment, waiting in the harbor, she knew dread solved nothing and only widened the gap between her and freedom.

All four of them heard the gargantuan splash of Triton's foot as it landed in the Seine just southwest of the center of Paris and they knew it was time. "Ten minutes!" the harbormaster shouted. Out of habit, he looked to his left for the Eiffel Tower. He'd always wanted to see it in person, but it was just 50 feet too short to clear the fog ceiling. It always had been, and unless the fog cleared, it always would be. But that didn't stop him from trying. As usual, he eventually tore his eyes away from their search, in muted disappointment.

Iris and Leon began their preparations to cross the ropeway. He crouched and began rummaging through his bag, removing his pieces of climbing equipment one by one. Iris emptied her bag of similar gear. Tonight she'd need a couple more pieces than she used the night she travelled down to Ghettobelly via Triton's support cable. She got it all out, but paused when saw her foot ascender.

The foot ascender was a simple set of nylon straps that could be tied and tightened onto one of her boots. Near the ankle, it had a small lever called a cam, through which the climbing rope could be threaded. The cam only opened one way, so when climbing uphill she could slide her foot up along the rope and then apply her weight to the foot, causing the cam to tighten and pinch the rope so firmly that she could push her body up on it like a rung on a ladder. Amazing, considering it wasn't bigger than her thumb.

"How tall is the rooftop on Hermitage?" she asked loudly enough that anyone could answer her.

The harbormaster knew why she asked. "It's shorter than we are, ma'am – all downhill from here."

She left the foot ascender – along with another piece of uphill climbing equipment – in her bag. Finally, she stood and got to work dressing herself in her rigging.

First was her harness. She put it on like a pair of pants – the most logical way, since it almost looked like a pair of boxers made of cloth framing like a hoop skirt. She put one leg at a time through each loop and pulled them up to her thighs, then snapped the belt at the waist around her stomach with a click. A pair of chest straps came up from the lower back and over her shoulders and snapped into the waistline like a pair of suspenders. She looked over at Leon; his harness was a simpler model without a full seat to support his backside while he climbed. He caught her looking at his equipment and took the opportunity to give hers a once-over in return.

"Hey hey, *some*body's fancy," he teased.

"Shut up, Leon," she replied.

She had left a locking carabiner fastened to one end of her short lifeline rope. She unscrewed its lever and hooked it into the loop on her harness near her bellybutton. She screwed this back in and gave the lifeline a firm tug to test its security. Everything was fine. On the opposite end of the lifeline rope – the end furthest from her – she secured another carabiner. Finally, she picked up the zip line trolley that would sit atop the rope she planned to traverse in a few minutes. She set it near the ballista. Leon finished preparing himself just moments before she did.

The time passed silently. Nobody else approached to disembark Triton. An immigration officer came out of the building to check their passports before returning to his desk. Triton approached Hermitage Plaza and stopped. Leon and Iris approached the ballista, fully dressed, their bags on their backs. The dock worker fired the ballista at its rooftop and it landed with a bang. He reeled in the long rope until it was almost taut and Iris picked up her zip line trolley from the floor. She stood on top of the balustrade and set her trolley on top of the ropeway and secured the carabiner at the far end of her lifeline to the loop on the bottom of the zip line trolley. It was a steep decline. Triton must be close to the skyscraper.

"Hey," Leon said. "You sure your gear's all set?"

Iris grabbed the handle on the zip line trolley, her fingers near the handbrake. She had neither the time nor the inclination to let him second-guess her. "Only one way to find out," she said. She firmed her grip and picked her feet up and she quickly sped down the line towards Hermitage Towers.

The wind rushed at Iris's face. When she felt she'd gone about halfway she applied pressure to the handbrake, slowing her descent. She kept her eyes trained on the grappling hook on the edge of the roof. She approached it and picked her feet up to the rope, using their friction and the handbrake together to slow her to a stop. She raised herself over the ledge with her arms, her biceps burning as she climbed, and collapsed on the rooftop. She caught her breath and retrieved her trolley from the ropeway, shouting up to Leon as loud as she could that she'd made it.

He barely heard her, but the harbormaster had been watching her descent through a pair of binoculars and told him when he was clear. Leon followed her lead, tying himself to his zip line trolley and making the quick trip down to the tower.

"Godspeed," the harbormaster said quietly as Leon rode the ropeway.

When he was on the rooftop and he'd dismounted from the ropeway, he pulled the grappling hook from its anchor point and shouted back up to the dock worker.

"*Reel it in!*"

He released the grappling hook and it swung towards Triton, under the titan's body. It was hard to tell at first, but as they watched, Iris and Leon could tell the line was indeed getting shorter. Eventually it was wound back into the ballista. In another 45 minutes, Triton would be on his way to London. *They should get to The Shard tomorrow mid-afternoon,* Leon thought. Once it left, it would be just him and Iris with three days to kill.

They unpacked for their stay. It was already close to midnight and both detectives had sleep on their minds. The raven-like Psamanthe had always been true to her appearance, adopting a maternal instinct towards her residents. Over the years, she made a habit of fishing materials straight from the surface in her mouth – makeshift birds' nests for the humans she hosted. In the end, the rooftops of her perches were domesticated enough to feature couches, Oriental rugs, even several dressers and tables. Leon and Iris each picked a couch with a nearby end table. Iris unrolled her sleeping bag and laid it out on the couch. She set out the gallon jug of water she'd brought with her. Leon did the same, then hung his hat on the corner of a nearby dresser and stripped his upper body to an undershirt before the two of them awkwardly undressed the rest of the way for bed with their backs to each other. It was a fast process; Iris slipped into her sleeping bag quickly in her shirt and underwear. She kept her gloves on, not ready to risk Leon seeing her without them. They said their goodnights and she put the top layer of the sleeping bag over her head – something she hadn't done in years. It was warm and uncomfortable, her breath reflecting off the fabric and back into her face, but for now she knew it was necessary. She still had her secrets to keep from him. He'd already seen her interrogation methods and knew of her birthplace; she didn't know what he was liable to do if he learned everything else about her.

Leon noticed her bizarre sleeping patterns. He didn't know if she had something to hide or if it was just an eccentricity but he saw no reason to stir the pot. He shook his head in resignation and rolled over, grabbing a cigarette from his bag. He reached for his curved glass before remembering it was the middle of the night. There were always campfire materials on the skyscrapers, left by ancestors and other travelers and Psamanthe's nomadic residents, but it didn't seem worth building. He sighed and left his cigarette for the morning, opting instead to look up at the stars.

Iris heard Leon's breathing get heavier and she knew he was sleeping for the night. She was left alone with her thoughts. She peeked out from her sleeping bag and looked at Triton, watching the ichor in his veins slowly pulsate an electric blue. Her whole life she'd heard it was because the colossi were happy. What was Triton thinking about? Was he glad to be back in France, or did he sense another colossus near him? Had he seen the nest Psamanthe had built on Hermitage Towers and been reminded of her existence? She was glad that the titan was in high spirits, but this train of thought led her to herself. The smile faded from her face and she thought back to her final days on Sao. A minute later, tears streamed down her face as memories of her mother clouded her mind. She retreated back into her sleeping bag and cried herself to sleep.

Morning came slowly. Leon awoke first, bleary-eyed, and looked for the sun. By his estimate it was between two and three hours after sunrise. He got out of bed and put his pants on, retrieving last night's unlit cigarette and putting it in his mouth. He looked out over the horizon. Just 50 feet below the rooftop that was their hostel for the next several days, the red-orange fog rolled by, as eternal as the stars in the night sky. Leon had forgotten how eerily quiet layovers were. Compared to the hustle and bustle of city life, the Paris skyline was utterly silent. It was hypnotizing – even imposing. He lost his focus, staring off in the distance for several seconds before catching himself. He checked his pockets for his makeshift lighter, then remembered it was in his bag.

He reached for his backpack and casually looked at Iris, still dozing in her sleeping bag on a neighboring couch. In her sleep she had emerged from her cover, her face largely masked by her hair. Her bare left arm was splayed out along the couch.

Leon's hand stopped rummaging through his pack. His lips parted slowly and his cigarette dropped from his mouth to the floor. His eyes widened. He couldn't believe what he was seeing – he blinked several times and shook his head to make sure, but the image remained. As plain as day, the veins in Iris's arm – and those on her face not hidden by her hair – were glowing. They glowed a pale blue; they brightened and dimmed in unison. Try as he did, Leon couldn't reconcile this with any reality he'd ever known.

Fear got the better of him. He was already traveling to the world's most dangerous city on the trail of an organized conspiracy involving ritualistic murder, and the odds of him leaving Sao alive were barely on the happy side of 50/50. Nash was dead, Allison was dead, Sean Bellamy was dead. He'd been partnered with this woman, about whom he knew so little, and this is what she must've been hiding from him – *intentionally,* he thought – when she crawled inside her sleeping bag last night. Something in him snapped. He reached for his gun in its holster by his bedside.

Iris woke to the sound of a click. She looked around and saw Leon pointing his gun at her. Much happened in the next instant. Without thinking, she threw off her sleeping bag and backed away from him in fear, her arms out. "Whoa whoa whoa, what the *fuck?!*" she screamed. She realized she was mostly undressed, then panicked as she looked at her own outstretched arms and saw the incandescence of her veins, slowly fading but still clearly visible.

While she rose, Leon looked her up and down. It wasn't just her arm – she looked electric from head to toe. Her arms and legs showed it the most, but the spidery veins reached towards her face and her belly as well. His heart raced. His thoughts raced through his brain in a moment. *Did Red Lung mutate? No, she'd have died from it. The colossi don't breed, unless I just don't know about it. Hybrid. No. Is everyone on Sao like this? No, someone would've noticed by now. New disease. Maybe. Next step of evolution, or infected by life on the colossi – no, we'd all be like this.*

Iris was thinking at the same time. She wasn't ashamed of her body, but she had worried the night before that something like this would happen. She must've unzipped and flapped open the sleeping bag in her sleep due to the heat. She cursed herself. Her first priority was convincing Leon to

149

stop aiming his gun at her. He was scared, almost to the point of shaking. Iris didn't want to hurt him. He was a good guy, overall. *But maybe,* she thought, *I could make a quick break for my escrima sticks. If I threw one just to make him dodge it, I could grapple and disarm him and* make *him listen to – No, that's no good.* She knew if she even looked at her escrima sticks he might shoot her. Besides, she could see out of her peripheral vision that they were well out of reach. The only option was to talk it out.

"Okay," she said. "Okay. Leon, I'm sorry; I didn't mean to scare you."

"What the Hell are you?" he asked.

"I'm still me: Iris, who is fully committed to bringing justice to the people behind the murders on Triton – your new partner who told your mayor that you shot Jeremai in self-defense. Remember?"

"W-What's wrong with you?" he asked, nodding towards her body.

"It's a long story, but if you take that gun off me I'll be happy to tell it to you."

He considered it for a moment but shook his head. "No. Not yet. First I want answers. W-What's that symbol we keep seeing?"

"I don't know," she said.

"Bullshit!" he said. He took a step towards her. "Stop lying to me!"

"Goddammit Leon I said I don't know! I swear I've never seen it before."

"Why are you so interested in this case? And don't tell me it's to keep Ghettobelly safe."

"It is," she said. His expression soured. "At least, it was until I got a look at our killer and could confirm where he was from." She spoke more slowly. "Now, I don't know why Sao would send someone over to Triton for the express purpose of stealing from its agricultural center and killing its chief botanist, but I do need to know why it was *Sao's* people who sent someone over. If this is a punishment to bring me back – if this is Sao's way of tracking me down and convincing me to return – then your friends' blood is on *my* hands. I can't live with myself until I know if that's true."

"What do you mean 'tracking you down?'" Leon asked.

Iris lowered her hands and looked away. The glow finished fading from her body and once again she looked normal. "15 years ago I left Sao. There were no fond fare-thee-wells, no best wishes or family-approved plans for me to strike out on my own and live my own life. I ran away."

"Why?"

She raised her eyes to meet Leon's again. "You mind if I put on a pair of pants before I tell you my life story?"

He paused then breathed deeply, lowering his gun. His senses were coming back to him and he realized she wasn't a danger to him. She dressed for the day and he found his cigarette on the floor. When they were ready, he spoke. "Remember, I covered for you too."

"So?"

"Just…make this make sense for me, okay?"

She recited the story from memory.

"At the time of The Great Ascension, when the whole world reset its calendars to Year Zero, Sao was a prison colossus – a convict colony," Iris said. "The politicians couldn't bring themselves to leave all the murderers and rapists and thieves locked in their cells on the surface, as much as the public wanted them to. It wasn't the law. So, the same as every other titan, there was a committee selection for some of the people who would be saved and a lottery for the rest. World leaders pardoned some of the criminals onto Sao at their own choosing, whether for favors or because they saw some merit or redemption in them. The fates of the rest – from drug users to mass murderers – were left to chance.

"There were only about 500 names pulled from a list of millions of convicted felons. Two of those names were Darlene and Jeremai Ewell."

"Jeremai?" Leon asked, retrieving the piece of curved glass from his pack.

Iris ignored him. "Darlene came from the Bedford Hills Women's Correctional Facility in upstate New York; Jeremai from Rikers Island. They were fraternal twins – both egotistical sociopaths. They were from somewhere in the deep south, but even they didn't know where originally. The Ewell Twins' parents lived a nomadic life bouncing from one state to another in rapid succession. Their juvenile records placed them in Mississippi, Kentucky, north Florida and at least one of the Carolinas for shoplifting, disturbing the peace, public intoxication and assault.

"When they turned 18 Jeremai was acquitted of manslaughter – and Darlene as an accessory to it – and they traveled north in a stolen car. Over the next couple years they tore up the East Coast on their way, wanted for charges of homicide, aggravated sexual assault, armed robbery and

152

manufacturing a controlled substance – and those were just the crimes the police could *prove*. The law finally caught up with them in upstate New York and it came out that they'd been living as man and wife for over a year, and they testified to having slept together since they were children."

"Jesus Christ," Leon said.

"And there was no death penalty in New York at the time, so the judge locked them up and threw away the key. He figured they were a volatile chemical compound. They riled each other up like a perpetual motion machine, always showing off and trying to outdo one another. So even though it violated some paperwork, he had them separated to Bedford Hills and Rikers. Seven years later, the fog and the colossi came from the sea.

"In his ego, Jeremai never doubted his name would be pulled from the lottery when they announced it. The way he saw it, all the announcements and legal papers and transfer processes were just time separating him from his new home – and his wife. So March 22nd, the night before the ascension, all the prisoners were escorted onto the comatose Sao in their shackles and chains and cuffs. They say the doctors who had induced the colossi's comas for ascension kept staring at their computers and monitoring the sleeping beast, too afraid to lock eyes with the killers and sex criminals passing by them to the twin prisons. The cons shuffled along in a straight line, their chains making a cacophonous applause of their extended lives, their orange jumpsuits like licks of flame, and Jeremai looked over to the line of female prisoners and locked eyes with his beloved sister."

Leon finally lit his cigarette. He was trying to space them out since it would be at least a week or two before he could get any more, but the craving had won out.

"In her first month on Sao, Darlene killed three inmates. Eventually she earned enough respect and trust from her other inmates that they started a large-scale prison riot. That first hour in the women's facility was the toughest, I hear. A lot of girls died, outgunned by the guards and having to work around locked doors. Eventually, though, they secured the guards' shotguns, rifles and – most importantly – keys and started to make quick work of the entire prison."

"You sound like you admire them," Leon said.

"I respect them," Iris said. "Once they took over the women's prison, they lived there for a few days unnoticed while they drew plans for freeing the men. The prisons were literally identical, which Darlene took as a sign from God that she and Jeremai were meant to rule over them both."

"Oh, bullshit."

"I'm not saying I believe it. Anyway, *since* the prisons were built the same, the women knew the overall blueprint of the building, they knew the quickest ways to get to the armory and the guards' quarters, how to lead the guards to slaughter and so on. They even tried a couple practice runs in their own facility. They crossed over Sao's hide under cover of night, lying prone and crawling through his fur to stay hidden from view. They infiltrated the men's prison and attacked in unison. It happened so quickly; law enforcement never had a chance. They freed the men, imprisoned whichever guards and doctors they didn't kill and collectively breathed the free air. They'd been on Sao under a year. Darlene and Jeremai

154

were reunited and had enough followers that they rose to the top of the pile soon enough.

"With nowhere to go and nothing left to steal, Darlene and Jeremai turned to appropriating their home to their own interests. What is it they said about Alexander the Great? 'When he looked upon his kingdom, he wept, for there were no more lands to conquer.' Yeah. They ran out of prison food before long, and they'd been forcing the guards to garden for them but it wasn't enough. They missed steaks and pork chops and chicken drumsticks; nobody wanted to live on salads and steamed vegetables. First they drew lots for who would rappel down to the surface and forage for food, liquor and drugs – much like Triton's fishing system. There were occasional territorial disputes, fights and murders. One night during Darlene's first pregnancy they threw a body onto a fire and a very stoned Jeremai stared at it for several minutes, sauntered up to it, hacked its arm off, cleaned the arm and ate it medium-rare.

"Then there was real panic. Most people won't accept cannibalism…but some did. Enough did that it gained traction, actually –"

"See, that I don't believe," Leon said. "How the hell do people just clear the hump and resort to eating folks?"

"Have you ever heard of the Milgram Experiment?"

"Sure. It was back in the 20th century. A guy puts on a lab coat and tells random people to shock other folks for making mistakes on a test – and the lab coat sees how far it goes."

"Yes. Plenty of those people ended up zapping the test-takers voluntarily. An authority figure told them to do it,

155

so they did it, and then some went that extra mile and actually did it without being told. Aside from just going along with the program, some of them even seemed to like it."

"That's messed up, sister."

"So if you're hungry and someone you practically hail as a king tells you to eat, what do you do?" Iris asked.

"Well, I imagine some people would object," Leon said.

"They did," Iris said. "They…didn't last long.

"The closest the twins ever got to a domesticated, quiet life was that each of them had many members of the opposite sex – and some members of the same sex – living with them in a harem. Darlene's first child, a boy named after her husband, was Jeremai's, but the others…who knows who their fathers were. At the same time, Jeremai sired several half-siblings for his son. The colony throve. Everyone looked down the barrel of parenthood as the population dwindled and meat became scarcer, but the occasional uprising and power struggles still made for enough cannibalism to…complicate things."

She stood and crossed to lean on the railing atop the tower. It was her turn to notice the deafening silence in the air. A soft wind blew.

"Bloodlines narrowed as Darlene and Jeremai repopulated the colossus with their own descendants. All that hedonism, all the unchecked drugs and violence and sex…I guess what goes around comes around. You ever wonder why, in the history books, cannibals all seem so insane?"

"Sure," Leon said, flicking his cigarette over the edge of the tower. "I always figured it took that insanity to make them eat."

156

"No," she said. "It's because of prions – proteins in the brain that can cause other normal proteins to fold abnormally and create mental defects. While the convicts were raising their kids, they noticed they themselves were suffering memory loss, difficulty chewing and swallowing, muscle failure and more. On Sao, it either manifested as Kuru or as variant Creutzfeldt-Jakob Disease; nobody really knows. Ignorance and pride kept them from admitting they were doing something wrong – The Ewells were practically messianic to them by then – so they just assumed it was a side effect of life on the titan, or life up in the air."

"How do you know all this?" Leon said.

"Books."

"I mean…*why* do you know all this?"

"The story of Darlene and Jeremai is taught to every child on Sao as history."

"No, why do you know everything about the diseases on –"

"Can I finish? Years ticked by. Dementia and schizophrenia were rampant. Darlene and Jeremai grew old and kept preaching their radical theories about pure bloodlines and Gemini omens and they sold it for so long they started to believe it themselves. Inbreeding became the cultural expectancy, like the Hapsburg Dynasty in the 16th century or Tutankhamun's family in ancient Egypt. Sao reveled in its creature comforts: they still had their solar panels and electricity; the raids on the other colossi were sheer chest-beating. But nobody was willing to admit their babies were being born deformed or that the parents were going half-crazy and dying young from whatever prion disease circulated on the colossus. How do you think the heads of the city would react if you complained that they were running Sao into ruin?"

"With a barbecue?"

Iris nodded. "By the third generation, most of the turmoil had settled down. The population had shrunk from over a thousand to just a couple hundred…and half the babies born had pretty radical birth defects as they whittled themselves down to just a dozen separate families or so."

Leon had heard about birth defects from inbreeding. He thought back on Jeremai from Ghettobelly. "Ok. I understand. Our killer…his underbite, his large nose and forehead – those are all results of siblings reproducing; that's how you knew who he was when we confronted him…"

Iris nodded again. Leon followed a train of thought.

"But there are other physical signs of incest-born children too. Some of them can't speak, right?"

"Right," Iris said.

"Or they have cleft palates, or facial asymmetry or –"

He stopped suddenly and looked up at Iris. She turned around and looked at him, her pale skin and colorless eyes ready for his judgment.

"…Or albinism."

It was a long time before either of them spoke again. Leon finished his cigarette and flicked it over the railing to the fog. "So are you a…Ewell?"

"No; I don't think so," Iris said. "My father was killed before I was born for dissenting from Sao's practices. Mother would've told me."

Iris turned back to look out over the horizon.

"But playing their game was the only way to stay alive on Sao," Iris said. "Be an eater or be meat. Keep your families from marrying other families or wind up on the menu. By the time Sao was four generations along, the original Jeremai Ewell was dead, and in his honor they named the boys Jeremai. Every boy was Jeremai, Ewell or not. The only way to tell them apart was to give them numbers as they came out instead of last names, since each family had several Jeremais apiece. And we start back at 'one' every generation."

"And the girls?"

"The girls of all the different families were named after their matriarch – kind of. Darlene Iris Ewell."

"That's why you wouldn't tell me your last name," Leon said. "You…don't have one."

"In a way, I do," Iris said.

"What is it?"

"13."

"Iris 13. That's your full name."

"Yeah. Specifically, if they had to refer to me instead of the previous generation's Iris 13, I'd be Iris 13, Generation Five, but that doesn't usually happen."

"So you're the 13th Iris born in the fifth generation of Sao's history."

"Yes."

"Wait," he said. "You mentioned you had to 'play along' with what was happening on Sao. How many people have you killed?"

"Only as many as I've had to."

"How many people have you…eaten?"

"That's really none of your business," she said. "But if it helps you sleep at night, I haven't in over 15 years."

Leon opened his mouth to ask if she'd been subjected to molestation, rape or other sexual acts when she was a child, but he stopped himself. He wasn't actively trying to judge her but his curiosity had gotten the better of him and he'd ventured into unsafe territory. And he realized it at least one question too late. It was equal parts habit from interviewing victims and male entitlement. He chose a more reasonable route of conversation.

"You still haven't told me why you…" Leon nodded upwards towards her general direction.

"Glow."

"Yeah. That."

Iris sighed. She was getting restless being under the magnifying glass, but she was past the point of no return.

"When we were born, my siblings and cousins and other kids our age were a little more genetically problematic than our parents, who in turn had more defects than theirs. The elders noticed it first. Now, either they couldn't tell that our city's diet and dynasties were the source of our problems or they just couldn't bring themselves to make it public – because by that point, the reigning families were so mixed together there's no going back. Personally I think they didn't know. I got the impression they still believe that it's because of the leviathans themselves. So what do you tell the straggling few hundred people? 'Sorry, we never adapted to life up here, so let's forget continuing our families and just die off.' No. We kids were different enough that the problem

160

wasn't going away, but nobody could say why it happened. So they decided to try and 'cure us.'

"My parents' generation of Sao-born once retrieved a cache of medical supplies from a hospital when Sao walked through Buenos Aires. It was the biggest score since my great-uncle looted an electronics warehouse and they loaded Sao himself up with 30-foot speakers pointing outwards in every direction. Typical braggadocio – they blast their fucking music so you can hear them coming from a mile away and have time to piss your pants before they kill and eat you. Anyway, so the descendants of the prison doctors – who had lost much of their reason from decades of living Sao life as well – found a soft spot on Sao and nicked a hole in him at a prominent vein. Nothing serious – just enough to siphon a couple gallons of his ichor into old plastic milk jugs. Then they gathered all us kids up and sat us in chairs and told us how we've been given a gift from the gods and from the original Ewell twins. 'It's medicine from the titans,' they said. 'Oh, remember your cousin whose muscle spasms killed him? Well these titans haven't aged a day in over 80 years; they *can't* get sick or die. Wouldn't that be nice? Roll up your sleeve; you're gonna get a little shot. It won't hurt; it'll just be a little pinch.'"

Leon dared not interrupt. Not to ask questions or lend his support. Iris began unlacing her left glove. She pulled its fingertips off her fingers before removing the glove entirely from her left hand. It was the first time he'd seen either of her hands. The left looked normal.

"It wasn't a little pinch. When they put Sao's ichor in us it was like fire erupting through all our veins. We

161

screamed and cried. Some kids vomited, a couple went into seizures. One died.

"The next day they did it again."

She began taking off her right glove. As she unlaced it the cuff near her elbow became loose. Leon thought he saw a scar of some kind on her forearm. Then she stopped.

"For a few weeks, our bloodstreams fought the titan's plasma. We fought and won. We knew we won because every time someone's circulatory system *lost* the battle, they lost the war and their corpse got thrown overboard – nobody wanted to eat tainted meat. But these doctors and the town elders had our folks convinced it was what was best for us. 'The titans' resilience and cell renewal is proof that this is a good thing to introduce to your daughter, ma'am. The other kids were just too weak but *your* girl is strong!' Piss. Nobody listened to them when they said to stop boning their siblings or eating one another but they're all ears when it comes to poisoning their kids.

"Then I turned 15 and received a birthday present from Sao himself. It was over a month into the treatment and I was given an injection and it didn't hurt. Not in the least. And compared to the pain of the previous sessions, its absence was enough to feel like bliss. The doctor called everyone's attention to me. In my shock and confusion I looked immediately to where they'd stuck the needle, in the vein in the crook of my right arm. I was just in time to watch the skin from the needle mark to the fingertips redden."

She removed her glove and held her arms up in front of her face for comparison. Her bare right arm was scarlet from the elbow down, a lively shade of crimson. The fine hairs on her forearm grew naturally – in fact, aside from the color, her right arm was a perfect symmetrical match of the left.

"Good lord."

"Relax, Leon. I was as freaked out as you were the first time I saw it, but this is just one reaction my body had to accepting Sao within me. Think about the heart pumping blood in and out of the body. Sao's ichor just changed the skin from the injection on outwards. I don't know if it pushed my blood out from the veins into the tissue or what, but there it is."

Leon was still uneasy.

"Also I grew a dick," she said.

"*What?!*" Leon shouted.

Iris laughed out loud. "I'm kidding! I'm sorry, I'm sorry; I couldn't help myself. Man you're too easy!"

Leon tried to laugh too. It was clearly fake, and forced, but it made him feel better. Iris rubbed her forearms a bit; they'd been stuffy inside the gloves.

"So we figured my hand was the only side effect until that night when I fell asleep. We lived in the prison – with the doors unlocked of course – and my mom said that night I lit up like a fluorescent light."

Leon thought back to the tube lights in Doc Frazier's clinic on Triton, when he'd remembered his parents telling him about losing power. "They're all crazy on Sao," his father had said.

"So did your mother explain to everyone what happened?"

163

"No, in fact she wrapped me in an extra blanket and covered my head with it so nobody would know. 'From now on, you sleep like this,' she said. 'Every night.' The transfusion didn't help with my skin or my eyes, so we agreed that whatever they'd tried to do to me was a fruitless endeavor. But if I suddenly stopped going to the therapy they'd find out what *had* happened. So I faked sick for a few days while my mother went nightly to Jeremai 1, Generation Four – who has been Sao's king since before I was born – and pleaded with him to order the treatments stopped."

"How did she try to convince him?"

Iris looked at Leon until he understood. The shift in his eyes from confusion to empathy spoke volumes.

"Then one night she didn't come back. She gave everything to him and he ended up feeding her to his fucking sycophants. And I couldn't save her. She died, and I lived, and…"

"Hey, hey," Leon said. "You were a kid. Don't be so hard on yourself. There's nothing you could have done."

"I don't know," Iris said. "Maybe. But now I dream of her several times a week, and most of *those* are nightmares. I can never save her. It never ends."

"What never ends? The dreams?"

"Everything I think about her – and myself. Sure, I drive myself crazy wondering if there's something I could've done. But also I wonder if I've lived the kind of life that would've made her proud. Was my life worth her death?"

The wind blew warm as Iris pondered her fate.

"Mom didn't come back and I knew they'd come for me, and if they found out I had a real symbiosis with Sao they'd likely perform every medical test on me they could for the rest of my life – or just kill me and eat me to gain whatever 'power' they think I have."

"What about the 'tainted meat' paranoia?" Leon asked.

"I didn't get sick and die from it like the others, Leon; I was thriving," she replied. "At any rate, Mom and I didn't want to take any chances." Leon could tell by the tone in her voice that she saw through him, looking for holes in her theory to determine she was really telling the truth. He let it go.

"We were near a skyscraper so I packed a jug of water and some food and disembarked at night. I rationed out my food and water the best that I could, but it was weeks before anyone found me. Malnourished and dehydrated, I woke up in Yuki Nakajima's house on Naiad."

Leon was once again surprised. "You've been to Naiad?"

"Yes. Nakajima-san rescued me from a cruel fate on that rooftop, nursed me back to health and took me on as an assistant for a while at Naiad's pharmaceutical production plant – the one that leaves the medicine drops for all the other colossi?"

Leon laughed. "Yeah, I know what's on Naiad."

"So chances are, if you took an antibiotic in the late 80s, it was made under my and Nakajima-san's supervision." She beamed with pride. "Over several years, she became like a second mother to me. She taught me proper English and enough about gardening, social norms and behaviors that I could get by in any city."

"When was that?"

"Back in…let's think…89. I spent the last 10 years island-hopping, working day jobs and spending my free time in libraries and bars."

"Really?" he asked.

"Yeah. I almost drove myself crazy in hematology, trying to find an answer for what was happening in my bloodstream, but ultimately it proved pointless. I broadened to studying other sciences to understand the short- and long-term physiological effects of the Ewell Empire and other inbred families. Of course all that learning makes one thirsty," she said.

"So where'd you learn to fight like you do?"

"Well, like I mentioned on Triton: a girl spends enough time in a bar and eventually someone's going to think they have a right to her. I've had to defend myself more than once from unwanted advances. The first time, I barely got out of being raped."

He sighed. "I'm sorry."

"Not as sorry as he is," she said. There was memory in her eyes and voice.

Leon changed the subject. "So, Psamanthe will be here the day after tomorrow. She'll take us to 432 Park Avenue in New York City."

"When do we get there?" Iris asked.

Leon pulled his notes from his bag and looked them over. "If she takes us from here to London and stays her four days at each spot," Leon said, "we'll leave here around midnight on the 21st and get to London between 2 and 3 a.m. on the 22nd. We stay on The Shard until *late* late night, maybe 3 a.m. on the 26th? Then it's…3,471 miles to Manhattan. That's close to 50 straight hours in the air, but with the time change it'll be just after midnight on August 28th."

"Okay," Iris said.

"The only problem is, nobody knows much of Sao's migration pattern besides his affinity for New York City. I mean, the Tlingits on Psamanthe will give us some food, but I don't know how much. You lived on Sao. How long will we have to wait for him to show up?"

"Not long," Iris said.

Iris and Leon spent their remaining time in Paris eating, talking, drinking and sleeping. They told jokes, toasted the lives of the departed from cups made of halved coconuts and played blackjack with a dog-eared deck Leon had brought. At night they lay on their backs and talked about the constellations and the planets they saw. The day before Psamanthe came, a thunderstorm blew east across France. They hurriedly gathered up their things and hid under one of the canopies built by Psamanthe residents years ago. The canopy was a plastic tarp that angled just slightly, causing a funneling effect for the rainwater, which gathered near one corner and drained into a non-functioning water heater. Iris and Leon caught water in their gallon jugs, filling them both. They didn't want to take water from the main supply, lest they accidentally cause a shortage for Psamanthe. When the water had filled their jugs, they filtered it through a clean rag into a small pot. Iris, much more the traveler than Leon, had brought a fire piston with her for their trip. She made tinder from bits of dried grass she'd found around the rooftop and packed it into the claw. With a forceful push of the piston, the tinder began to ember. She added it to a bundle of coconut fibers she placed in the fire pit under the canopy and they boiled the pot of water to sterilize it. It cooled and they stored what they didn't drink.

The next night was overcast. Psamanthe was due any minute but between that night's campfire and the cloud coverage, she'd be next to impossible to see with much notice. It took her distant caw – a warning and salutation upon seeing the fire – for them to realize she was flying in from the horizon. Psamanthe was far smaller than the other coloss:, measuring just 150 feet from head to tail, but when she perched on the top of one of the towers at Hermitage Plaza, Leon and Iris almost expected the building to buckle under her weight.

She seemed to be a cross between a bird and a dragon with just a pinch of human. Her massive wings hung down by her sides like sleeves on a straitjacket, curving backwards like great sickles alongside her legs. Psamanthe had an underbite and her jaw was halfway between a pigeon's and a pelican's. She settled on the rooftop and shook herself out like a dog, careful to minimize the motion on her back. Finally, she straightened her back and crowed once more, loudly and with pride. Iris and Leon looked at her with wonder – neither had seen her before and she was a marvel. The magnificent beast brought smiles to their faces and they laughed when she bellowed.

Soon, long ropes uncoiled from her and dropped to the skyscraper. They heard the frictional sound of cloth nearing them from above and saw people sliding down their ropes to greet and inspect them. Pair after pair of feet landed with a thump on the tower and the citizens of Psamanthe spread out around the two detectives. Within minutes, 100 had dismounted Psamanthe and were unpacking and setting up camp around the towers.

Many of the men and women wore aviator goggles, raising them from their faces and resting the goggles on their heads when they landed. Most of the population was descended from Pacific Coast Indians from between Alaska and Washington State – predominantly Tlingit and Haida. Their light brown skin was accentuated by prominent cheekbones and black hair. Most of them looked Iris and Leon over just once before going about their own business. Many crossed from their landing tower to the other via a wooden bridge connecting the two. Finally an old woman, accompanied by a much younger woman, approached the two whites. The old woman's face was tanned, wrinkled, ancient. She was draped with a bright and intricate raven's robe – a Chilkat-woven, poncho-like garment with a mythical animal depicted across it. The young woman wore a small but loose t-shirt and faded brown shorts. The old woman smiled at Iris and spoke.

"Yakíei yee y·t · xwal geini," she said.

Iris hesitated. The young woman stepped forward.

"Sprichst du Deutsch?" she asked.

They didn't respond.

"Ellos hablan Español? Que diriez-vous Français? No?"

Iris put her left hand on her own chest then patted Leon's shoulder. "My name is Iris. This is Leon."

The young woman's expression changed to satisfaction. "Ah, you speak English! Forgive me; you never know. My grandmother said, 'It is good to look upon your faces.' She speaks only Tlingit, no English, but if you'd like, I can translate between you."

It was an artful and deliberate-sounding language. Just as the granddaughter, who introduced herself as Kenai,

170

had promised, the old woman spoke only in the Alaskan language. She talked to Leon and Iris with a familiarity as though they spoke it as well, but she waited for Kenai to tell them in English what she'd said. In turn, Leon and Iris responded in English and awaited the translation to Tlingit for the elder. It was slow, and required much patience of all parties involved, but with Kenai's help they were able to hold a conversation.

"I'm a police officer from Triton; this is my partner," Leon said. "We'd like to accompany you on Psamanthe until New York."

"What awaits you in New York?" the old woman asked.

"A man who needs to be brought to justice."

The old woman shook her head.

"A man was sent to Triton to steal from our public supply of plants," Leon said. "He murdered two people, including one policeman. We had to kill this murderer, but the man who sent him must also be stopped."

As Kenai finished telling the old woman this, Iris interrupted Leon. "The man behind this plot is Jeremai 1 from Sao."

At the sound of his name, the old woman perked up and raised her hand to Kenai, stopping her from translating. She called out for a young man and he began to approach from the opposite rooftop. He moved slowly, limping on a crutch. When she resumed speaking, her tone had darkened dramatically.

"I was born on the rooftop of Kingkey 100 in Shenzhen, China, the year Psamanthe took flight. When I was a small child, my father told me about the genocide, the false treaties, the broken promises made by the Americans – all the tragedies the Indian people suffered for so many centuries. Every time a white man needed passage on Psamanthe, my father refused them food or water, even urinating on them as they slept. In his old age he tempered his anger, resigning himself to occasionally cursing at your people or spitting on the floor as they walked past him. He died so long ago I can hardly remember his face, aside from how twisted with anger it was. His only satisfaction was successfully appealing to the American government – and, later, a global council called the United Nations – and attaining citizenship for the Tlingits, the Haida and Tsimshian on Psamanthe. We're one of the only cultures on Earth who have ever worshiped birds as deities, you see. My father argued that for all that had been done to American Indians, the least the Europeans and Americans could do was to let us be one with a living embodiment of one of our gods. My mother said he laughed as Psamanthe flew for the first time, leaving so many to choke on the mist."

The young man who she'd called over was getting closer, slow as he moved. As she spoke of the past, her eyes shone with distant memory and decades-old triumphs and tragedies in the light of a nearby fire. Kenai continued to translate for the old woman.

"What my father failed to see was the extraordinary responsibility with which we were burdened. He saw our emigration as a victory over his ancestors' wrongdoers – surviving where they died, outlasting them in some imagined contest. In fact, our dwindling numbers were like a crucible, the luckiest and strongest of us living on. Aren't we all the sum of our forefathers' experiences and destinies? The fewer of us there are, the more precious each of our lives are. I believe we have a duty to look out for one another – to hope, to dream, to stumble and rise and stumble again, to help others who have fallen regain their footing and try once more. Surviving isn't the only thing left for people, young man, but it is of great importance."

The young Tlingit man reached them. In the dim light, Iris saw that he had large eyes and tousled black hair. He used a crutch because his left leg was missing below the knee. He only used the one crutch, and he used it with his left arm, because his entire right arm was gone. He was shy; he looked at the floor except to occasionally steal a glance at Iris. When she returned his gaze and smiled, he looked away quickly.

"This is my grandson Kiviaq," she said. "He was taken in the middle of the night by your Sao-born on a layover in New York several years ago. He and two of his friends liked to sleep on the scaffolding left hanging on the side of the building. The morning after our first night in New York, they were all gone. His father – my son – ran down 85 flights of stairs to the ground to see if the boys had fallen or snuck away to the surface, against my protests. I was foolish to think a father could be talked out of risking his life for his child. He was gone for two days, frantically searching for Kiviaq and his friends. He returned alone, to his wife and their daughter, Kenai. Psamanthe was devastated for us, crying out into the night. The evening before we departed, as the sun set, we heard an unpleasant noise. It was some kind of chant, or music, and it grew to a horrible volume. It was Sao, his sound machines trumpeting his arrival. We didn't think much until they approached the building just long enough to throw Kiviaq overboard onto the rooftop, dismembered and disfigured for life. They threw him like a bag of garbage, laughing as they did so. My only grandson. They had sewn up his wounds so crudely, one of our doctors had to open the sutures and fix them or surely Kiviaq would have bled to death.

"You've heard the rumors about that cursed giant," she said. "I don't need to tell you what happened to his limbs or his friends. Some nights he still wakes screaming. His father died of the Red Lung last year, a complication of searching in vain for him on the streets of the city."

Iris and Leon were silent. Kenai had become emotional relating the story about her brother. She was able to continue translating for the old woman, though tears fell freely from her face. The old woman wrapped one arm around her shoulder and held her close. Iris's ears burned.

"When a leader fails to value every one of his followers' lives, they become disconnected and cruel," she said. "No other boy or girl should suffer the way our family has, or the families of Kiviaq's friends. We will take you to New York, and you will make those monsters pay for what they did to your friends and our families."

They spent the next four days meeting some of the families of Psamanthe. Much like Leon and Iris's time alone, they were halcyon days of joking and laughing and storytelling. On the fourth night, everyone packed up their camps and boarded Psamanthe again. Leon and Iris retrieved their hand and foot ascenders from their packs and strapped them on, using them to climb up to the middle of Psamanthe's

174

back and work their way over along one of the many heavy belts that ran across her. Some of the residents teased them a bit, having themselves spent their lives practicing this routine and finding no use in most climbing gear. The citizens of Psamanthe climbed the ropes with their bare hands and maneuvered into Psamanthe's middle with deft hand- and footwork. Leon and Iris hooked themselves into their belt with carabiners and lifeline ropes, their backs to Psamanthe, their hands slipped between her body and another thick strap that was level with their heads. In a flash, she leapt from the roof of Hermitage Towers and they plummeted several dozen feet before her enormous wings began beating and raising them back up. Iris's heart was in her chest; Leon put on a face that was braver than he felt. They took their time and looked around as Paris receded away from them, but with the wind blustering about they had to yell in order to hear each other talk.

"What did you think about the story she told us about Kiviaq?!" Iris asked.

"Damn kid's lucky he ain't pushing up daisies!" Leon replied.

"But she said Psamanthe cried for him! Do you really think the colossi care about us that much?!"

Leon snorted and nodded his head towards the ground below. "Well, right now I think it's very important that we believe they do!"

The flight to London was only three hours. They arrived around 2 a.m. BST and disembarked Psamanthe with shaky legs on The Shard, London's tallest building. Psamanthe's residents took great joy in seeing Leon and Iris regain their footing on solid ground. Leon wanted to be angry at them laughing as he composed himself, but he knew it was all in good fun. The next flight would be far longer – over 49 hours from London to New York – so they enjoyed the sturdy ground while it lasted.

Their first morning in London, Psamanthe took off. It startled Leon and Iris for a moment, but Kiviaq told them that Psamanthe would be back soon and they remembered the stories they'd heard about Psamanthe feeding her residents. Often when they stopped near coastal cities, she flew out several miles to the ocean and nosedived into the water, her plumage waving a brilliant show of her acrobatics as she headed towards the icy blue sea through the loathsome red-orange fog. The shock of the impact stunned hundreds of fish. Psamanthe swam back up and circled around for a second approach then, opening her great beak like a pelican and scooping up as many of the fish as she could. Still dripping with sea water, she beat her great wings and soared back up above the fog ceiling, releasing the fish from her mouth onto the rooftop for all her people.

Leon still found it hard to believe, although he couldn't imagine where else Psamanthe would go. Just as he was starting to wonder what she was really doing, Psamanthe returned to thunderous applause and cheering from the others. True to Kiviaq's word, she perched atop The Shard and lowered her head as close to the rooftop as she could before opening her mouth wide. The roof flooded with ocean water and countless fish shimmering silver in the sun. The children shrieked with joy and ran around, splashing one another with water and trying frantically to catch the flopping, slippery ocean creatures. Several of the adults laughed at their efforts and excitement; even Kiviaq's and Kenai's somber grandmother emitted several deep chuckles. Iris noticed that just before she delivered her cargo, several adults had gathered at Psamanthe's mouth with plastic containers.

Iris leaned over to Kiviaq to ask a question. "Why did those men rush to Psamanthe's mouth and catch the ocean water in those large plastic basins?" Kiviaq, still enjoying the children's fervor, answered without looking at her. "We boil it down and make salt with it," he said. He realized he must've sounded too matter-of-fact as Iris feigned disinterest. He let it go. They watched as several children and adults lovingly rubbed Psamanthe with both hands, patting her with affection. Again, Psamanthe cawed with pride.

The adults got to work trawling the rooftop with nets and plastic bags, scooping fish into them and hanging them on anything above floor level. Once the fish quieted down, they were cleaned. Some of the fish were cooked and eaten, but not before several dozen fish were rubbed with salt and hung to dry, beginning the process of being preserved. Kiviaq didn't want his conversation with Iris to end where it did, so he struck it up again as they sat to eat lunch.

"In two days, the fish should be dried out enough for the next leg of the journey," he said. "We don't always get enough to survive on fish alone, though, so we trade with other leviathans for fresh fruits and vegetables."

"Who do you trade with?" Iris asked.

"Anyone we meet," he said. He looked down at his amputated leg. "Well, almost anyone. We trade with Galatea, and I *heard* that we used to trade with Laomedeia before I was

born but nobody's seen them in 20 years. They either went
off-course or…"

"Yeah," Iris said. Neither of them wanted to think of
the alternative. It brought Iris's thoughts back to Triton and
the murderer Jeremai. She wanted to change the subject to
keep her mind off it. "So you get a lot for your fish?"

"Oh yes," Kiviaq said. With pride in his voice, he
added, "We're the last earthly source for fish, as far as I know.
We don't make problems for anyone else, and they don't make
problems for us." He jokingly waved his right shoulder at her.
"Usually. I'd say we charge an arm and a leg, but I guess it's
the other way –"

Iris became upset. Her kinsmen were responsible for
it, even if nobody knew it except her and Leon. She stood,
throwing the rest of her lunch to the ground. "That's not
funny, kid. Those sons of bitches on Sao turned you into a
goddamn cripple and in all likelihood ate your friends, and
you're sitting here with me joking about it like it doesn't
matter. Thanks to them you'll never run again, never climb
or…you're gonna spend the next however-many years of your
life *without* your father because of them and, and you just
think it's some kind of game?!"

"Iris, I'm sorry, I –"

"Forget it," she said. People were staring; she felt her
ears burning again. "Just forget it."

She left him and found Leon on the other side of The
Shard, eating alone. He opened his mouth to speak.

"Don't."

He tore off some of his fish and offered it to her. After
a silent moment she took it.

178

That night, Iris sat on the edge of the rooftop, her feet hanging off the side. Her eyes were raw from crying; her breath came in tiny gasps. Kiviaq, her journey, the Triton murders – Iris had been trying to sandbag her emotions but now the dam was breaking. She heard footsteps approaching from behind her and she did her best to clean herself up, wiping her tears and sniffling, then clearing her throat. Iris turned to see who was coming, but as soon as she saw who it was she swiveled her head again in the direction from which it had come, not wishing to show her face to her new company.

Kenai sat without looking Iris in the eye. She put her left leg over the edge of the skyscraper but pulled her right foot in towards her rear and rested her right arm on the knee. They stared out over the horizon and watched the fog roll and shift along the London landscape, fires crackling and families speaking behind them. Kenai found it serene.

"What do you think is down there?" Kenai asked, offering a gentle upwards nod to the city below.

"A whole shitload of double-decker buses," Iris said.

They laughed.

"Do you think there's still anyone living down there?"

"No," Iris said. She picked a pebble up from the rooftop and rolled it between her fingers. It may have spent millions of years on this planet and it ended up passing its days atop one of the few safe havens mankind had from the fog. She thought it was funny.

"Why not?"

"This isn't Dublin."

"What's that now?"

"I don't think the British are as stubborn as the Irish," Iris said.

"Seriously, though."

Iris scoffed and tossed the pebble ahead, surrendering it to the fog. Kenai wasn't dropping this conversation. "Piss.

"Look," Iris said, finally locking eyes with the young woman, "I've been a lot of places the last 30 years and I've seen a lot of strange shit. If you're asking about the urban legends of the child warriors –"

Kenai interrupted her. "Child warriors?!" Her eyes had lit up.

"Oh, for Christ's sake – forget I said anything, ok?"

"No!" Kenai said. "Tell me!"

Iris's scalp itched. She scratched it and ran her hand through her hair before wiping her face down with it. "Okay.

"So you know that back when the fog came up from the ocean with all the colossi, there just wasn't enough space on all 13 for everyone, right? And everyone had different ideas of where to go to escape the haze."

Kenai nodded a bit impatiently.

"Well, post-Ascension there were still billions of people left on the surface. We've always taken it for granted that they all died from Red Lung, and usually the prisoners or desperate people who make runs back down to ground level say the same. 'Oh, there are skeletons everywhere; it's a global cemetery, totally.'"

"What do you mean 'usually,' Iris?"

Iris stood to stretch her legs and paced slowly as they talked. "Every so often someone will come back up insisting they saw a bunch of kids walking around down there, foraging for food and supplies, baby brothers and sisters in tow. Of course these sightings are always off in the distance. 'I couldn't get too many details; the fog was too thick. But I know what I saw!' No one ever gets a good look, conveniently enough."

Kenai caught herself looking down at the fog, squinting intently. *Maybe,* she thought. Iris saw her staring and laughed a bit.

"Kenai, think about it. Where could they have come from? How could they possibly live down there?"

"You said yourself there were people left over after the exodus," Kenai said, standing to meet her and dusting off her rear. "Maybe some of them were immune and –"

"*Nobody's* immune," Iris shot back. "Besides, where are their parents?" She could see Kenai's eyes darting around, grasping for answers.

"The older children *are* the parents," Kenai finally said. "The Red Lung kills at random, right? It would cut the average lifespan down dramatically – almost past the point of puberty, but *not quite.* If the surface children came of age and immediately had offspring, they could be on their eighth or tenth generation by –"

"Bullshit!" Iris barked. She was uncomfortable by the implications of child brides and such a radical society. Her temper was getting away from her and Kenai was insulted. "Grow up, Kenai; it's a fucking fairy tale."

"Does it remind you too much of your life on Sao?" Kenai asked.

Iris stopped dead in her tracks, her eyes like saucers.

"Yeah," Kenai said. "I know where you come from."

181

"Whatever Leon said to you –"

"It wasn't Leon," Kenai said. "I could tell by the way you reacted to Kiviaq this afternoon."

Iris looked away.

"And you used 'piss' as a curse," Kenai said. She was walking towards Iris and getting uncomfortably close. "The only other time I've heard that was when they dropped Kiviaq back off. We demanded justice. 'Piss,' they said, laughing through their crooked teeth."

Iris could feel Kenai's breath on her face.

"Did you do it?"

"No!"

"Were you there?"

"No," Iris said. "I…I ran away, back in 84."

Kenai shook her head and scoffed. She turned and walked back to the edge of the building and resumed her former sitting position.

"So why yell at my brother?"

Iris begrudgingly joined her on the edge again.

"Those are my people who did that to him. I don't know which of them did it, but I grew up with every single person who lives on that creature. I was born and bred on Sao, raised to further our own interests and to look at other people like rabbits."

"Rabbits?"

"Or…y'know…fish," Iris said.

"And now I look at all those years and…you know, I fought like hell to learn to live a good life away from all of them, all of that. I told Leon about how I learned to do everything properly on Naiad and in libraries – reading, writing, speaking, behaving and taking care of others. I learned to be sane, to be normal. Then I started learning about mortality and life and death and for the first time I really considered how my life on Sao had impacted myself and those around me. I've eaten…I took part in all aspects of that life, okay? Can I really tell myself or anyone else that now I'm a changed woman so we can all just forget how I used to live? How many lives have I destroyed? How many of my countrymen did I enable and cheer over the years for their cannibalism, their predatory hedonism? I drove myself halfway back to crazy thinking about it. Which half of me is really me – the Sao-born or the wanderer?"

Kenai put a hand on Iris's back and a gentle wind blew in their faces. It felt good. Iris shut her eyes as it rippled through her hair, which caressed her warm cheeks.

"My great-grandfather took pride in the subtle malice he bestowed on whites," Kenai said. "Grandmother encroached on him to make amends. 'Leave it down in the mist, papa,' she told him. 'We all made it. We're all safe now.' Yet until the day he died, he remained bitter and burdened with his hatred. He carried such weight with him, she told us she half-expected it to sink Psamanthe and all the Tlingit people with him.

"In case you can't tell, he didn't," she added, provoking an empty laugh from Iris. "But my grandmother told me he looked older and more worn down at 60 than she does at 90. Your hatred is internalized. It's self-inflicted. Someday you must ask yourself when you've punished yourself enough. This question of 'which half of you is you' is garbage. Both halves are you. The poisoned earth below us is

183

still our home, but so are Psamanthe and the other giants. We simply let go of who we used to be. You can do the same. With time."

"It sounds a lot easier when you say it," Iris said.

"I know; it's probably going to be a real bitch," Kenai laughed. "But don't ignore it." She rose and began walking away. Iris called after her.

"Are you sure it's not too late?"

"Not yet," Kenai said. "But the time is coming, Iris. Cloud and poison your soul with your old life or come up and breathe the free air. The choice is yours."

Iris sat back down and looked out at the mist-covered London. *That's what I was afraid you'd say*, she thought. She reflected on the brutish society to which she'd been born. She knew children were more impressionable and naïve than adults. It didn't excuse her from the responsibility of the lives she'd taken or whose flesh on which she'd dined in her youth, but once her mother had died, Iris had a hard wake-up call. She was slapped in the face with the value of the innocent people whose paths she'd crossed. She cried for and mourned the lives whose lights had been snuffed out by her own hand. When she'd run away from Sao and awaited another colossus to come along, she spent days wondering if her own life was worth saving. She couldn't even save her mother. Now, 15 years later, she was headed back to help her new home, Triton, find justice for its departed and heal its wounds. Looking out over London, Iris felt optimistic about which half of her would win out – until she remembered how easy and natural it had been to take Jeremai's fingers off him in

Ghettobelly. Her smile faded and her heart felt heavy. She went to sleep.

The rest of their time in London passed quietly. Iris and Leon stuck together; Psamanthe's residents took Iris's conversation with Kiviaq as a sign to leave her alone. The night before they flew to New York, she made a quiet apology to Kiviaq, Kenai and their grandmother for how she'd spoken, but she remained distant. She still found it hard to look at him.

The flight to New York was 49 hours straight. Leon and Iris were provided with small bags of pre-cooked fish and dried, jerky-like fish to keep them from going hungry during the trip. They slept as much as they could to pass the time. A Haida man near them sang; the children occasionally got bored and whined to their mothers about the trip. And always, far below them, the red-orange fog stretched endlessly away, a poisoned blanket covering the entire globe.

Leon became lost in thought as he stared hypnotized at the mist. He wondered what Earth must look like from space, the big blue ball now another red planet – Mars's twin, perhaps. No one living on a colossus today had ever known anything *but* life in a theriopolis – or, in Iris's case, in several of them. *If it ever dissipated,* he thought, *would we go back down? If we did, who would we meet?* Leon had heard the stories from his grandfather about humanity's final days on the ground. There were people swarming the titans by the thousands, trying to buy themselves passage with anything they thought would be valuable. They tried desperately to give the armed guards sacks full of money, the keys to their cars and houses, anything and everything they owned, just to make it to Ascension.

"Hey. Hey buddy. Parked outside I have a 2003 Ferrari Enzo with your name on it. This is the key to the ignition; I have a bill of sale drawn up for anyone who lets me onto that thing. This car costs up to $2 million at auction – turn the other way and I put the key in your hand."

"Listen – it's a 4,000 square foot, two-story lodge high up in the Rockies. Here's the deed and the key to the front door. Take it – take it! Just get me and my kids on that creature and it's yours. Easiest money you'll ever make, pal."

While some people had rushed the theriopolises, there were other ideas to escape the surface. Teams of miners and builders worked overtime to construct hermetically-sealed underground shelters for several families. Little was known about them nowadays, because whether they were alive and thriving – or if the fog had gotten into their subterranean homes – there was no way to contact them. Even if there were anyone still alive underground, why would they be willing to open the airlock and expose themselves to the fog if someone knocked on the door?

Several extravagant aviators and engineers invested in incredibly lightweight dwellings the size of ranch houses that were topped with four sets of rotors and solar panels. Leon's grandfather had called these latter units "Flying RV's," which had amused the man to no end, though Leon didn't understand the joke. Leon didn't know if the people in the floating houses were still alive, but once or twice a year, someone on a theriopolis would claim to have seen a distant flying object far in the sky. The momentary excitement and

186

longing to contact them – however impossible that would be – always faded when logic took over and the theriopolitans considered that they may just be flying coffins now, pilotless air tombs who would only cease their voyage when their propellers or solar panels shorted out. Between the floating homes, the underground neighborhoods, the missing leviathans, the urban legends about the child warriors and the rumors that some governments had invented their own solutions to the vapor, it was impossible to tell if there were 20,000 people left alive on Earth or ten times that amount. If they existed, they may as well be on the moon.

Remembering the anecdotes of people bribing theriopolis guards with the deeds to their mountaintop houses reminded Leon of another story his grandfather had told him – the story about the people who fled to those mountaintops and other high places. They'd believed the early, unsupported rumors that the 1,000-foot fog ceiling that rolled in from the seas would become thinner at high altitudes. "You wouldn't believe how stupid these sons of bitches were, Leon," his grandfather said. He mocked them shamelessly. "'Oh, the air in places like Mount Kilimanjaro and Everest is so thin, there's *no way* the fog could creep very far up them,' they all said. 'You wouldn't have to go up to where you couldn't breathe – just a few thousand feet from the base would do it.'" He shook his head and took his own voice back on. "Some of them even built greenhouses as a failsafe to get fresh oxygen further up there, sonny. You had whole swarms of folks just trying to buy up land and build housing further and further up the sides of Makalu and Mont Blanc and Denali." He sighed.

"But it didn't work," his grandfather had said. "None of it worked. Of course it didn't. We'd pass nearby a mountain a couple times a year and there would just be less and less of it visible. The families who stayed down there realized it, too. They crept higher and higher up the mountainside every few months. They knew what was coming. Imagine. Imagine a mother and father looking down and seeing that, that gloom, marching towards them like a sentinel – towards their family, their children. Now think about this. You know the mountain climbers used to have to bring oxygen tanks with them just to climb up and down the mountains because the air gets so thin. You know that, right? The air is so sparse tens of thousands of feet up that there isn't enough to support you. And even those oxygen tanks only lasted a few days. So you've got desperate families – parents, trying to protect their children – relocating further and further up the mountain now to escape the fog that they'd believed would never get up there in the first place. At the same time, they know they can only go so high before they run out of oxygen. Stay and catch Red Lung, trudge up the slope and asphyxiate. What do you think they'd do? What would they tell their kids?"

His grandfather paused to let the thought sink into Leon's head.

"Now I said some folks opted to buy higher and build these big greenhouses to try and get fresh air from plants they brought," his grandfather said. "Well, how long do you think they'd last with every one of their goddamn neighbors breaking down their doors to get in? If the fog was moving up the mountaintop, it would get to the greenhouses eventually, but desperate times bring out equally desperate and irrational behavior. Some people kept their civility and migrated as high up as their lungs allowed and just waited it out, but for the most part…"

"What happened to all the people on the mountains, Grandpa?"

"Nothing good, kid," he said. "Every time we passed by, it was a little worse. First you'd see people living on the mountainside in new houses, their kids playing outside. After a couple more passes the houses would be swallowed up by the fog, campfires burning and tents pitched a few hundred feet higher. Into the second year you could tell how much smaller the visible summit had gotten, and fewer fires and fewer tents were set up, and they were closer to the greenhouses. Once we went by and I looked through my binoculars and the tents surrounded the greenhouses, which were busted out, glass shattered everywhere, streaks and pools of blood surrounding the properties. Eventually…"

"Yeah?"

"…No more tents."

No more tents, Leon thought. He knew it meant everyone was dead, and it was a phrase that stuck with him. Whenever the story came to him, Leon found himself unable to stop thinking about how many skeletons must lay below them. Most of those who died after the Ascension were likely buried or cremated, in keeping with societal customs, but at some point there would just be too few people to conduct – and attend – regular funerals. It always saddened him, knowing that there was no one left to care for them, to remember them, to properly lay them to rest and pray for them. No more people. No more tents.

They arrived in New York on schedule, just after midnight on August 28th. Iris and Leon disembarked Psamanthe on the rooftop of 432 Park Avenue and immediately began keeping an eye out for Sao. He was one of the only theriopolises with an uncharted travel route; Iris even confessed to not knowing his exact migration pattern. The Psamanthe residents unpacked their things as their titan patiently waited until morning to dive and find them more fish. It was a sleepy and slow-going process, yawns and groans accompanying their small talk.

"It gets like this when we take too many night flights in a row," a voice said behind Leon and Iris. They spun around to see Kenai looking out at her friends and family. Iris made an excuse to move several feet away, beginning her unpacking as Kenai and Leon conversed. Leon spotted a small, newly-built fire and lit a cigarette on it before Kenai continued. "When we leave for Chicago on September 1st, Psamanthe will fly through the night as we all sleep. We should touch down on top of the John Hancock Center in the middle of the morning, well-rested and eager to start the day."

Leon nodded towards the great bird. "Where's she headed in the morning? The East River ain't ever been known for its cleanliness, even before Ascension."

Kenai laughed. "We think she flies southeast, over Queens and past Rockaway Beach, to the Atlantic Ocean. Of course you're welcome to share in whatever she recovers," she added with an inviting look towards Iris. Leon cleared his throat to get her attention. She turned just halfway around,

190

thanking Kenai curtly before returning to her work. Kenai excused herself and Leon unpacked near Iris.

"You ought to say something to him," he said.

"Leave it alone, Leon," Iris said.

"Look, the kid was just trying to be friendly. I don't know what's going on in that brain of yours, but whatever it is –"

"I said 'leave it alone!'"

He decided to change the subject.

"So how long does Sao stop wherever he goes?"

"He doesn't."

"So how do we get up onto him? Do they have lookouts we can hail?"

Iris stopped unpacking her things and hesitated before standing and turning to Leon.

"Look…I know I've asked you to trust me a lot since we left Triton, but I was wondering if you'd consider it once more. It's a big one."

"What do you have in mind?"

"You saw what they did to him – to Kiviaq. They value outsiders' lives about as much as we did Carol Lee's rabbits'. And you know they're not going to give much consideration to your badge if they're really involved in some massive conspiracy."

He didn't want to admit she was right, but he'd felt increasingly unsure of himself every day since they left Triton. Seeing the results of their ghoulish practices up close – and the looming mystery of the theft – had started to wear down his confidence.

"So what do you propose?"

"Let me take the lead when we get there. I'm one of them. I know how they act, how they speak and how they fight. Let me get us to a meeting with Jeremai 1 and you can grill him as much as you want. I won't interfere."

An uncomfortable silence permeated the air.

"Listen," Leon said. "About you and this Jeremai 1…"

"I know."

"If I can prove he ordered the Mackey hit, we can bring him in – alive."

"I know."

"But if he's clean, you can't…I mean, I believe you about your mother, but I don't know how we could prove he greased somebody 15 years ago."

"Jesus, Leon, I said I know!" Iris shouted. "You don't have to worry about me. I won't shoot him on sight and I won't do anything that could jeopardize the Mackey case."

"Okay," Leon said. "I'm sorry. I am."

"I'm not fucking like them, Leon. I'm not gonna give in to some bloodlust and take some kind of revenge on him. I'm like you Triton residents, I…I mean I want to be like you guys…"

"Okay," he repeated. He could tell she was being honest.

"So look. You have my word. I know you've learned a lot about me the hard way, but I think we're getting to be friends here and I'd like you trust me. Can I take the lead?"

Leon thought it over. No matter which angle he considered, she knew more about the people and the place than he did. He and Iris *were* becoming friends, and he didn't want her to risk her life – much less relinquish the control of the case to anyone else – but he couldn't come up with any alternatives. Not to mention he felt bad for giving her such a hard time about Jeremai 1.

"Okay, fine," he said.

"There's just one catch," she said reluctantly.

He started laughing as soon as she said it. *Of course there is.*

"I can promise you they snatched and subdued Kiviaq quickly, silently and on-sight," she said. "We should probably get on Sao without being seen and stay out of sight until we can get close enough to the men's prison that we can work our way to Jeremai 1 with the least involvement from the locals."

"How in the Hell are we supposed to board a theriopolis without anyone seeing it? Let alone set up a meet with its top brass?"

Iris sighed. "Do you really want to know?"

He rubbed his eyes with the butts of his hands, mulling it over.

"I guess not," he said. Taking the passenger seat on the case, Leon felt sullen – and a bit like a failure. After a while, he added another thought. "I guess you're the boss here." He regretted saying it instantly.

"Listen," she said. "This isn't a man-woman thing, okay? I'm not trying to emasculate you here and I'm not your boss. I know that both our victims are more your responsibility than they are mine, and they're your friends. But I have a stake in this too. Like I told you, if Jeremai 1 set this all in motion because of me, I'm as responsible for their deaths as he is. I need to know. I just want us both to survive this in one piece."

"Yeah," Leon said. "I'm sorry."

They passed their final days with the Tlingit. Leon and Iris remained quietly friendly with the Psamanthe locals, asking questions about their remarkable host and telling them about life on Triton. They learned that the rumors of Psamanthe's nesting habits were true: the well-adorned rooftops on her route were originally bare, but she had soon made trips to the surface and stuck her massive beak into glass-walled storefronts to obtain sofas, beds, oriental rugs, dressers and other furniture. *So that's why everywhere we land looks like a showroom from a furniture catalog,* Leon thought. Kiviaq's and Kenai's grandmother told them about Psamanthe's first residential journey around the world as her father had explained it to her. When Psamanthe perched herself on the Makkah Clock Royal Tower in Mecca, she had planned on clenching her talons along its vertical moon-topped spire, but under the weight the spire broke and fell to the earth. It had offended the Islamic population greatly; the grandmother empathized with their reaction despite the obvious accidental nature of the incident. Although any physical conflict was narrowly avoided, relations between the Muslims and Psamanthe had been tense ever since. Iris was surprised to hear that nobody knew exactly why Psamanthe chose the buildings on which to perch that she did. They were all over the fog ceiling, providing a safe rest stop for Psamanthe's population, but it remained a mystery as to why she landed on 432 Park Avenue instead of One World Trade Center, for example, or the John Hancock Center in Chicago as opposed to the Willis Tower nearby. "She just likes them more," one Haida man joked, patting Psamanthe's leg.

The night of the 31st came and Leon and Iris sat idly as everyone else packed up their belongings and boarded Psamanthe to fly to Chicago. Kenai's grandmother wished them well on their journey and entreated them once more to bring justice to Kiviaq's attackers. Leon promised her. Midnight came and went; Kiviaq was one of the last to leave. He needed help from his sister and another woman to get onto Psamanthe. As the line progressed and he ambled towards the giant, Iris became increasingly fidgety. Finally Leon looked over to her and raised an eyebrow.

"Okay, fine," she said. "I'm going."

She stood and walked briskly to Kiviaq just before he left the rooftop, calling out his name.

"I'm sorry for what I said to you, back in London," she told him. "I was wrong. You should be proud of who you are, not angry about it. You're a great guy and the people of Psamanthe are lucky to have you."

He bashfully looked down. Psamanthe started stretching herself.

"I have to get going," he said. "But thanks."

"No problem," she said.

There was a pause. She looked him in the eyes. She doubted she'd ever see him again.

"Oh – fuck it," she said. She grabbed his face with her gloved hands and kissed him on the lips. Not by way of apology and not under any pretense of love or romance. She kissed him because his unbroken spirit and his perseverance in the face of such adversity were beautiful and he was beautiful and she wanted to kiss him. His whole body stiffened with surprise and it was all over at about the same time that he'd gathered his wits enough to kiss her back. Iris turned and walked back to Leon. Some of Kiviaq's older friends teased him a bit, cheering him in falsetto and clapping. A wide grin stayed on his face as he finally got on Psamanthe's back and strapped himself in. He gently touched his face with his only hand and looked at Iris. The moment she looked back at him, Psamanthe took off.

The massive boom of her beating wings diminished to silence, her nomadic population disappearing in the night sky to the west. For the first time in two weeks, Iris took off her gloves to let her hands breathe. With another ounce of peace in her heart, she laid down in her sleeping bag. She was asleep immediately.

The next couple days drew out slowly. They were out of what food they'd brought and were sustaining themselves on fish. They knew they wouldn't starve – Iris had vaguely but insistently reassured Leon that Sao was coming sooner rather than later – but to be safe they'd rationed their supplies out thinly enough that they spent much of the day hungry. It was hard resisting the temptations of hunger and thirst, but they managed. Without the Psamanthe citizens in sight, Iris was able to keep her gloves off all day and sleep with her head and chest outside her sleeping bag. It was, she decided, the best thing about Leon knowing her secrets.

On their third afternoon alone, which was also the third of September, she was rummaging through her bag and checking its inventory when Leon called her name.

"What?" she asked.

He was pointing at her with a mystified look on his face. She looked down at her torso and arms. Her circulatory system had begun glowing again. For the first time in 15 years, it hadn't been brought on by sleep. She looked at Leon to offer an explanation but a distant sound interrupted her.

It was a boom, followed a second later by another – and another. Footsteps. The two looked to the source of the sound. A roughly spherical shape headed straight towards them, its long, thin legs moving at a rapid pace. Its face was just the front of its torso, the mouth spread in a grin and its pitch black eyes stared fiendishly. Its upper legs seemed to point backwards. Leon imagined its knees were inverted, like Psamanthe's or a chicken's. Iris dove into her bag immediately, retrieving various items and stuffing others into it.

"Pack your bags, Detective."

Leon couldn't take his eyes off of the approaching menace. The closer it got, the more ominously it loomed. Several slipshod buildings adorned its back, and just as Iris had described, stacks of speakers 30 feet high faced outward from all sides of it, near the buildings. Only half-listening to Iris, he took a step or two backwards towards his belongings. He could hear sounds coming from the speakers. *Rapid screaming – English, but so much slang,* he thought. *I know that accent – Jamaican, isn't it? Unnatural drums and trumpets – it's music.*

"Detective…"

As it got closer, he could see long objects dangling down its sides by ropes. He squinted and focused on one – it was a skeleton. They were all skeletons, adorning the figure like dozens of thick strands of hair. It was only a few hundred feet away now and every step it took, Leon became more frightened. His breath became shallow and his heartrate increased; his mouth went dry. It had bizarre lines, curlicues and bullseyes painted on it in white, a stark contrast to its dark fur and the even darker brownish-black lines that complemented the white. The music got so loud it was hard to hear anything else.

"Detective!"

He turned and stared blankly at Iris. In his terror, he couldn't imagine what she'd possibly want to talk about. Depending more on reading her lips than hearing her voice now, he focused on her as best he could.

"It's time to go," she said.

"Is…is that…?"

"It's Sao."

He took one last look at the colossus, seeing all the pieces as a whole for the first time even as new aspects of it came to light. He saw the speakers blasting their deafening music and the ramshackle neighborhood on its back, the war paint - *Is that darker paint blood?!* he thought – and the ornamental corpses bouncing with each massive step, the creature's glistening oil-black eyes and what could only be dozens of human and animal skulls strewn along cords that pierced its featureless face. Sao was an eldritch nightmare, a 1,500-foot island of unbridled malevolence and he was louder than God.

"Leon!!!"

His body kicking into autopilot, Leon packed everything into his bag in seconds. Iris was ready to leave; she ran to him and her hands held something that looked like small daggers. For just a moment Leon wondered if it had all been a setup, a trap to get him to Sao for some unspeakable purpose. Then she was shouting in his ear over the din. Apparently she had been for several seconds.

" – out of their sight behind that air conditioning unit, wait for the rope and bring the end of it with you off the rooftop! And don't forget my bag!"

His eyes wide, Leon nodded at her, not knowing the full extent of their plan. He'd heard what she said but he hadn't processed it yet. She grabbed him by the shoulders and shouted "Don't worry!" He ran to the back side of the large, blocky a/c unit and he opened his bag to get his gear. Sao came up alongside the building, 20 feet out from it, and slowed to a stop. The first things Leon saw in his bag were his standard foot ascender and his hand ascenders, which locked like little more than staple guns with cam devices where the staples would come out. He pulled them out of his bag and set them on the ground and realized Iris was slowly backing away from him, away from Sao.

Time to go home, Iris, she thought. She adjusted the grip on the piton she held in each hand. At this size, she doubted Sao would even feel them. Doing her best not to overthink it, she ran as fast as she could to the edge of the rooftop and leapt off it, her arms and legs still cycling like they were searching for ground. As the distance closed between her and Sao, she began to fall, the wind rushing past her face. She steadied all four of her limbs, bending her knees to bring her feet back as she crooked her elbows and flexed her biceps to brace for the impact. *Please don't die, please don't die,* she pleaded of herself, raising her elbows and preparing to stab her hometown.

As the Jamaican hip-hop track ended and another song waited to come out of the speakers, there was a brief moment of silence. Leon heard men's voices emanating from Sao's back. They spoke to each other in the same dialect that the hateful Jeremai had used back in Ghettobelly. Then he heard them calling to someone else in the distance, and though he couldn't make out the words, the tone of voice seemed to be giving an "all clear" of sorts. More of the aggressive hip-hop began blaring out of the sound system. After the momentary silence, it seemed even louder than the previous song.

What did Iris say? he asked himself. *Wait for the rope, bring the end of the rope with me off the rooftop, don't forget her bag. What rope – from Sao? Where did she go? Does Sao have a Ghettobelly-like town too?*

Then he saw her. Hand-over-hand, she was climbing up Sao's hip towards his side, her feet pushed against Sao's hide. *They were pitons in her hands,* he thought. *Possession of them alone is enough to land someone in prison for 10 years; they completely undermine the immigration process. Of course, I guess her unsanctioned climbing rope did too, but –*

It suddenly occurred to him that the reason she went first was to help him get in quietly. *Does she have that same climbing rope from Ghettobelly with her? No; I would've seen it by now.* He looked up and saw a ballista pointing out towards the horizon from Sao's back. Iris was climbing straight towards it.

Oh shit.

He hurriedly returned to tying on his foot ascender. As he reached for his bag to retrieve his harness and lifeline rope, Sao began to get restless, stretching his legs. *She wasn't kidding,* he thought. *He hasn't been stopped more than a moment.* At the same time, something landed with a large clank not 10 feet from Leon. It was a grappling hook on the end of a rope. His eyes followed it up to the ballista and saw Iris waving him up and looking behind herself to see if anyone had seen her.

Oh shit, he thought again. *No time. No time.*

He picked up his hand ascenders and fastened his bag, throwing it over his shoulder. He started for the rope when he realized he'd forgotten Iris's bag. He doubled back and picked it up and began sprinting for the rope again. Sao began to walk. The rope was dragging away from Leon as fast as he was running towards it. Leon was finally thankful for the music: loud as it was, it was driving his fears about this moment from his head. The grappling hook caught on the edge of the building and the spool of rope began unraveling from the ballista. With one hand holding Iris's pack and both his hand ascenders, Leon grabbed the hook with his other hand, yanked as hard as he could to get it some slack and unhooked it from the rooftop. He wrapped the rope around his hand once and jumped.

homecoming

Iris was lying on her stomach, both her bare hands tightly gripping the rope she'd shot from the ballista, her ankles locked around the low railing behind her. She was almost completely upside-down. The blood rushed to her head and it began to throb. Her long black hair hung straight down and obscured her vision of the far end of the rope to which Leon clung. She knew he was still alive down there, though. She could tell it by the weight of the rope. She daren't mount the ballista and reel him in, lest she be spotted by Sao's residents. Instead, she pulled the rope hand-over-hand, the slack dipping down Sao's hide in front of and below her. It burned her palms; her biceps howled in pain. She tried not to think about it and she kept pulling.

The detectives' upcoming confrontation with Jeremai 1 popped into her head. *No,* she told herself. *Don't think about that. Not yet. Just pull the rope and push the rest away. Ignore who and what await you in the city. The people, the sights, the sounds, the last place you saw mom – no. Stop it. Just pull the rope. Get Leon up here and plan your next move. One step at a time, girl. Keep pulling.*

Leon was jolted when the line pulled taut and nearly broke his right hand. Once he'd recovered, he lifted his right leg up to try to thread the ballista's rope through his foot ascender. He was swinging forward after his leap and crashed against Sao's side, nearly losing his grip on Iris's bag and his hand ascenders. Then he swung back after his impact. He tried again to thread the rope through his foot ascender. He kept his wits about him despite the circumstances, rotating his ankle around gently to catch the rope. It slid in. The fog below him seemed to be blowing ahead at an unheard of pace in contrast with his locomotion. Leon reached down and closed the gate on his foot ascender just before his momentum steered him back into Sao. He pushed down hard, the cam fastening shut firmly on the rope below him, and kept pushing until he'd locked his knee. In the same instant, Leon struck the beast for the second time, closer to its rear end than the first impact. This second collision with the behemoth sent him spinning at a furious rate. He was standing, though he wasn't secured to anything beyond the tiny clasp strapped to his shoe. He let Iris's backpack slip onto his left arm and drew it up to his shoulder with the same hand. Everything hung by a thread, both literally and figuratively. Leon was getting dizzy and nauseated, but thankfully his rotation was slowing. He brought his hands together and shifted a bit more weight to his foot. It was just enough that he could use his free left hand and two fingers from his right to fasten both hand ascenders to the rope. Again and again he crashed against Sao, whirling about at various speeds in either direction. Finally, after what felt like an eternity of delicate maneuvering and searing pain in his arms, the detective steadied himself and began to climb.

Leon felt motion sick from his journey; he hadn't ascended more than 20 feet before he felt overwhelmingly queasy. He turned his head to the side and leaned over and retched several times while reflecting on just how much he'd always hated doing so. *And me without a free hand to get a drink,* he thought. After a momentary pause to catch his breath, Leon continued to go up. Soon he reached a point where he could push off of Sao with his free foot, almost walking up his side. Leon doubled his efforts when he saw a long loop of the same rope slowly drooping towards him. *Jesus, she's pulling me up. No wonder I'm moving so quickly.*

They got him to the top and he heaved himself over the balustrade, throwing his hand ascenders over first and unfastening his foot ascender to free himself from the rope. Iris let it go and rolled onto her back, being careful not to lose her feet's grip on the harbor railing. Leon reached down and grabbed her arm and pulled her up over it. They collapsed on the ground next to the ballista, panting and gasping for air, their arms sharply aching. In fact they'd exerted so much energy they each realized their arms were shaking uncontrollably. Iris spoke first.

"You want to arm wrestle?"

They both laughed.

"Let's never, ever do this again," he said.

"Yeah. I think once was good."

After recuperating for another moment, the two got up and returned the harbor to normal, reeling the ballista rope back in together and putting Leon's climbing equipment back into his bag. He grabbed his jug of water and took a swig, rinsing his mouth out and spitting over the edge. Iris placed her pitons back in her bag and put it on and they found cover behind a small home from which to survey the corner of town.

For the second time in an hour, Leon struggled to reconcile the scene in front of him with the world he'd known his whole life. Rusted sheet metal shacks lined the beast in uneven and awkward rows. This kind of housing had been added on to Ghettobelly and even a couple houses atop Triton, but something about these seemed eerily askew. There were few real streets. Instead, Leon saw wide paths that had been trampled into Sao's fur by years of foot traffic. They all seemed to twist and stretch one way or another, suggesting a trail to the mammoth twin prison buildings Iris had described to him over a week ago. Trash barrel fires burned every 60 to 80 feet and around each one stood several men and women eating, drinking booze and shouting over the deafening music that still came from the speakers. They were all underdressed, by Leon's judgment. Many of the men wore no shirts; some even ran around naked and filthy, old and new cuts and bruises adorning their bare skin. One nude man stumbled down the row, inebriated, for several seconds before tripping and falling. He tried to stand again but eventually he gave up, opting instead to stay on the ground and slowly gyrate his pelvis on Sao's fur.

The women were the same. Some wore full outfits, but many wore tattered rags or miniskirts with no underwear, or they wore nothing at all. One topless woman at a fire cackled loudly, leaning on her mate, taking large swigs from a bottle, her swollen belly indicating impending motherhood. *The rags on that dame are bright orange,* Leon thought. *It must be the remnants of a first-generation prisoner's outfit. All that hooch came from somewhere too; maybe they have a fishing system like Triton, just as Iris mentioned.*

Leon stopped himself. He knew he was desperately searching for answers, reason, logic where there was none – a vain and Gestalt effort to rationalize and quantify pure chaos. It was one thing to put down Nash's killer back on Ghettobelly, but here, seeing hundreds of people living in some kind of Hedonism with its edges frayed by sociopathic malevolence, the city was overwhelming.

He knew his fear accomplished nothing, so he doubled down on stopping his frantic thoughts, and thought about their next move.

"We have to move," he said quietly. "They could come back to the harbor any second."

Iris surveyed the area. The row of shacks ended far before the prison complex. For a moment she thought about taking a cue from her foremothers and going prone, crawling along the high, unkempt fur of the titan like a soldier in high grass, but she decided it was too bright to risk it. *Shit*, she thought. *We have to get closer one way or another, if only to get a better look at our surroundings. Things may have changed since I left.*

She and Leon walked quietly, hunched over, along the backs of the residences. It was a narrow fit between the houses and the railing at the edge of Sao's back. They got to the end of the alley and saw the prison compound, two armed guards standing near the closest entrance.

"Okay, how do we get in there?" Leon asked.

"We can't take out those guards," Iris said. "They're too far away."

206

Leon squinted at them. "Agreed. But we can't just head out with a white flag, hands in the air, asking for parlay like refugees. We're too much of an odd couple; you look more like one of *them* than –"

Iris spun around and looked at Leon intently. A wicked grin spread across her face.

"Oh, you gotta be shittin' me," he said. "No. No way, sister."

"Yes," she replied. "I know how to speak Sao, and I'm shorter than you – I can hide behind you so they don't recognize me."

"There has to be something else," he said, although he already knew there wasn't. "Let's just…think for a little bit."

"There's no time!" she said. "You said it yourself – any minute, one of them could come walking around and see us hiding back here. Look, I'll rock-paper-scissors you for it," she said. "I win, we go with my plan. You win, we stay here and come up with something else." She seemed almost giddy.

"We are *not* going to rock-paper-scissors this," he said.

"Oh come on."

"No!"

"Pleeeeeeeeeease?"

He looked back at the guards, then back at her. She already had her hand out, palm up, her other hand in a fist on top of it. He winced. In unison they whispered "Rock, paper, scissors, *shoot!*" and they played their respective hands.

Jeremai 9, Generation Five, had been at his post for several hours. His assault rifle was heavy in his hands. His palms sweated in the hot sun. He stared out over the horizon as Sao ran down the coast, the fog rolling in undulating blankets underneath him. He always thought the Earth looked like it was on fire. It contrasted strangely with the blue sky above it, not to mention Sao's dark brown fur like high grass blowing in the wind. Jeremai 9 had always been able to tune out the noise of the other Sao-born as they laughed, drank, screwed, killed and got high. He had to, lest he fail at his post and be eaten by his family and friends. He didn't understand why it was okay to kill and eat people who didn't do what Jeremai 1, Generation Four, said to, but he was the boss so it must be alright. 9 was interrupted from his inarticulate ponderings by a female voice that rang louder than anyone else's. He turned and looked at the source of the sound. A woman was shouting from behind a strangely-dressed man, who seemed to be her prisoner. They were walking towards him slowly. *Woman speaked like Sao, stay eater,* he thought. *Weird man enemy. Weird man stay meat maybe?* He raised his rifle and pointed it at the man, finally focusing on what she was saying.

"Jeremai, heard?" she said. "Me find meat Triton law man stay climbing Sao. Jeremai 1 Generation Four speaked me 'Bring non-Sao-born prison, Jeremai stay decide send home or cut off dick.' Seen?"

Jeremai 9 hadn't heard anything about it. He tightened the grip on his rifle and tried to think of what to say. Some of the other Sao-born in the streets had stopped and were looking at Iris and Leon. Jeremai 9 knew they were looking at him too and it made him nervous. *Fuck up job, turn meat, no eater,* he thought. *Disgrace family, forsake Sao privileges.*

Leon's heart pounded. His own handgun was in Iris's left hand, pressed against his left temple. His hands were handcuffed behind his back and with her right hand, Iris had one escrima stick pushing his hands against his spine. It was painful, but they had to maintain their image. She had even gone so far as to remove her shirt, bra and gloves to give the appearance of the native Sao women. Iris had no desire to show her breasts to these people but she knew clean clothes were rare enough to raise suspicion in the city and she didn't have anything ragged enough to blend in. Fortunately, her hair was long enough and Leon was so close in front of her that one covered what the other didn't. Her red right hand was even buried against his back to avoid scrutiny. She imagined she could dress again once they were in the prison.

Leon glanced to his left and saw a man squatting and picking the last meat off of what appeared to be a femur. Just past that, a man was having sex with two women at the same time, in the middle of the street, and they seemed to be enjoying it despite it looking rather violent. One of the women was pouring alcohol into the other's mouth while all three of them copulated. A man ran across their path in front of Leon, pursued by another man who tackled him from behind and lay on top of him, getting both their pants down as the first man tried and failed to escape him. Leon knew what would come next and turned his attention back towards Iris. He didn't understand. What had become of subtlety, of modesty, of empathy? This leviathan was a veritable Roman orgy of sex, violence, drugs and loud, angry music, and through it all was their detestable invented speech that seemed equal parts American south, Cajun, Jamaican and some other dialect he couldn't identify. He felt so far from Triton. He kept his fists clenched.

Jeremai 9 thought something seemed strange. "Bitch, what your name stay?"

"Dumb fuck Jeremai, no recognize I after take long gander?" she said.

"Iris 9?"

"Piss," she said.

"14...?"

As they got closer, Leon could tell their subterfuge was beginning to fail.

"Clock me," he said quietly.

"What?" she whispered.

"Right in the noggin – you have to hit me, kick me, do *some*thing."

"Okay. Sorry," she hissed before flipping his gun around in her hand and pistol-whipping him in the back of the head. Cheers and laughter came from several spots around them. All eyes were now on Leon and he spoke to Jeremai 9. His mouth ran dry.

"What's your name, son?" asked Leon.

"Jeremai. Jeremai 9, Generation Five," he said.

"Jeremai, my name is Leon and I came here from Triton," he started. The crowd didn't seem happy with that. "I caught Jeremai –" Leon realized he didn't know the dead Jeremai's number. Iris didn't either. "I have a man named Jeremai in custody at the jail on Triton." The crowd got angrier.

"Return Jeremai Sao, meat law man!"

"Suck dick Triton bitch; throw overboard!"

Even Iris growled at him and spit on the floor near him. Leon raised his voice and spoke over them. "Please!

Listen to me! The mayor – the boss – of Triton…sent me here to talk to whoever it is who's in charge of Sao –"

"Jeremai 1!"

"Jeremai 1, Generation Four! Meat cocksucker."

"Okay!" Leon said. "Okay. Jeremai 1, Generation Four. I've come halfway round this ball of fog to speak with Jeremai 1 of the Fourth Generation of Sao about returning this other Jeremai here, to his home. He hasn't committed any serious crimes – just some minor theft – and we can work this out as friends or as enemies. But know this – if I don't return to Triton alive and in one piece, and if nobody ponies up a damn good yarn for our prisoner's actions, he will be killed. What do you think Jeremai 1 will do to you then?"

Everyone listening cursed and shouted and spat more, but none of them approached him for fear of feeling Jeremai 1's wrath. Even Jeremai 9 wavered. He lowered his rifle a bit and looked around at the crowd. *I got you, you bastards,* Leon thought. Jeremai 9 spoke up.

"Meat Leon speaked truth? Proof. Proof Jeremai 9, Leon know other Jeremai. Jeremai 9 ask boss Jeremai 1. Truth, Leon seen Jeremai 1. Lie? Leon stay dinner."

The crowd laughed and catcalled Leon.

"I kinda figured that much, pal," Leon said. "Tell Jeremai 1 that…the Jeremai in the big house on Triton…has a new tattoo on his arm: three straight lines, a filled-in circle and the head of a trident."

Jeremai 9 turned to his partner at the prison entrance and said something softly. The partner disappeared inside the prison and things got tense. Iris took the pistol away from Leon's head and readjusted her hair, making sure it covered as much of her face as she could manage. Jeremai 9 kept his eyes focused on Leon for several moments, but as time dragged on, it occurred to him that he still didn't know who the woman behind this stranger was.

"Iris 4?"

This time Iris didn't answer.

"Iris 4, Generation Five?"

He raised his rifle back up and started to approach them slowly.

"Leon," Iris whispered.

"Just a little longer," he said.

"What name stay, bitch?"

"Leon, do something," Iris whispered more urgently.

"Me? I'm the hostage here," he responded.

Just then, Jeremai 9's partner came bursting out of the prison.

"Boss Jeremai 1 speaked once time 'Girl take meat Leon Jeremai 1 prawn toe.' Fast now Jeremai 9, seen?"

Without a word, Jeremai 9 and his partner stepped aside and Iris escorted Leon into the prison. Jeremai 9 walked several steps behind her. She kept her face down, hidden from view, but she'd lived on Sao for so long that once they were inside, she could've gotten him there blindfolded. They walked in the doors to the air-conditioned prison and kept up their façade as they passed some people living in unlocked cells and others who Leon assumed were guards' descendants, working as slave labor and near starvation. Iris got chills as she passed one of the cells. It was twin to her and her mother's room in the opposite facility – the same floor, the same number of cells in from the catwalk.

Still not now, she thought. *The time will come. Forget about it. We're almost there.*

They moved up a set of stairs, along a platform, up another set of stairs and around a corner to the warden's office. At long last, they reached the warden's enormous door. Leon pushed it open, entering Jeremai 1's dwelling and leaving 9 outside.

Jeremai 1 was a giant man. Years of unchecked excess had piled weight on him and his long dark hair was stringy and greasy. He wore an open robe made of irregular stitched-together leather. Leon considered what it might be made of before making himself abandon the train of thought out of fear. Jeremai's teeth were yellow and brown. He sat behind an old oak desk with his eyes closed, a full bar on a mantle behind him. One hand was flat on the desk; the other was in a fist near his crotch, gripping a woman's hair tightly and guiding her mouth violently along his erection. They were surrounded by men and women in various states of undress – some enjoying one another in groups, others splayed out and asleep, exhausted from Jeremai's previous whims. The room was lit by fluorescent tube lighting above them, which bathed the scene in a sickly pale blue. The smell was nauseating.

Once again Leon felt a pang of culture shock. He'd seen criminals in their natural elements before. Some were crimes of passion or spur-of-the-moment doings, their perpetrators crying and shaking and utterly loathing themselves. But others...others were completely at ease with themselves and the questions Leon had asked them, pinning them to crimes. They offered him drinks, stayed calm, never lost their temper or nerve, all while describing the ways in

213

which they'd stolen or raped or killed. It took him years to figure out how someone could do those things without being racked by guilt, and the search for an answer paled in comparison to the harrowing despondence he felt when he finally reached a solution.

They just didn't care. Like Adolf Hitler, they saw the people they harmed as being so different from themselves that the criminals felt no empathy or compassion towards them. They told themselves it wasn't killing a fellow human being; it was more like swatting a fly. It wasn't violating a woman; it was just exerting one's power over something else. It took a frightening disconnect from humanity to be able to act so maliciously towards a completely innocent person. It took the same kind of sociopathy necessary to kill Allison Mackey and carve a symbol into her arm, to idly watch a man rape another in the streets, to forge an empire built on cannibalism and drug abuse and sex. Leon had seen this haze of self-serving indifference before, but never on this scale. He was overwhelmingly disgusted by the man in front of him, but his heart was pounding, having traded in his momentary shock for a gnawing anxiety. He'd traded away so much this summer. His worst fears about Sean Bellamy and his own inaction to prevent the man's suicide had come to bear fruit. Triton's horticulturist was dead, her replacement likely still struggling to keep the colossus's emergency food stock full to this day. Leon had felt the Wandering City Blues creep up around his neighbors in the days since the murder. He himself had shot a man – who was likely a family member of the gluttonous monster he now faced – in cold blood. He'd lied to the mayor on multiple occasions to get off-titan and go

214

on an investigation that led him here. Now he was on Sao, full of boogeymen and deformed psychopaths, and he didn't even know where the beast was running or where he and Iris could next make berth, if they lived long enough to do so. Nevertheless, this was the confrontation Leon had been awaiting since Allison's body was found over a month ago and he wasn't leaving this room without answers.

It took every ounce of control Iris had not to aim the gun at Jeremai 1's face and pull the trigger. Literally every second that passed she pictured how it would happen, over and over again. Without ever knowing who she was, with his eyes shut and his mind focused only on the pleasure he was receiving from his slave, Jeremai would never see it coming. Iris would simply extend her arm straight ahead, aim Leon's gun at the king of Sao, look down the barrel with one eye closed and commit regicide. The man who raped and killed his mother would dye the far wall red with his blood before he knew what hit him. There would be the roar of the pistol, a sickening splatter and the ding of the shell bouncing on the floor, drowned out by the screams and frantic fleeing of the harem.

In the end, Iris's common sense won out – but just barely. She knew Jeremai 9 and the other soldiers would likely fill her and Leon with bullets before they got out of the building, let alone off the titan. If by some miracle they lived, Leon would have to arrest her and maybe she'd be executed. She considered that Sao's remnants could either fall impotent without their leader or rise up and declare open war on Triton. The gamble was more innocent lives on Triton. She wasn't the one to make that bet, nor did she wish to. One instant of her vengeance meant a lifetime of consequences for thousands of people. For as long as she and Leon lived, he'd never know how close she came.

Jeremai 1 felt Leon and Iris looking at him and he opened his eyes and met their gaze. They could see the gears turning in his brain as he shifted stupidly from his id-driven carnal greed to the people in his presence. Iris was still mostly hidden by Leon, aside from her bare left hand still holding the gun at his temple. Jeremai blinked quickly several times before shoving the woman at his feet away from him. She lost her balance and fell on the floor, rejoining other members of the harem in a huddle in the corner. They rested together like a litter of new puppies. They looked pathetic to the point of Leon nearly crying for them. Jeremai swiveled in his chair to face them directly.

"Show face."

Iris hesitated. She reaffirmed her grip on the gun and pushed it just a bit harder against Leon's temple. She tried her luck again at buying some time while she thought.

"Meat Leon leave Triton, speaked have Sao-born prison. Meat Leon stay law man plenty year, big friends Triton boss and Triton law boss. Trade Jeremai 1 answers for Sao-born prisoner. Jeremai 1 kill meat law man, want I kill? Eater boss Jeremai 1 gone speak secrets to meat Leon?"

Jeremai 1 paused before speaking insistently. "Show face."

Iris looked down and shut her eyes for a long moment before releasing her right hand from Leon's back and stepping out to his left. She kept the gun on his temple to maintain the illusion of Leon's captivity, but she felt it begin to fail the moment Jeremai 1 looked at her face. There was an almost imperceptible change in his expression. Iris was less confident in her camouflage of nudity and wary of how little hair may be covering her face. Their subterfuge was ending. It had gotten them an audience with Jeremai 1 but now –

"Leave," he said.

Nobody moved. He turned his head and stared at the nearest pile of humans.

"*Leave!*" he roared before turning back to look at Iris again.

All of Jeremai's human pets came to life, scurrying out of the room. Some ran, some stumbled, some covered themselves, some didn't. Jeremai 1 watched their naked asses and bare feet as they fled. Eventually the three were alone, the door still cracked open behind them. The room seemed twice the size it had when it was full. Under the tube lighting it glowed a sickly sea foam green. A slow, wide grin crossed Jeremai 1's face. A rumble grew from within him, eventually rising to the surface and erupting into a low, terrible laugh. He spoke slowly, as though every word pained him greatly.

"Iris. 13. Generation Five."

Jeremai 1 rose from his seat, his massive frame even more intimidating while he stood. He closed his robe as an afterthought, covering his genitals and stomach, the hair matted down with sweat. Finally he walked around his chair to the bar behind him on the mantle.

"Whiskey."

"No," Iris said.

Jeremai 1 turned his head halfway around to her.

"Wasn't asking."

Leon's mood shifted again. He'd been shocked, scared and anxious; now his intense dislike of Jeremai 1 was taking hold and his worry was being replaced by anger. Jeremai poured three drinks as Leon and Iris traded glances. Jeremai 1 set two down on the desk and held the third and began sipping it. He finally raised his free hand towards Iris.

"Dress."

After another pause, Iris reached into her bag and retrieved her shirt and bra. She set the gun down and dressed hastily, glad to know no one could see her breasts anymore. Her body was hers to share with whomever she decided; this ruse had made her uncomfortable. She had moved her hands quickly in hopes of preventing Jeremai from getting a good look at them. Finally she put both gloves on. When she was done, she put the gun back on Leon, but Jeremai 1 laughed at this.

"Iris…will no kill law man. Law man…is Iris friend."

Leon only spent a moment pondering why Jeremai's tone had changed. Iris lowered the gun and stowed it in the back of her pants and retrieved both whiskey glasses from the desk. She went to hand Leon his drink only to realize his hands were still bound. This amused Jeremai 1 greatly. She looked to him to question freeing Leon, but Jeremai was already a step ahead of her – he again stretched one hand outward in a gesture that seemed to be granting permission. She fingered the handcuff key out of the fifth pocket of her jeans and undid the bracelets. Leon rubbed each wrist with the opposite hand and reattached his handcuffs to his belt loop, pocketing the key and taking his drink from Iris. He found the nearest wall and leaned his shoulder on it, his limbs still sore from the climb up Sao's flank. He took a sip of his whiskey.

"Clever disguise," Jeremai said. "Why…is…Iris here?"

"Jeremai 1, Generation Four – I've returned home after 15 years to seek an audience with you regarding a murder in South Africa. Last month, a fifth-generation Sao-born man arrived on Triton. He had this symbol tattooed on him." Iris produced the paper drawing of the mysterious sigil from her back pocket and handed it to him. He gave it a quick look and set it down on his desk. "This man traveled to Triton and killed an innocent woman in the town square in the middle of the night."

Jeremai interrupted her. "What woman?"

"Her name is Allison Mackey."

Jeremai snorted. "Piss."

All of Jeremai's slow speaking, his towering stance, his sexual indulgences and arrogance finally triggered something deep within Leon. Deciding it was all bravado and showmanship, he couldn't hold back anymore. *The devil with Iris taking the lead here,* he thought. *I'm ready to nail this goon.* Leon rebuffed Jeremai's derision.

"No, not piss, fat man," he said, standing and approaching the man. Iris winced at his insult. "Leon…"

He held his hand up to silence her and he kept talking to Jeremai. "The fact of the matter is, your boy was on a con. Thought he could glaum a whole mess of seeds from our local gardener. Too bad for him, she caught him picking the locks and she tried to run to the cops. He knew he was behind the eight-ball, so he chased her down, tripped her up and choked her. Figured she was out for good. That was when it came to him – she had the key. So he picked her pockets for 'em, but here's the rub: she wasn't dead yet. She woke up, rolled over and tried to crawl to safety and your button man grabbed her by the hair and cracked her noodle into the pavement. Over and over, he came down on her like The Wrath."

As Leon laid out the scene, the three of them sipped their drinks. Leon pulled a cigarette from his case and patted himself for a light, which he knew he didn't have. Jeremai 1 opened a desk drawer and pulled a genuine lighter from it and flicked it open before thumbing the flint wheel. The spark set and the flame lit. Leon had never seen a working lighter before. It was beautiful. He leaned in and lit his cigarette on it and took a drag, nodding in thanks.

"Once he'd zotzed her, he finished the theft and replaced the keys, hoping to make a clean sneak of the whole job. But he figured he had to throw us for a loop so he took his shiv out and carved up her arm with the same marking he'd just gotten inked on *him*. Drew up a decoy and tried to put us on a wild goose chase. But we caught up to him, see? Then I get a good look at this guy's ugly puss – and when I say ugly I mean *ugly*. This goon's got a face fit for a plastic bag." Leon stopped and gestured towards Jeremai 1 with his cigarette before taking another drag. "Well, look who I'm talking to."

Iris protested again. *"Leon…"*

Jeremai smiled an idiot grin, amused by Leon's presumptuousness and disrespect. Leon continued.

"Anyway. He tells us he's connected, and my new best friend here spills it: the two of them are from *this* dive: a walking big house. So I gotta hop two crossovers and come all the way to the Big Apple and gab with *you*. So start singing, your highness; where's the rest of the stash, what's it for and how's this skirt involved? Did you send him after her?"

Time drew out like a blade. Finally Jeremai 1 spoke. "Iris 13…lives on Triton?" He burst into laughter and clapped his hands together once. "What are odds?"

Iris breathed a sigh of relief. The deaths – Allison, Nash, the other Jeremai – weren't because of her. She could've cried, but she knew she had to keep herself together. The Jeremai who Leon had killed was still Sao-born, and she knew this could turn ugly. Leon's untimely swagger had belied his promise to keep a low profile here. *What was he thinking?* she asked herself. If he stayed this insensitive, there's no telling how Jeremai 1 would react.

"Where…is Jeremai 21, Generation Five…now?"

"Oh, you know him?"

"Jeremai 21…is…my child," he said. "Where…is he?"

Bingo, Leon thought. He took one final drag of his cigarette, exhaled the smoke and put the butt out on Jeremai's desk.

"Most of him landed outside Johannesburg."

Much quicker than Leon thought possible, Jeremai 1 leapt over his desk and shoved him against the wall, choking him with his forearm. Leon's whiskey glass fell to the ground and shattered. Iris retreated from the broken glass out of reflex but then ran to Leon's aid. Before she could do any good, Jeremai caught her and shoved her back with his other arm. She fell to the floor and knocked her head against it hard. She blacked out for several seconds. Jeremai seethed at Leon, his foul breath smothering the detective's face.

221

"21 was…naïve. Just stupid boy, gathering last of castor beans for –" He stopped himself from saying any more. He thought of his son dying and being heaved over the side of another colossus, alone and uncared for, and he was ready to kill Leon where he stood. Leon involuntarily gasped for air, choking on Jeremai 1's forearm. Each second felt like a full minute. Leon noticed that he'd been grasping at the oppressive arm with both hands, attempting to pull it away from his throat. His heels kicked out and away from him. He saw stars. Things started to go white, and all the while, Jeremai's eyes burned with the rage of a parent's worst nightmare. That and the insanity of Kuru or Variant Kreutzfeldt-Jakob Disease or whichever ailment tormented his crippled mind. Jeremai 1 was going to kill him, consequences be damned. Iris was rousing herself but not quickly enough to save him.

Then something happened in Jeremai 1's brain. His face changed from fury to epiphany. Jeremai 1 let go of Leon and turned away from him. Leon collapsed to the ground and caught his breath, coughing uncontrollably, fully regaining consciousness. Iris gathered herself together enough to crawl to him and help him recuperate.

Jeremai spoke slowly, mulling something over in his head. "I think…meat law man Leon is right," he said. "Yes. Leon dies here, then war comes. Hmm. Leon and Traitor Iris want answers, yeah? Maybe Jeremai...'points in right direction.'" Again his loathsome cackle emanated from his body. He reached for the drawing of Jeremai 21's tattoo that Iris had handed him. Standing over the detectives, he gave it another look, crumpled it up and threw it at Leon's face. Then he squatted, getting as close to Leon as he had been when he was choking him.

"You look for reasons, for…explanations," Jeremai said. "You found them."

Jeremai 1 rose and leaned out the only door. *"Nine!"* he screamed. In moments, Jeremai 9 entered the room and detained both Iris and Leon. Under Jeremai 1's orders – delivered in his native dialect again – Jeremai 9 took them to a cell and locked them in. Leon rubbed his throat and looked at Iris.

"Could've gone worse."

Detective Leon Adler was falling through the sky head over feet, high above Miami Beach, Florida. His arms and legs flailed wildly, a reflexive action that did him no good. His view was of the damnable fog below, followed by the cloudy Floridian sky above, the fog again, the sky again, seemingly without end. The crisp mid-September air rushed all around his body. All the while, the cacophony from Sao's speakers assaulted him with unlistenable music, but it was fading into the background as he tumbled. Any second he'd plummet through the fog ceiling and everything around him would be seen through tauntingly limited visibility, the miasma blanketing the empty city which was racing up to meet him at breakneck speed.

As a boy he'd heard stories about the origins of the mist. It came rolling up right out of the ocean, they said, and government agencies from all around the world reported it within a few days of one another. It crept up shorelines and grew to 1,000 feet high even as it slunk inland from the coasts. None of the land dwellers knew if it was related to the goliaths or not – it all happened so fast that no one knew which to focus on first. Sooner or later, though, it covered the surface of the planet, both land and sea. The rest was history – Red Lung, the theriopolises, The Ascension and all the rest happened in just a few years. As unsettling as the quiet could be, Leon couldn't imagine life in that circus. The panic and chaos alone killed millions. There were riots, looting, murders – total anarchy. It reminded him of the colossus that was receding away from him as he tumbled to the ground.

Please God Jesus not like this, he thought. *It'll break every bone in my body. How did it all go so sideways?* He thought back to the last week and tried to put the pieces together.

As soon as Leon and Iris reached their cell, Jeremai 9 took their bags away from them. He locked the door to their cell and left. Immediately Iris crossed the cell and slapped Leon in the face. "How could you be so stupid?" she asked. "He was going to kill you!"

Leon put his hand to his reddening cheek, which felt afire from the blow, and grimaced. Speaking was still an effort after being choked out by Jeremai 1. "Yeah; it was a gamble."

Iris was furious. "What?! Then why in the Hell did you put yourself in that position?"

"I…knew you wouldn't let him."

She stopped herself short of yelling at him more, but she growled and ran her hands through her hair.

"One way or the other, I knew I could…you know…trust you."

"Can you? Can you trust someone like me?"

"What's that supposed to mean?"

"Forget it," Iris said. She looked out the barred window at the horizon as she detected the sound of footsteps approaching. The fog looked a bit different than it did most days – almost blurrier. *A dust storm must be kicking up on the surface,* she thought.

Jeremai 9 appeared again and handed Leon the lighter from Jeremai 1's office through the bars. "Eater Jeremai 1 speaked meat Leon need. Jeremai 1 speaked 'Get comfortable.'"

Neither prisoner liked the implication of how long they'd be in their cell, but Leon stayed with the conversation. "Sorry pal; I just smoked my last one in front of your boss."

A snort of contempt escaped Jeremai 9. "Jeremai 1 order Jeremai 9 give meat Leon present." He reached in his pocket and retrieved a small paper box with a shining foil top. The color had drained but Leon recognized it immediately. It was a pack of real cigarettes. He looked at Iris, who had been peeking over her shoulder at him.

"And you said nothing good would come of this trip."

Leon hungrily tore the foil off the pack and pulled out a cigarette, eyeing it like the artifact of a lost civilization that it was, and put it to his lips. He lit it with the lighter and nodded his thanks at Jeremai 9. "Hey fella – tell him he ain't all bad." Without another word, Jeremai 9 left them alone.

Leon took a drag. It was a fascinating flavor – hardly better than the theriopolitan smokes to which he was accustomed, but his curiosity had finally been abated. He held the pack towards Iris, offering her one. She waved him away.

"Fine," he said. "So where are we?"

She turned and looked through the barred door from which they'd entered. "Cell Block 2 of the men's prison. The hall we passed on the right on the way here is –"

"No," Leon said with a chuckle. He nodded towards the window. "I mean where *are* we?"

Iris sighed and looked out the window again. "Eastern Pennsylvania."

"So we're headed west. Wait, we already passed New Jersey?"

"Probably when you were getting tuned up," she replied with a smirk.

"Okay, okay," Leon said, taking another drag. "So you still haven't told me anything about Sao's route. Why the hell are we riding into the sunset?"

"You know how nobody has ever pinpointed an exact migration pattern for Sao like they have for seemingly every other titan?"

"Yeah…"

"It's because no one here really seems to care about where he goes. As you saw today, Sao-born are mostly happy to sit up here and enjoy the ride while…indulging in other pleasures in life."

Leon thought back to what he saw earlier that afternoon – the drinking, the drugging, the sex, the violence. It made him shudder. He sought comfort in his cigarette.

"And nobody has ever come to study it," she added. "We're not too keen on guests."

"No shit," he said, rubbing his throat.

"So when I was a kid I tried keeping track of where he went. New York, Los Angeles, Toronto, London –"

"Those are all Triton stops."

"But not *only* Triton," she said. "Sao also goes to the Canary Islands, Nuuk, Reykjavik and plenty of other cities –"

"Reykjavik?"

"– that the other colossi visit. In fact everywhere Sao goes, another titan has been first."

"Don't tell me he has some cockamamie psychic bond with them and always knows where they're at…"

"No, no. If I had to guess, maybe he can smell them? Or he just has a feeling. You ever get that feeling that someone's looking at you?"

"Sure."

"I think it's like that. He's just always trying to catch up, I think."

"And when he doesn't find them…"

"He just keeps walking," Iris replied. "That's why he didn't stop in New York."

"So what happens when he *does* find one? Kiviaq's grandmother didn't mention anything about Sao himself approaching Psamanthe, or attacking her."

"From what I've seen, he stops, but he keeps his distance."

"I don't understand," Leon said.

"Nobody does," Iris replied. Each of them thought about what it could mean.

"Say, Iris, you don't put any stock into that Therioanthropic Coupling Theory nonsense, do you?"

"You mean Dr. Mills' hypothesis about the behavioral congruencies between the leviathans and their residents?"

"Yeah."

"I think it definitely has its merits, but we'd still need more evidence before –"

"Bunch of malarkey and mumbo jumbo," Leon said dismissively.

"You're a career detective, Leon; you're supposed to keep your mind open to the idea until you can prove otherwise. So why not consider the possibility? Did our ancestors pick the colossi or did the colossi pick them?"

"I work with clues and hard evidence, Iris, not metaphysics and witchcraft."

Iris rolled her eyes. *Witchcraft? Really?* "Okay, but you have to admit it's a Hell of a weird coincidence. Triton and Proteus are two of our biggest colossi. They choose to stop in highly-populated areas – Pre-Ascension of course – and they end up with the most diverse melting pots we have."

Leon shook his head. "But there's no evidence saying one is *because* of the other."

"Well, no, but –"

"And you heard Kiviaq's grandmother talking about how they ended up on Psamanthe," Leon said. "Her father and the other Pacific Coast Indians *petitioned* to get on Psamanthe specifically because of their spirituality."

"Yeah, but they were successful; those government leaders could've given the space to anyone. Why suddenly have a heart? Or maybe the Tlingits' faith in avian deities originated in a place of reality and Psamanthe really is here *for them.*" Iris knew it was a stretch but she was starting to feel cornered. Her whole life she'd dealt with men who assumed they were smarter than her and it made her anxious. She moved on. An idea reached her at the same time it came out of her mouth. "In fact, look at Sao."

"What *about* him?" Leon asked.

"He's a good fit for Mills' theory."

"How so?" Leon asked. "Initially he was peopled entirely by criminals – men and women who for the most part planned and executed schemes to commit crimes and skirt the law. Does planning and foresight sound a lot like this big lug running around chasing his tail all day to you?"

"Say that again: what did Sao's first residents do?"

Leon was reticent to repeat himself for fear he'd said something that would cost him the debate, but he knew there was no backing out now. "They…planned and executed schemes to skirt the law."

"Exactly!" Iris said. "They reached outside the boundaries of order and society and did whatever they wanted, refusing to follow what's expected of them and their peers."

"So?"

"Every other behemoth that came from the sea over 100 years ago developed a strict, unchanging pattern – a specific ritual to roam the earth seemingly for eternity. That's order – you could set your watch to it. Sao defied the expectations and norms set by his peers and to this day walks an incalculable, chaotic path. In a way, Sao-born are disorder riding atop a vehicle of disorder!" She beamed.

"I ain't buyin' it, sister."

"Well shit, Leon; you've got all the answers. Why is Sao such a misfit just like his residents? Why does he live outside the rules by going wherever he wants whenever he wants, and why have an impersonal disconnect from his own kind – just like his residents – that makes him avoid direct contact with the other titans when the rest of the titans do the exact opposite?"

"Jeez Louise, I don't know," Leon answered. "I just don't think fate or some mystical influence caused all these cities to end up how they did. If anything else, it's the other way around."

"What do you mean?"

"Well, let's consider Triton again. He's got maybe the biggest square footage of any of the theriopolises, right?"

"Right."

"More space means more people. More people means you probably have different *types* of people. It's more a matter of practicality than a cause-and-effect. Proteus is the same way. You ever been to Proteus?"

Iris nodded.

"His front two legs are longer than the hind two, so his whole city is on a slope. To compensate, The Founders built short stilts onto one side of each building on Proteus to even their foundations out. The people have spent their lives – as did their parents, and *their* parents and so on – walking up and downhill day in and day out. According to Mills' theory, Proteus would've somehow attracted people with strong ankles." He laughed at the thought, stood and flicked the butt of his cigarette through their barred wall into the open pavilion in the middle of the cell block.

Iris was quiet. She liked the Therioanthropic Coupling Theory but she didn't know that it was foolproof and she couldn't prove its claims. It was vexing to consider that they may never understand Sao's behavioral patterns like the others, or why the residents' societies seemed to correlate with the titans' personalities, but in the end she had to let it go.

Neither of them spoke for some time. The sun slipped into the fog like a hot bath as Sao chased it across the Midwest. Impending darkness in the prison waited for them like a hangman.

"What do you make of Jeremai 1's slip-up?"

The cessation of silence startled Leon. "About the castor beans," he said. "I noticed it too. It's nothing good. He mentioned that his son was getting 'the *last* of them' for something, which implies that there's a stockpile of castor beans out there somewhere."

"I agree," Iris said. "Castor plants make beautiful decorations, but somehow I doubt gardening is what he had in mind."

"Especially if he was willing to travel to Triton, break into our agricultural hub, steal the beans and kill two people for them," Leon said.

"What else are castor plants used for?" Iris asked.

"The plants themselves, not much," Leon said. "I mean they don't grow any food or medicine. In fact they're so toxic that just eating a few could – oh shit."

Their trains of thought arrived at the same time.

"With the quantity of castor beans he probably had, he was going to poison a *bunch* of people," Iris said. "But how?"

"It couldn't be via drinking water. Every house has its own filtration system. He'd have to go house to house mixing a dozen seeds' worth of castor oil into their water supply at a time."

"There's no way he could pull that off; he'd be caught immediately."

"Food?" Leon asked.

"If he were going to poison people's food, it would be the same scenario –"

"– unless he snuck his castor oil into a restaurant like Carol Lee's and threw it into a pot of grub or something. Then he could take plenty of folks out. Of course it could be a moot point; I iced him myself."

"I don't know," Iris said. "In the time we talked to him, did Jeremai 21 seem like he could concoct some kind of terrorist attack like this?"

Leon grunted.

"And the way Jeremai 1 said he'd show us what we were looking for…I think there are too many pieces still missing from this puzzle."

"You know what, Iris?"

"What?"

"You're becoming a real gumshoe."

"Well it helps to have someone around who's an expert – but since I don't have that, I'll make do with you," she said a smile.

Jeremai 9 approached with two plates of food – their dinner. He eased the first plate through a slot in the door and looked at Leon. "For you."

"Good grief, pal; you're still here? I'm starting to think you're sweet on me," Leon said, taking his plate. Jeremai 9 spat on the floor as they laughed. Iris approached the door and took the other plate from Jeremai 9.

"Next I stay home, seen? Sleep under stars. Meat prick."

He turned and left. In the dark it was hard to make out the food at first glance, but Leon saw he had a small portion of quinoa and mushrooms. He looked at Iris; her face had fallen. She shouted after Jeremai 9. "Hey, I'm not eating this! Do you hear me you son of a bitch I'm not eating this!"

She could just barely see him turn around and put his arms out. "Orders, bitch. Stay hungry; Jeremai 9 not care."

She threw her plate at the door; the clang echoed throughout the prison ward. "Are you fucking kidding me?! Get back here! *Get back here!!!*" She screamed more, her eyes tearing up and her hands trembling, but he was gone. *I'm not eating it,* she thought. *I'll starve first.* She knew her meal was just a show of power by Jeremai 1 but she cried herself to sleep on the stained prison mattress anyway. Leon stayed silent. When Iris awoke the next morning, she found that sometime during the night, her plate had been placed on the floor next to her, adorned with a small portion of Leon's vegetables. No guards had come back after Jeremai 9's shift ended. She looked over at Leon, asleep on his mattress. His back was to her.

Most of the following week passed uneventfully. They were given meager amounts of water and less food. More than once, guards stopped by and urinated through the bars onto their floor, howling with drunken laughter. The sheer volume of the music drowned out the street noise outside their window except for the seemingly random hours at which it was shut off. Early in the morning on the sixth of the month they reached a city. Iris and Leon peeked out the window just in time to see that they were circling the John Hancock Center, its stygian roof home to two antenna masts, one of which still stood defiantly, the other broken off before either detective's parents were born. *Chicago,* they both thought. Iris remembered Kenai telling her it was Psamanthe's next stop, but the Tlingits had left before Sao arrived and he found none of his companions nor whatever it was he sought from them. With a deafening bellow from his great maw, he turned around and headed southeast.

On the eighth day of their imprisonment, Leon awoke before Iris. She slept until a guard whose full name was unknown to Iris and Leon brought them their packs. He unlocked the cell and dropped the bags on the floor, uttering just one word. "Time." He even dropped Leon's gun and Iris's escrima sticks on top of the bags. Leon looked at Iris in uncertainty before taking his belongings and exiting. She did the same, though she wouldn't look him in the eye.

Neither of them had changed clothes or bathed in over a week. They smelled abhorrently. Leon had a fair amount of scruff on his face that would be a beard before long if he left it alone. Leon and Iris followed the guard through the dismal building and out the front door.

"Leon, I have to tell you something," Iris said.

"Shut face, cunt," the guard ordered.

They were both sunblind and it took some time for them to open their eyes. Even when they could force their eyelids to draw, they involuntarily squinted. Several Sao-born pointed and laughed at them. Both detectives shielded their vision from the sun with their hands, but they still found themselves suffering headaches from the brightness. As their vision adjusted, they realized a huge crowd had formed around them and only grew thicker as they walked. The guard was leading them to the front of the great two-legged monster where Jeremai 1 waited for them, his back turned. The guard stepped back behind Leon and Iris. Jeremai raised his hand in the air and everyone in the crowd fell silent. At the same time, someone stopped the music.

"Twin Ewells maked free all Sao-born. Speaked truth: re-destiny, eaters' new Babylon, Jeremai 1 stay god-king Sao. Perfect world, seen?"

"Piss, Jeremai," Iris said.

"Sao perfect world all eater families. Jeremai 1 maked happy. Eaters sad, city dies. Eaters have...what name? 'Blues.' Jeremai 1 keep eaters happy. Then...Iris 13, Generation Five forsake re-destiny."

Jeremai 1 turned around and faced them. Leon heard another man approach them from behind. Jeremai 1 reached his massive arm between Leon and Iris and grabbed a backpack from the man before stepping back near the edge of the plain and dropping it to the ground.

"Should be, Iris 13 find cure Sao children. Was, Iris 13 abandon perfect world Sao. Iris 13 gone meat seen 15 year. Sao think Iris 13 dead."

Angry murmurs surfaced from the crowd, which continued to grow ever larger. Leon wouldn't have been surprised if it were every man, woman and child who lived on the titan.

"Piss," Iris said. She spoke loudly, clearly and in her native dialect to ensure that they all heard and understood her. "Jeremai 1, Generation Four maked doctors put Sao blood in children. Sao babies die, Jeremai not care!"

Jeremai laughed. "Lies. Brave child eaters give lives make cure Sao-born sickness. Jeremai 1, mothers and fathers, grieve. Seen? No. No seen; Iris gone. Iris lose hope cure."

"But eat meat maked Sao-born sickness!" Iris protested. She had to shout over the din of people calling for her to be punished, raped or killed. "Fuck sister, make Sao babies sick! Me read mess of books. Cure? Cure eat vegetables, cure make no sex family, cure pregnant woman not drink 'shine. Eater mothers seen babies die. How many babies? Eater mothers know. Eater mothers remember. Sao children not choose. Children not choose make cure, make dead. Mothers remember."

By now the detectives were being spit on. An empty liquor bottle crashed at their feet.

"Mothers remember," Iris repeated.

Jeremai 1 calmly waved the crowd down again. He was in high spirits.

"Yes, Iris 13 forsake Sao re-destiny. Iris leave Sao, ruin cure. But Jeremai 1 kind. Jeremai 1 give Iris and meat law man Leon bed, food, gone one week. Jeremai 1 not kill Leon, not kill Iris – Jeremai 1 give bags back. Jeremai 1 help meat Leon and traitor Iris, bring Florida."

Florida, Leon thought. *What the Hell is in Florida?* In the notebook he kept in his pack, he had a page of all known leviathan migration routes and patterns, but he didn't dare pull it out and study it. His biggest concern was that he couldn't think of any buildings or structures over 1,000 feet in the whole state. Nothing was above the fog ceiling. A dark feeling in his heart blinked to life and swelled over the next several minutes.

Iris wasn't ready to give up. She broke into more proper English. "How many babies, Jeremai? How many Sao-born children died from the ichor? And how many mothers did you kill for trying to stop you?"

It was of little use. A few pairs of eyes glanced sideways at others, hearing her words, but ultimately nobody spoke up. Iris knew most didn't believe her. They had an easy life, albeit unstable. They mated, drank, killed and ate whenever they wanted. Even the mothers of the children who had died so many years ago either didn't believe her or were too afraid to stand up against the venom that Jeremai spewed.

"Iris 13 leave friends," Jeremai said. "Now Iris see other side. Come."

Leon felt a rifle's muzzle in his back. Out of the corner of his eye he saw Iris go stiff as well. They walked towards Jeremai, who picked the mysterious bag up from the ground. The guards walked Leon to the edge of the titan, past Jeremai. They only walked Iris half as far. Leon turned around and faced everyone, turning his back to the edge of the leviathan. His heart was racing. He knew what was coming but couldn't bring himself to face it.

"Making me walk the plank, boss?" Leon asked, mustering as much courage in his voice as he could. "You keep saying you're going to let me go. I guess you're not a man of your word."

"No," Jeremai replied. "Jeremai not kill meat law man. Jeremai promise not kill Leon. Jeremai give Leon choice –

238

Jeremai ask Leon one question once time. Jeremai ask, Leon speak truth.

"Who…is…Iris 13, Generation Five?"

"This a trick question, Ahab?" For his impetuousness, Leon was stricken in the gut by the butt of the nearest guard's rifle. He doubled over, coughing repeatedly, and staggered. The crowd roared.

"Who is Iris 13, Generation Five? Jeremai speaked once already. Boring. Iris lived 15 year eater, 15 year meat. Half, half. Who Iris stay?"

The air was muggy. Leon had a headache and he felt a vile cocktail of panic and dread welling up within him. The pang in his heart had come to fruition. Leon looked to the guard who was on him to make sure he wasn't risking another blow from the rifle before he spoke again. The guard nodded towards Jeremai. Leon locked eyes with Iris. They both still had their hands up. Leon was only there to be humiliated and mocked but he spoke.

"She's…she's a good person. I've seen her be kind, personable…empathetic and just. Even if she can't hold her corn liquor worth a damn," he teased. Iris brandished a Mona Lisa smile at him.

"Who Iris stay, Leon?"

Leon smiled back at Iris. "She's my partner."

"Leon trust Iris?"

"Yes."

"Sure?"

Leon looked at Jeremai.

"Leon trust Iris? Think Iris wish stay meat, stay law man? Leon seen Iris take Jeremai 21 fingers, try kill Jeremai keep quiet."

"Yes, even though she –" Leon stopped. *How the Hell did he know that?* He looked at Iris and her face gave it all away.

"Iris meet Jeremai 1 once time Leon stay sleep. Iris tell Jeremai all."

"Iris, this is a load of bull, right?"

"Leon, I –"

"Iris speaked take Jeremai fingers, meat law boss Triton trust Iris, meat Leon throw Jeremai fingers in fire, meat Leon lie to boss…"

"You had some kind of secret meeting with him? Iris, did you bring me here on purpose?"

"No, Leon; listen to –"

"Jeremai 1 best story: Meat law man head explode, hero eater Jeremai 21 kill!" He laughed heartily, as did the crowd. Leon started to rush him but was stopped short.

"You son of a bitch!"

Jeremai 1 turned sharply to Leon and raised the bag he was holding high in the air. The crowd fell silent again. Leon stopped resisting his captors.

"Could be, Iris Sao-born stay Sao-born, eater. Iris not care law, order. Could be meat Leon know shit, Iris forsake law man life. Jeremai think…Jeremai think Leon, Iris go home. Fuck off. Leon quit case; go home failure. Leon write letter Miami titan, warn law boss: Jeremai 21 friends cause mess of trouble. Iris go home Triton, hands clean. Iris forget law man life. Iris speaked wishes; Sao leave Iris be."

Leon didn't answer…yet. Jeremai wouldn't have brought them to Miami if he simply wanted them to turn back. *He wants to humiliate me, send me back to Mayor Davis with my tail between my legs and let whichever approaching colossus's local law enforcement take over this case,* he thought.

"Or Leon take Jeremai bag. Leon use 'pair of shoot' Miami, chase answers. Jeremai give Leon pair of shoot, Leon wear, Leon leave Sao."

"There's nothing over 1,000 feet in Miami," Leon said. "The fog…You leave me there to die it's as good as killing me."

"No," Jeremai said. "Choice. How bad meat Leon need answers? Could be Leon, Sao return New York, Leon leave truth. Leon return Triton safe."

Leon nodded towards Iris. "What about her?"

"Iris go with Leon. Sao finished Iris. Iris life Leon hands. Iris hands clean Triton murder: Leon think Iris want go home, Leon speak once time. Iris selfish, only want 'clear con shuss.' Seen? Iris learn hands clean, Iris betray Leon. Leon want Iris go home Triton, Iris Leon go Triton. Leon think Iris want law man life, meat life? Leon speak once time, Iris Leon go Miami. Leon choose: both Triton, both Miami."

Now it was Iris's turn to object. "Goddamn you Jeremai, that wasn't our deal!"

Jeremai ordered her to be silent and simultaneously struck her face with the back of his hand. He wore a ring and when her face came back from the blow, a razor thin line across her cheek grew red and began to drip blood.

"Sounds like you had other arrangements," Leon said. "I don't think she's interested in *me* deciding if she gets Red Lung or goes back to Triton."

"Choice stay Leon," Jeremai said. "Leon speak Iris 13 traitor, Iris selfish coward? Iris go Triton, life shame. Leon speak Iris 13 meat law man, Leon need chase answers? Iris, Leon go Miami." He paused then took on a mocking tone. "But...Jeremai only bring one pair of shoot."

The Sao-born broke into hysterical laughter, cursing at Leon and Iris.

"Leon answer question. Last time Jeremai 1 ask. Who Iris 13?"

Tears welled up in Leon's eyes as he looked at Iris. Who is she? She was the Sao-born traitor Iris 13, Generation Five. She was a short-tempered, emotionally troubled loner with a scarred body full of colossus plasma. She was a 30-year-old inbred former cannibal. She was an admitted torturer and liar who told her supposed sworn enemy classified information about the murder case they were working. Or maybe she was the sole success of the ichor experiments. She was the woman who made friends with Carol Lee and trusted Leon with all her secrets. She was a repentant refugee who caught the man who murdered Mackey and Nash before covering for Leon when he killed him in cold blood. She was –

"My partner," Leon said. "And we're solving this thing together." No sooner had the words escaped his lips than a guard kicked him hard in the chest. He fell backwards and rolled off Sao's edge. Someone started the music back up and Leon's speed increased as he tumbled down the side of the creature's face.

Iris's eyes widened as she saw Leon go off the cliff. Jeremai held the bag out to his side for her to take. Leon was hers for the saving if she could catch up to him. She didn't want to risk Jeremai playing keep-away with the bag, so in one motion, she drew an escrima stick with her red right hand and began running. She cracked Jeremai 1 so hard in his hand with it that it broke three of his metacarpals. She grabbed the bag with her other hand, replaced her weapon in its holster and ran without thinking to the spot from which Leon had just fallen.

Iris did a swan dive and put the parachute on. She put her arms by her sides and put her legs together, the wind rushing at her face. She could see Leon flailing below her. Thankfully she was catching up to him, though she knew they had nowhere to go to escape the fog. *Think about that later,* she thought. *His life is in your hands.*

She was getting closer.

He believes in you. You have to make it.

Closer. He could see her now, even if it was just for a fraction of a second at a time as he spun.

Almost there.

He disappeared into the mist.

So did she.

The visibility was terrible. He was almost within arms' reach but she could barely see him. She reached out to catch his ankle and get his spinning under control.

Gotcha.

She forcefully pulled him by the ankle, then used her other hand to grab his waistline. They just missed landing on the roof of the Four Seasons.

Shit. Maybe 750 feet. No time. No time.

Iris embraced her friend and wrapped her legs around his hips so she wouldn't lose him. She reached for the cord and pulled, grabbing him again before the parachute caught the wind and ripped him from her grasp. The chute opened and the pair decelerated with a jerk. Iris almost lost Leon despite her hold on him and they clung to each other for dear life as they came down to the earth.

As soon as the parachute opened, Leon could tell it wasn't built for two. They were still falling too fast. He found little reprieve in his escape from the freefall as his thoughts quickly turned to the danger that remained – and the impending injuries he'd incur. A string of curses ran through his mind and he pictured broken bones and torn skin. The street entered their field of view and approached quickly. Leon remembered something he'd read in an old textbook once and he shouted to Iris, futile as it may be.

"Try to land on your back!"

In the last moment before impact, he let go of her and did his best to fall backwards. He knew to keep his knees limber so as not to break a metatarsal – or worse. His heels hit the cement of the street first, and he tried to let them give but he felt a pop in his left ankle and a sharp pain from it shot up to his brain like a bullet from a gun. When his back hit, it knocked the wind out of him.

Iris had the parachute and was able to pull her knees up a bit and put her shoulder out to brace for impact. She was still falling too fast. She tripped over her feet and landed on her side and rolled over several times before stopping. She could see that she'd scraped both her arms to the point of widespread bleeding. Her right shoulder and ribs were in agony. She laid still and the parachute crumpled down on top of her.

Neither of them moved for several moments. They caught their breaths and took a moment to appreciate that they were still alive. Everything had happened so quickly that neither detective had considered their present situation. Leon sat up first and tried to stand but his left ankle took no weight on it. He sucked air in through his teeth and balanced on his right leg. He heard Iris rustling through the parachute and was about to look at her and joke about her struggle when he caught sight of their surroundings. The city of Miami, Florida, nearly a century empty, silent. Ivy overtook several buildings as well as the street. Several cars sat vacant around them – they were lucky not to have landed on one. But above all, enveloping everything, was the fog. Leon's heart sank. From the moment Jeremai presented him with his options, he didn't really think he'd end up on the surface – at least, not alive. He knew what it meant to breathe in the red-orange miasma even for a few minutes, let alone how many hours or days they'd be stuck in it. There was no way around it – if he hadn't contracted Red Lung already, he would by the time they found somewhere to get topside.

"Fuck," he said. Then he thought of Jeremai doing this to him, and how he'd never see old age, or grandchildren, and that one day he'd die coughing up blood in fits. He took a deep breath in and screamed.

"*Fuuuuuuuuuuuuuuuuuck!!!*"

Leon was shaking with anger. He repeated himself, just as loud and long as before. He heard Sao's footsteps receding and he swiveled around to curse the entire creature, but without thinking, he tried to use his bad ankle and ended up falling onto the street. He quietly murmured other obscenities about Jeremai 1 as he came face to face with his own mortality.

Iris crouched behind him and put a hand on his shoulder. He needed time to process the day's events. He was in shock. He'd never been within 200 feet of the mist before, let alone wrapped in it. Everything was masked by it. It made the city look desolate and forgotten. Ultimately he turned around and faced her. He looked at the parachute, rippling in the gentle sea breeze.

"Thanks," he said.

"You wanna go again?"

He scoffed and shook his head.

"He killed us, Iris," Leon said. "The son of a bitch killed us."

She didn't respond.

"He played me for a fool. And *you*…"

"We could've gone home," she said.

"You know I can't do that."

"…Yeah. I know."

"And now, we're both –"

"Don't…don't think about that right now," Iris said. "You still need to wrap this case up, right?"

"What other choice do I have?"

"Right. Wait right here a second," she said.

Iris rose and walked across the wide street to the nearby hotel, crossing into the lobby and emerging a minute later with a map of Miami. She sat next to Leon and unfolded the map. They found their location after searching for several minutes.

"Okay, we're here," she said, pointing at the hotel on the map. "It's probably six or seven walking miles to South Beach."

"South Beach? What's in South Beach?" he asked. He hadn't looked at his sheet of leviathan migration patterns and had no clue where they were headed next or who they'd meet when they arrived.

"Answers."

"What?"

"I'll tell you when we get there."

She helped him up and moved to his left, slinging his left arm over her shoulder.

"Is that broken?" she asked, nodding at his left foot.

"I don't think so," he replied. "It has a hell of a sprain though. I'm lucky."

They turned north and she started walking. He had to hop along with her for several blocks until they found an old pharmacy. She broke in and found some supplies in the storeroom – a pair of crutches and bandages for Leon's ankle; rubbing alcohol and gauze for her arms. There was a liquor store next to the pharmacy and Iris took a bottle of whiskey before returning. Leon removed his left shoe and sock and stuffed them in the top of his backpack without looking. Iris wrapped his ankle.

"Alright, you're set," she said. "Now I have to ask you a favor."

"What's that?"

She pulled the cork on the whiskey bottle and took several gulps. Then she showed him her injured shoulder.

"This is dislocated; you need to pop it back in for me."

"Oh, shit…"

"I know, I know," she said. "Let's just do this without thinking about it or else it's gonna hurt like a son of a bitch."

"It's already gonna smart, doll."

"You know what I mean. And don't call me 'doll.'"

Iris stretched out her arm and clenched her teeth, grimacing from the soreness when she moved it. Leon took her arm in his hands and gripped it. Her flesh was soft and cool. He popped her arm back in and she screamed, her colorless eyes glazing over from the horrid sensation. Her legs went weak and she ended up on both knees, her right hand on the street, holding her up.

She opened the bottle of rubbing alcohol and unpacked the gauze for her shredded arms, handing them to Leon.

"Now for the painful part."

Several minutes later, both their wounds were fully dressed and they were on their way north on Route 1. It was almost two miles from their landing zone to I-395, and in their condition it took them over an hour to reach the exchange. When they did, they stopped for a rest, sitting atop old newspaper vending machines. Leon looked at the fog that blanketed the landscape.

"I'm sorry," he said.

"It's okay," she replied. "We'll get there soon enough."

"No, I mean I'm sorry I chose this. Jesus, I should've argued or bargained or something – told him you should go back safely and I could go on alone."

"We're in this together, Leon," Iris said.

"But at what cost? Look around; you *know* what happens to anyone who breathes in the fog."

"Leon, it's alright."

"No it's not. I bought a lead and it cost you your life."

"Leon, listen –"

"That bastard killed us both. He really did it. You just wanted to clear your own damn name and now thanks to me and this case we're both –"

"I'm immune."

Silence.

"What?"

"I'm immune, Leon."

"What do you mean you're immune? Immune to what?"

She didn't answer.

"Nobody's immune."

Iris looked around uncomfortably.

"The ichor," he said. "The tests."

Her heart was palpitating. She could hear it and feel it.

"I told you how long I waited for Naiad when I escaped Sao," she said. "I…didn't spend all that time on the rooftop."

"Oh my God," he said.

"After Nakajima-san picked me up, I was in quarantine until she could test me for Red Lung. She waited out its incubation period and checked me out and it came back negative."

"I don't believe it."

"Neither did I," Iris said. "I even made her re-test me. But that was 15 years ago, Leon. Nobody born up above lasts 15 years after exposure, and even if anyone were born on the surface I doubt they'd make it past 20."

"So when you jumped off Sao today to get me, you –"

"I knew the fall would kill you. And me. And that's that."

Iris retrieved the bottle of whiskey. They passed it back and forth several times until Leon abruptly froze.

"What?"

"Shhh," he said. "Do you hear that?"

It was a distant thunder that seemed to be getting closer.

"What is that?" she asked.

They crouched behind the newspaper dispensers, away from the street, and stayed still. The sound got louder and louder. Finally a team of wild animals entered their view, galloping along the road at a healthy clip.

"What are those?" Iris asked.

"I've read about them," Leon said. "They're horses. The wild ones are called 'mustangs,' I think."

The horses whinnied and kept galloping. They passed the two detectives. Either they didn't see them, or they did but paid them no mind.

"They're beautiful," Iris said.

Leon smiled. "Yeah. They're not bad, huh?"

"What do you think they're running from?"

"I don't know. Something might've spooked them. Or they could just be roaming, running around the city."

When the mustangs were out of sight, Leon and Iris resumed their trek. They headed east. It was a quiet walk. They only spoke to check their position at intersections. The only sound was the metal clink of Leon's crutches with every step he took, the rubber stoppers at their bases muted by the grass and ivy on the highway.

They arrived at South Beach in the afternoon and Iris gathered wood for a fire. Leon built it at dusk and Iris lit it with her fire piston. The two of them sat and stared out at the ocean. Neither of them had seen it before. The orange of the fog and the campfire mixed with the blue of the ocean and the white moonlight, turning the seashore a deep olive green. The crackle of the burning fire and the lapping of the waves crashing against the beach were hypnotic and peaceful. Leon desperately needed it. Iris may have seen Sao's behavior for 15 years of her life, but it was too much for him. He'd spent as much time trying to understand Jeremai 1's Hedonistic kingdom over the last week as he had thinking about the case. *This is not my world,* he often thought. The sounds of the beach calmed him some, but he would never be the same. He knew that much. He turned his thoughts back to the matter at hand.

"Okay," Leon said. "I think it's fair to say that you owe me one hell of an explanation."

Iris sighed.

She was silent just long enough for him to wonder if she'd heard him.

"Last night I woke up in the middle of the night. Jeremai 9 had one hand over my mouth; the other was by his

251

face, the side of his index finger pressed against his lips. I was terrified. I thought he was going to rape me until I realized he couldn't get away with it while you were in the next bunk. The door to our cell was open and he made me stand and walk out. He led me to Jeremai 1's office, which was empty save for the man himself. 9 left us alone. I sat and Jeremai 1 asked me questions about myself, you, the case…getting information while pretending to give a damn about my well-being. Obviously all he wanted was to see if we'd found anything that could damage him, but I thought if I gave up enough information he'd let something slip."

"Jesus, Iris; what the Hell were you thinking?"

"Probably the same thing you were when you bragged to him about murdering his son," she shot back.

"Well, yeah, but that was…" Leon compared the two situations. "Okay, I guess I gotta give you that one."

"Counting on his sexism, I did my best to play the innocent, soft-hearted little girl. 'Oh, I'm so sorry about 21's hand; I was scared he was going to kill me! Then that crazy detective made me cover for him and go on a wild goose chase up here to Sao. If he and I can each just go home…' He may have wanted to kill you in the heat of the moment when you told him you'd killed Jeremai 21, but he must have realized the consequences once he saw you starting to lose consciousness. If killing you risked war with the other colossi, he had to come up with another way to punish you. He told me that for as much information as I gave him, he'd let you and I both go our separate ways. We'd each be free to choose our own destinations."

"Do you think he bought your story?"

252

"For the most part," Iris said. "At the same time, I think he saw an opportunity there: if I was pleading for your life then you and I must have some kind of rapport. He could free himself from any liability by allowing you to pick whether you went back to Triton or stayed here. If we go back, who knows if we'd ever get to the bottom of this; if we kept on, there's Red Lung. Either way, he wins."

"And he knew I wouldn't give up," Leon said. "He gambled on my conviction to see this thing through.

"Son of a bitch."

"I warned you not to underestimate him," she replied. "I should've taken the lead on this like we agreed; why didn't you let me?"

He shook his head and stared off into the distance. *Because you have no experience with working a case,* he thought. *Because I have to be the one to solve this for Nash, for Allison.* He refused to admit to himself that some of it was because despite how close their ages were, Iris still seemed like just a young girl to him. She knew when she asked him about it on Psamanthe that he didn't like handing the ship's wheel to someone else. At the same time, being a woman didn't inspire much confidence in him. He was embarrassed to say it, let alone feel it, but there it was. In the end he said nothing, but she could read his face like an open book.

"Okay," she said.

"Okay?"

"Yeah."

"You're not mad?"

"Of course I'm mad," she said. "But after you pushed me out of the driver's seat in our Jeremai 1 interview and after a week in prison, you still stood in front of that bastard and told him you believed in me. You told him I was more like your people than mine. And I think you did it knowing what was coming next."

He felt embarrassed again, though this time because she noticed how much he cared. "So you played 'babe in the woods' for this goon and he said he'd take us back to New York or wherever the Hell Sao goes next, giving up on the case," Leon said. "And you were okay with that?"

"No," she said, "but I thought it would buy us time to learn more about our next step."

"I guess that didn't work out so well."

She laughed. "Give me a little credit, you ass." She reached into the fifth pocket of her pants and pulled out a small, folded scrap of paper and handed it to Leon. "I swiped this from his desk when he was walking around his office grandstanding."

"What is it?"

"Our lead – the reason we're here."

He unfolded the paper and flattened it on his knee. It was another rendition of the infamous symbol that had been plaguing them since the beginning of the case. He was about to ask how that helped them when he saw the writing below it. In a childlike script it read "the ordr of terin reklamashin." Leon slowly read it aloud, sounding out the nearly phonetic handwriting.

"The Order of… Terran…Wreck, Recla – Reclamation."
Iris nodded.

"What the Hell is The Order of Terran Reclamation?"
"I don't know," she said.

"Well I'd like to find out. How are we supposed to find them?"

"Flip it over," she said.

Leon looked at the back of the note.

gallutia.

"Galatea?"

He pulled his notebook from the small pocket of his backpack and thumbed through it. When he found the titans' schedules he studied them for a minute, reading aloud from the book.

"Galatea – This seafaring goliath travels counterclockwise and spends 24 hours each at the North Atlantic's nicest beaches. Her route begins at Praia de Santa Maria, Cape Verde; and then takes her to Playa de el Bollullo, Canary Islands; Horseshoe Bay, Bermuda –"

"Followed by South Beach, Miami," Iris said.

"It won't be here for 11 days."

They gravely considered how they'd acquire enough food and water to last them a week and a half. It made Leon reflect again on the day's events.

"In a way, he actually tried to help us," Leon said.

"I know," Iris said. "But why?"

"The same reason we didn't stop when we got our hands on *our* killer," Leon said. "Jeremai 21 killed Allison and Nash, but there were other players involved – just the same as I may have shot 21, but the kid wouldn't have been behind the 8-ball if this 'Order' hadn't sent him to Triton. I think Jeremai 1 wants them to go down too. If he'd sent us back home and I mailed it in to Galatea, odds are they'd get some kind of collar sooner or later. If we kept on the case, we'd find them ourselves."

"So when he said 'Jeremai 21 was getting the last of the castor beans *for*' something, it wasn't for a purpose, but –"

"– for The Order," Leon said.

"So if Jeremai 1 wanted to humiliate *you* and punish *them,* where do *I* fit in?"

"I think you embarrassed him when you left," Leon said. "Then you came back, on your own terms, without anyone knowing, and with a cop in tow. By telling that crowd that *he* and I could pick whether *you* and I gave up or kept going –"

"He was trying to publicly display his – or your – power over me," Iris said. "Typical macho bullshit."

"Look, don't take this the wrong way, but whatever neurodegenerative disease they have up there is really taking its toll," Leon said. "Bunch of damn loons."

Leon looked through his bag for the first time since they'd left New York. Remarkably, everything was still there. Jeremai 1 had even filled up his water jug and given him a couple packs of cigarettes. *Son of a bitch,* Leon thought. He offered to share the water with Iris. She thought back to their first night in prison, how he'd left out food for her.

"I don't need you to take care of me," she said.

He rolled his eyes. "This is not chivalry," he said. "You're my partner, and my friend, and it would be nice if we both lived long enough to actually solve this case."

Iris thought this over. She took the jug and took several gulps of water from it. He took out a cigarette and lit it with the lighter.

"You know those things'll kill you," Iris said.

Leon laughed. It was absurd. Red Lung would take him long before cancer. It reminded him of her immunity.

"But they're the only smoke in the air that could harm *you*..."

"Don't be mad at me," she said. "You said back at the newspaper vendors this was your choice."

"That was before I knew you're fine down here," Leon said. She groaned audibly but he continued. "I thought this was going to kill you!"

"And it still might!" she shouted. "Have you thought for one minute what it took for me to go back to that town? I had no guarantee I'd be leaving alive, but – in your words – I came along to clear my name. Now we're on the trail of who knows what kind of organization that sends Sao-born to do *its* bidding, and we're just biding our time for the next week and a half *on the surface* with no food and less than a gallon of water! Do those odds sound good to you, Detective?"

"No, but –"

"No! You don't get to interrupt. After I learned that 21's murders on Triton had nothing to do with me I could've given it up, jumped ship and made my way back to Triton without you. But I didn't! Instead, I stuck with it through *three* confrontations with Jeremai 1 and a jump off a fucking titan. And now there's impending starvation or dehydration and whatever awaits us on Galatea. So yes, this could kill me. Or you. Any of it, all of it could kill us both. But I'm not stopping. Do you know why?"

Leon kept shaking his head. He hadn't considered much from her perspective since they met. He promised himself this would be the last time he spoke so carelessly in front of her.

"Because I'm too much like you," she said. Her tone was coming back down. "I have to know. I have to peel off the mask and see what's underneath all this insanity. But unlike you, I have to do it without some long-standing clout as law enforcement. I have to work harder to earn everyone's trust and respect. And I'm tired, Leon. I'm so goddamn tired of fighting for every inch of credibility with Davis, with Nash, with Jeremai 1, with you. I meant what I said earlier – that I knew you were being honest when you told Jeremai you believed in me. Just…don't stop."

He paused to compose his words and he spoke softly. "I'm sorry," he said. "Yeah, my life is cut short now. It's always a possibility, living up on the theriopolis, that something will go wrong and…you know. But every time you drop one of these bombs it's like it's the last one, the last time. Then there's one more thing, and one more thing. And I know your past ain't all my business, sister, but good grief. You don't mean to, but you make me feel like a real sucker."

"You're the only one who can choose how you feel, Leon."

"But this trust, this is a two-way street," he said. "I thought we were on the same page when we covered for each other back with Mayor Davis. Look at what I knew about you then compared to now. There's so much you didn't tell me."

"I know," she said. "But would we be this far along, working together, if I had? Or would you have shipped me off to someone, somewhere, on your authority?"

"You didn't give yourself the chance to find out," he replied.

They were silent a long time. They knew they were at an impasse and it was getting late.

"Look," he said. "Do I need to know anything else about you?"

"No," Iris said.

"You're not a spy, or creature from outer space, or you can fly?"

She laughed. "No; I said no."

"Is that a promise?"

"Yes," she said.

"Alright. Now I'm going to take your word for it. Please, though; no more secrets."

He laid back on the sand and looked up. She did the same. The stars were probably out, but they couldn't see them through the mist.

"You know, if you can spontaneously conjure food and water out of thin air, now would be the time to tell me."

"Good night, Leon."

The next morning Leon rationed their water out to last three days and tended to the camp. In the meantime, Iris went out to find other sources for food and water. She first returned from a hardware store with a hammer, nails and a rolled-up plastic tarp that she washed out in the ocean and laid to dry. She also had a replacement pair of pruning shears. When the tarp was dry enough, they folded it like a hammock and nailed it to the two barest palm trees in walking distance. If she could find a vessel to transport any rainwater it caught, they knew they could boil it and drink it.

Food was another matter. There were palm trees, but the coconuts that hung from them proved to have contracted some kind of disease that neither Leon nor Iris could identify. Iris went to find a pot or pan and returned later with two fishing poles and a saucepan full of earthworms she'd harvested from further inland, under the soil. They walked to a pier and fished properly. They cleaned and ate what they caught.

The following ten days passed slowly. The fish were scarce, the rain scarcer still. Further journeys into South Beach proved largely fruitless. Leon found a flare gun with which to signal Galatea, but even the most irradiated and tightly-sealed canned foods had entirely decomposed. Leon had nightmares of being back on Sao, of sexual assault and being forced to eat people. More than once he awoke screaming in the middle of the night.

Iris awoke on September 20th knowing they had just a day and a half until their next massive beast-city would find them. It hadn't rained in so long they'd run out of water on the 18th – and they hadn't eaten since two days before that. Debilitating stomach cramps had set in the day the water ran out, followed by dizziness, and now she had a splitting headache. She looked up at the detestable haze and wondered if they'd have the strength to hail and board Galatea.

"Iris…"

"What?"

"Iris…"

She rolled over to look at Leon. "Leon, what do you –"

When she saw what he was staring at, she shot up like a bolt.

"Did you do this?" he asked.

"No!"

He spun around. "Iris, be straight with me –"

"Leon, I promise I –"

"If this is another one of your bullshit secrets, I swear –"

"For Christ's sake, Leon, I was going to ask *you*…"

They looked again. There were two gallons of fresh water in milk jugs not 50 feet from where they lay. Just behind that, there was a lone buck tied to a stake. At the base of the stake there was a machete. Someone had brought it to them.

Iris stood as quickly as she could and drew her weapons, looking around. "Did anyone come off of Sao after us?"

"If they wanted to ice us, they would've done it in our sleep," Leon said.

"Then who the Hell did this?"

"Someone who wants us to eat," he said.

They gave the deer some water to see if the water had been poisoned, but when its health and behavior remained constant after an hour, their hunger overcame their caution. Leon agreed to slay the deer while Iris covered him with his service pistol. He approached the animal and petted it, thanking and apologizing to the creature before doing it in with the machete. He had never killed an animal himself, but he found cleaning and portioning its meat the greater challenge. Once he'd broken it down as best he could, he hobbled back over to their campfire and started it up. While he was rebuilding the fire, Iris boiled the new water to be safe and let it cool before returning it to its original containers, all the while keeping an eye out for a trap.

They made a spit over the still-burning fire and roasted a large flank of venison after washing off as much of its blood as they could. While it cooked, Leon cleaned his hands in the ocean. It was lunchtime before they ate any of the deer. They stored some of the uncooked meat in the rainwater tarp, covering it with their fresh water in hopes of staving off bacteria. They spent the rest of the day with their backs to the Atlantic, debating over the identity of their mysterious benefactor. Iris dried and cooked some of the leftover meat for their dinner and they ate again. They agreed to sleep in shifts, though no one came.

The following evening, the sun sank on the horizon and the detectives packed up their belongings. They heard a deep disturbance on the water and turned towards it. After several moments, a monster with 100-foot claws and feet came into view. It was as ugly as a lobster and larger than life, though its body was the color of seaweed, all dark green with shimmers of light reflecting along it. They retreated up the shoreline lest it trample them, but it stopped on the beach. Looking straight up, they could just see the bottom of its conical slit shell.

"Galatea," Leon said.

She was a magnificent creature. Her forearms were like crab claws, her thin legs scurrying until she stopped. She had two eyes at the ends of pole-like tentacles, like a snail's, that looked around and inspected the beach. Then she saw the two of them. When Galatea made eye contact with Iris, Iris's veins lit up again, glowing a bright, pale blue.

262

"What the Hell…" Iris murmured, inspecting her arms.

Galatea made an excited bellow and the ichor in her own bloodstream illuminated. But something was wrong. Galatea illuminated a sickly purple from her veins, like a blacklight.

Leon turned from the creature to Iris and back again. "Iris…"

"I don't know," she replied, anticipating his question.

"I thought you only glowed when you were asleep, a- and the one time when Sao approached…?"

"So did I!"

"What's it doing?"

"I don't know, Leon."

"What does it…" The question caught in Leon's throat. It was absurd. "What does it want?"

"I don't know!"

In another moment, it was over. Iris and Galatea faded, returning to their normal appearances.

"Something's going on up there," Iris said. "There has to be."

Leon drew the flare gun from his belt and fired it straight up into the air. After several minutes, four ropes fell to the ground. No one would descend into the fog.

"I guess that's our cue," Iris said.

"Don't tell them anything they don't need to know," Leon replied.

The two strapped into their climbing harnesses and fastened them to the ropes. Leon slung his crutches over his shoulder and the two began the climb to Galatea's harbor. Almost as soon as they started climbing, they heard a rustling on the beach behind them. Leon was 30 feet in the air when it happened. He stopped and did his best to spin around. It was dark, and he had to squint, but then he saw it.

"Oh my God," he muttered.

Iris had stopped too. They both stared, motionless. Over a dozen teenagers, all clad in differing outfits of black and red, had stepped out of the woodsy shoreline and onto the sandy beach. Some carried weapons; others carried infants. All of them looked at Iris and Leon cautiously. One of them, apparently their leader, raised his hand high above his head, slowly. It was a gesture of good will, of blessing.

"It's all true," Iris whispered.

Leon returned the gesture and slowly the children returned to where they came from, fading from sight into the trees and the fog.

the seafarers

When the detectives arrived on the harbor, several Galateans awaited them. At least two citizens were armed, pointing their guns at them. The harbor was dimly lit by sparse torches affixed to the walls of buildings. The detectives put their hands up.

"No sudden movements," Leon murmured to Iris.

"Good evening," Leon said to the crowd. "My name is Leon Adler; I'm a detective from Triton. This is my partner Iris. I first want to thank you folks for lowering down ropes for us; we've been stranded in Miami near two weeks and you saved our lives. May I ask who's in charge here?"

A man from the middle of the small crowd stepped forward. He was a white man of exceptional height and average weight, his blonde hair balding and the thin wireframe glasses on his face reflecting the torchlight. He dressed more formally than the others and his big, hollow voice resonated throughout the scene.

"I am. My name is William Buckley, governor of the state of Galatea."

"How do you do, Governor," Leon replied. "My partner and I have been working a case for near three months now and we've got cause to believe some mug's been hiding out in your fair city – uh, state. I got a letter in my bag from Greg Davis, the mayor of Triton, if you want me to grab it."

Leon pointed his thumb at his back and one of the armed Galateans tensed his grip on his rifle.

"Or not."

Governor Buckley rested his hands on the raised rifles and gently pushed them down. "You'll have to forgive us; we don't get many visitors from…" He nodded downwards towards the fog. "Please, go ahead."

Leon slowly removed his bag and opened it, producing the letter and handing it to Governor Buckley.

"Why didn't you tell me you've had that this whole time?" Iris asked him in a whisper.

"You didn't ask," Leon replied with a wink.

Buckley read the note, folded it again and handed it back to Leon. He had a stern look on his face.

"You're not welcome on Galatea…" he started. Leon's heart skipped a beat. "…until you tell me if Greg Davis is still the smug son of a bitch he was when I saw him back in 89."

A smile crept across Buckley's face. Leon coughed out a nervous giggle. The governor and several Galateans broke out into laughter. Leon and Iris lowered their hands and Buckley patted Leon's shoulder heartily several times. He addressed the crowd with a jovial shout, wrapping one arm around Leon's shoulders.

"Everyone, relax! These two people are law enforcement from Triton. Mayor Greg Davis is the one who sent them here, although we won't hold that against them." There was more laughter from the crowd. "Please tell your friends and family to treat them with respect while they conduct their investigation. This is Detective Leon Adler and his partner, Iris…" Buckley looked at Iris to get her last name.

"Just Iris, Governor."

Buckley shrugged. "Alright! Iris it is. These detectives will be with us for some time and will stay as guests in my home."

Iris interrupted him. "Oh, we don't want to impose –"

"Nonsense, nonsense," Buckley said with a wave of dismissal. "You two are welcome to stay as long as you like; we have the space." He spoke more quietly to the two of them. "I'm sorry to have to do this, but I'm afraid you'll both have to be quarantined until we can determine –"

"We were down there a week and a half, sir," Leon interrupted. "We know what's coming to us."

The mayor cleared his throat and quietly expressed his condolences.

"We all know it's not contagious, but if you don't mind we'd like to undergo some…safety measures, just for my people," Governor Buckley said.

"We're happy to take any precautions you'd like," Leon replied.

Governor Buckley consulted with some other Galateans, who appeared to be their city council, while Leon and Iris waited. It was decided that baths would be drawn for Leon and Iris and each be given new, clean clothes from residents who matched their sizes as was needed. Their bags and current clothes would be hung out to air in the harbor. Leon and Iris objected but Governor Buckley assured them that a guard would be posted at all times to protect their belongings and that anything they required immediately would be replaced on Galatea. In return for the clothes, safe passage, room and board, Leon and Iris agreed to keep the governor informed of any developments in the case immediately, doubly so if the suspects posed a clear threat to any Galateans.

"You feel like we're getting the short end of this stick?" Iris asked Leon quietly.

"Yeah; where's the common courtesy of dragging us out to a public shaming and throwing us to our deaths with just one parachute between us?" he asked.

She grunted at him.

They were finally welcomed into the city. They didn't like leaving their things behind – it reminded Leon too much of Sao – but they had no other choice. After they washed themselves and redressed in new outfits, they were brought to the governor's house, which had spare rooms for each of the detectives. On the way, Governor Buckley told them about the city's landmarks and important buildings as they passed them, though it was dark and they couldn't see much. Iris discerned that Galatea was quite similar to a 1,500-foot hermit crab, though its shell stood straight up. The town was built along the outside of the shell, above the fog ceiling. It was like an enormous spiral staircase that wound around the beast's conical casing, houses constructed alongside it. Every house faced outwards, their rear walls actually part of the shell itself.

They reached Governor Buckley's house at the top of the city and the crowd of curious onlookers dispersed.

"So," Governor Buckley said, "Do you two want separate rooms, or…"

"Separate," Leon and Iris said in unison. It brought another soulful laugh from the governor. They were directed to their rooms, which were at the front of the house. They could see the street through the windows in their rooms. Foot traffic was moderate, and occasionally a local child would peek in to see the new people. Iris closed the curtains to the window and fell into a deep sleep, the most comfortable she'd had since Psamanthe had left them in New York.

They spent the next several days recovering. They were still on the rebound from ten days' malnourishment and dehydration, despite the gift from the land-dwelling teens two days prior, and Leon's ankle was still sore. They were offered free meals by countless Galateans but they insisted on working or trading for their food. Governor Buckley had Leon looked at by Galatea's doctor, who assured the detective he'd be fully healed in the next few days. They met Governor Buckley's wife, Lilian, a vivacious and curvy woman with wavy dark red hair. She wore formal attire, like her husband. They made quite a pair, he in his suits and she in her silk dresses. Leon would've thought they were sucking up all the town's wealth and extravagances with their spacious home and wardrobe, but as the days passed, they saw that Galatea didn't suffer the economic disparity of Triton or the desperation of Sao. It was by all appearances an affluent and prosperous colossus of people who were truly happy. All the while, the detectives kept an eye out for suspicious activity and the sigil of The Order, but they failed to develop the case any further.

Galatea took the detectives to Clearwater, Florida; Playa Paraiso in Cayo Largo, Cuba; West Bay, Honduras; and Playa Manuel Antonio in Manuel Antonio National Park, Costa Rica. The salty sea air blew in their faces whenever they were outside, the titan below them swimming her way across the North Atlantic. It was a fond reminder of life below, the residents told them. Life on the open sea felt like freedom. Galatea never passed skyscraper rooftops that had been repurposed for Psamanthe's nests, nor the gloomy OKO South Tower in Moscow that served as a deathly monument of theriopolitan life.

Once Leon and Iris were fully recovered, Governor Buckley invited them to a formal supper at his house with other Galatean officials. Leon and Iris borrowed a suit and an evening gown, respectively, from a family with whom they'd struck up an acquaintance. They dressed in their rooms and greeted each other awkwardly in the entryway before going to dinner.

"Iris in a dress," Leon said. "There's something you don't see every day."

She nodded at his clean-shaven face, noting a spot on his right cheek where he'd nicked himself with the razor. "You catch the guy who sliced up your face?"

"You ready to do this? Breaking bread with stuffed shirts?"

"I think sitting down for smoked fish with Kiviaq and Kenai was a little more in my comfort zone," she said.

270

"You'll do fine. Remember when you said Jeremai kept asking you about the case, seeing if you could finger him for any cons?"

"Yeah, so?"

"Same idea, but more discreet. Buckley's the top brass around here, so this cat's gonna bump gums until the wee hours, grilling us on the sly to make sure his keister ain't in whatever fire we're here to put out. Suppose word gets around he's blind to a conspiracy involving a double homicide and a knockover of the strongest poison on Earth, *and* it's happening on his doorstep. Buckley goes from the Big Cheese to the big house."

"So what do we tell them?"

There was a knock on the front door and Lilian Buckley appeared from the next room to answer it.

"Less than they tell us."

Lilian opened the door and welcomed in the guests. She introduced Leon and Iris to Marcus White and his wife Aniyah, a middle-aged couple of African descent; Kabir Ghadavi, a middle-aged and soft-spoken Indian man in glasses; and Angúo Leung, a large Chinese man whose manner was warm and engaging. The detectives recognized them from the harbor the night of their arrival. Leung reminded Iris of their hosts, whereas Ghadavi and the Whites were reserved and polite to the point of seeming out of place. Mrs. White emanated an air of snobbery towards the detectives, which they chose to ignore. The seven of them walked in through the entryway to the large, open dining room where Lilian had just finished setting their places. Governor Buckley came from the kitchen with a bottle of wine and poured glasses for everyone. Leon and Iris sat on one side of the table with the mild-mannered Ghadavi and the boisterous Leung; the Whites and the Buckleys sat across from them.

"Leon, Iris, I wanted to thank you both for being our guests tonight," Governor Buckley said. "Misters Leung and Ghadavi and Missis White are Galatea's aldermen – they're in charge of different parts of Galatea, and as you know, I have the pleasure of serving as her governor."

"Between the aldermen and the governor, isn't there usually a mayor?" Iris asked.

Aniyah White picked up her wine glass and put it to her lips. "I've been telling you you need to change those titles, Bill."

Governor Buckley laughed warmly, slapping his right hand on the table. "Too right, ladies! Very good! Truth be told, Iris, I like to think of my aldermen's collective jurisdictions as beginning and ending with the residents and the livable part of our great beast – the city. Since Galatea herself extends above and below the quarters our forefathers built, I consider her entirety to be my responsibility."

"I understand," Iris said. "I'm sorry if I offended you."

"Nonsense!" Buckley replied. "Now, the city is built along the outside of Galatea's shell. It winds around her a full four times. From the lowest point of the city to the spot directly above it is Mr. Leung's district. From that spot, the next circuit around Galatea is the area over which Mrs. White and her husband preside. Mr. Ghadavi is in charge of the rest of the city from that point upwards."

"So Mr. Ghadavi governs *two* rings around Galatea?" Iris asked.

"They're much smaller than my colleagues', Miss," Ghadavi said. "In reality it's a quite negligible difference in population."

"Makes sense," Leon said.

Leung chimed in. "Of course, that means Kabir gets the nicest view."

"Here we go," Lilian said.

"Would you like to trade, Angúo?" Ghadavi asked him.

Leung laughed. "And leave the harbor in *your* hands? No sir; I like for my city to keep running *smoothly*."

"You'll have to excuse them," Lilian said to Leon and Iris. "This little one-upmanship of Angúo's and Kabir's goes back to their election 20 years ago. Men and their penises, right Iris?"

Marcus White shifted uncomfortably in his seat but Iris smiled and nodded in agreement with the governor's wife. A young woman emerged from the kitchen with a rolling tray of plates. On each of them was a wedge salad with tomatoes, cucumbers and vinaigrette. She served all eight of them and returned to the kitchen without a word. The party tucked into their salads, their silverware quietly dinging against the bowls. A second bottle of wine was served to the guests, who drank steadily.

"So," Leung said. "You're both here from Triton. Have you lived there your whole lives? Or were you born on another Terrible God?"

"Terrible God?" Iris asked.

"I'm sorry," Leung said. "I was born on Neso; sometimes my native dialect slips out a bit."

"I'm a lifelong Triton resident, Alderman," Leon answered. "Born and bred. Iris is a bindle punk."

"Is that so?" Leung asked, turning to Iris. "Tell us, miss; where are you from?"

Iris had no interest in pursuing the conversation. She didn't look up from her plate. "Oh, you know, all over."

"Shall we guess?" Governor Buckley asked. He was being lighthearted and half-joking, but Alderman White chose to pursue the topic. She wasn't one for coyness.

"Well, we can use process of elimination, Bill. Mr. Adler, tell me if you like my detective work. She isn't from Triton *originally*, and we've never seen her around *here*. Laomedeia has been missing since probably before she was born and the only inhabitant on Naiad is that...that pharmacist woman."

"Yuki Nakajima," Iris said curtly. "Doctor...Yuki Nakajima."

The room got quiet, the atmosphere a bit uncomfortable.

"She doesn't have the tan for Psamanthe either," the alderman said. A snobbish laugh escaped her.

"Dear..." Marcus White said.

"I'm only asking, Marcus," she replied. "And I'm sure she's not from Sao. Do you know why?"

Marcus sighed. "Why's that, dear?"

"Because they're all mutants and cannibals on that shithole."

"Oh, are we?" Iris asked loudly. The room fell silent.

"Iris, let it go," Leon said.

"No, it's okay," Iris said, looking around quickly. "I'm just saying, I don't *feel* like a mutant."

"Iris."

"I mean do I look like a mutant to you, Leon?" Iris asked.

"…No."

"Well *there* you go," Iris said with a glance at Aniyah.

"Then are you a cannibal, young lady, or am I misinformed about your…lovely hometown?" Mrs. White asked.

A dark grin spread over Iris's face. "If you're curious, why don't you go to Sao and see it in person, Alderman White?"

"Well, I'm sure that –"

"No, no; just for a quick drop-in. I'm sure they'd be happy to have you for dinner."

Mrs. White was embarrassed. She turned her nose up at Iris and looked away. A long, quiet moment passed. Governor Buckley burst into a deep, loud laughter; Leung followed suit. Even the timid Marcus White and Kabir Ghadavi failed to hide devilish smirks. It seemed that someone standing up to Alderman White was a long time coming.

"Bravo, young woman!" Governor Buckley exclaimed. "Bravo. Always assert yourself! Excellent!"

Alderman White took a sip of her drink and continued pretending it had never happened. Leon awkwardly changed the subject.

"So! Ghadavi, that's an Indian name, right?"

"Yes, Detective; my ancestors hail from outside New Delhi."

"Aces. What does it mean?"

"It comes from the words 'ghad visa,' which means 'twenty forts.' The Ghadavis were responsible for the security of the small villages and forts in which ancient Indians lived."

"And now you're an alderman with a ward of people to protect," Marcus White said.

"Yes; I admit it's quite a fitting name," Ghadavi replied.

"Wow; it's like Galatea wanted you to be here," Iris said with a wink at Leon.

"So tell us about this case, detectives," Governor Buckley said. "That is of course if you're able to discuss it."

"There isn't actually much to tell," Leon said. "Our chief botanist caught some palooka dipping into her goods and he gunned her down. We caught him, but it turned out he was just the trigger man for a larger scam, so we followed a lead to Sao, and a witness and another clue brought us here in search of our killer's bosses."

"And you trust that this source from Sao is telling you the truth?" asked Leung.

"He seemed pretty cheesed off that the kid who iced our horticulturist had gotten involved in the whole thing, so he pointed us in the right direction," Leon said.

"But Sao isn't exactly known for its honor and forthrightness," Leung said. "No offense, Miss Iris."

"None taken. Actually we found a clue that predated our arrival on Sao and this source didn't mean for us to see it."

"I see. And what was the nature of this clue?"

"Unfortunately, *that* part we can't tell you," Leon said. "Now it's nothing personal – you all seem like fine folks. It's just sensitive information that we can't risk leaking until we've put shackles on the crooks behind all this. For your safety, and that of your people, we'll have to stay mum for the time being."

"I think we can all agree that that's fair," Governor Buckley said. A murmur of agreement sounded from the table.

"We *will* find the people responsible for this," Iris said, "quickly, cleanly and with the minimum of danger to Galatea and her citizens. You have our word."

"Hear, hear," Governor Buckley said with a raise of his glass. The rest of the table followed suit.

The remainder of the dinner passed without incident. After they ate, the entire company retired to another room where they continued drinking. Iris thought of her mother. Eventually she made an excuse to leave and bade everyone a good night. She needed fresh air. She walked from the top of Galatea to the bottom and back again. On her way back up she came across a small pavilion where music was being played. A young man had a violin and was accompanied by a boy with an acoustic guitar. Iris listened to them for nearly an hour, the wine still ruminating in her head. She felt warm, even tingly, and now that she had gotten away from the loud party and Alderman White, she felt at ease. She closed her eyes and listened to the sweet sounds of the band, the salty sea air kissing her face. *This is such a better life for me than on Sao,* she thought. *If mom died to get me away from there, maybe it was to enjoy life after all. This is good. For the first time in my life I'm doing things on my own terms and without hiding. I could've let Leon sort all this out by himself but I chose to help him – and now it's not just to clear my name or my conscience, but for justice, for the good of Triton and the rest of the theriopolises. I'm doing it, mom. I'm living.*

After Iris left, the Galateans decided to continue the party at a nearby bar. Leon decided to stay in his room and look over his notes to see if he'd missed something that could lead to the location of The Order of Terran Reclamation. There was nothing there. He became frustrated and threw his notes onto the desk at which he sat. There was a knock on his door; he assumed it was Iris.

"*What?!*"

The door creaked open and a beam of light spilled in. Lilian Buckley leaned on the doorframe. She still wore her evening dress and held a glass of wine.

"Evening, Detective."

"I'm sorry, Mrs. Buckley; I didn't mean to shout at you."

"It's Lilian, Detective, and don't worry. William's shouted at me plenty worse than that before."

"Well I'm sorry to hear that."

"From the sound of things, you need to take a break."

"I don't know," Leon said. "I feel like I'm so close on this. It's right in front of me and I can't see it."

"You ever think of stepping back for a minute and taking a fresh look at it?"

Leon laughed. "Easier said than done, Lilian."

"I could help take your mind off things," she said, stepping into the room.

He turned in his chair to face her. She shrugged the thin straps of her dress off her shoulders and the outfit fell to the floor. She wore nothing underneath.

"What about your husband?"

"He's out with his underlings, trying to recapture his youth," she said, walking slowly to him. "He won't be home until dawn."

"I don't know if we should –"

Lilian leaned down and set her wine glass on his desk with one hand and grabbed his crotch with the other. "Shut up and kiss me, Leon."

He couldn't help responding to her hand, but he had a choice in kissing her. *Fuck it,* he thought. He grabbed her wide, naked hips and kissed her, standing up so they could embrace. Her mouth tasted like the wine they'd been drinking. So did his. Leon's heart pounded. In moments, he was undressed, feeling the electricity of their skin touching. He took control of the moment and playfully pushed her onto his bed. She looked up at him with hungry, lustful eyes. They both knew what was next.

Iris walked back to the governor's house with a faint smile on her face. She'd decided at last that her mother would be proud of her for escaping Sao and living her new life. Iris had made quite a name for herself the last 15 years, helping to manufacture medicine for all the theriopolitans and now pursuing justice for the victims of a crime committed by her own people. It showed impartiality, she knew. She'd even come out of her shell enough to flirt a little with the young man playing the violin after his performance. The early autumn evening had fallen quite well on her and she had a spring in her step and a song in her head. When she arrived at the governor's, she thought she should apologize to Leon for causing a row at dinner. She took a quick peek into his bedroom through the crack in the curtains to see if he was asleep.

After a moment, Iris turned around and walked back to the area where the concert had played. Near the pavilion was a small bar still serving drinks to its patrons. She pulled up a stool and sat and ordered a glass of the homebrew after the owner described it to her. She cast glances around at the men at the bar. The violinist was there. He recognized her and they smiled at each other. He seemed to be a nice enough young man. Her drink came and she sipped it moderately.

"Buy you a drink?" asked a middle-aged man seated next to her. He was lean, with rich brown skin, a shaved head and neither attractive nor unattractive.

"You can pay for this one," Iris replied with a smile. The man caught the bartender's attention and motioned to him that he'd pay for the drink in Iris's hand.

"I don't think I've seen you around here before," the man said.

"I'm Iris."

"That's a beautiful name. I'm Joel."

Iris nodded politely. "So are you local?"

"Born and raised," he said. "Where do you come from?"

"Proteus," she lied.

"You live there with your…husband?"

Iris laughed and sipped her drink.

"Would you go away if I said 'yes?'"

"I...I guess not," he admitted sheepishly.

She leaned in a bit. "I'm not married."

"Oh really?" he said. "That boy over there seems quite keen on you."

Iris looked and saw the violinist wearing a saddened, lonely look on his face.

"I just met him at a concert he was playing. He's a nice guy."

"I think he's a bit jealous of me," Joel teased. Iris finished her drink.

"Then maybe we should go someplace where he can't see us."

Five minutes later, Iris and Joel were kissing deeply in the entryway to his house. He barely got the door locked behind him before they made their way to his bedroom. They undressed themselves between steamy kisses and fell onto his bed. He began taking her gloves off.

"These stay on," she said.

"Okay," he said. His tone was genuine and with concern for her.

Joel began to climb on top of her but she put a firm hand on his chest.

"No," she said. "You lay on your back."

He obediently did as he was told and she climbed on top of him, straddling his hips on her knees. He looked up at her with anticipation and arousal, and even a bit of concern, for in her eyes he saw no love and precious little lust. She could feel him pressing against her, just outside, and with one hand she reached down and put him inside of her. The encounter lost its pre-coital urgency and they slowed down to a comfortable pace. It took Iris a minute or two to find her rhythm, but when she did, she controlled her and Joel's movement with her pelvis. Iris looked down at Joel with a relaxed curiosity, an almost scientific study of his sexual behavior. Over time, his breathing changed, his hands changed positions to massage different parts of her body and his eyes kindled a small fire that built slowly but surely.

Okay, she told herself. *This is sex. This is how it looks, how it feels, smells and sounds.*

Physically it felt good to her, and Joel was a gentle and respectful partner, but she easily maintained emotional distance from it all. Iris certainly wasn't in love with Joel, nor was she lonely or looking to fill some need within her. She had been curious about sex since she was an adolescent on Sao and tonight she had decided she would act on that curiosity, at her own discretion, in control of every aspect of the act.

When it was over, she stood and redressed while he recovered. She put her shoes back on and he realized she was leaving.

"Wait, where are you going?" he asked.

"I'm leaving," Iris said.

"Just like that?"

"Look, I'm not looking for anything long-term…"

He scrambled to compose himself. It seemed very sudden.

"But…can we go out to dinner sometime?"

"I think this was a one-time thing," she said.

"Look, that was great, but…why me?" he asked. "I mean call me old-fashioned but, why go home with someone if you're not interested in seeing him again?"

She thought about her response for a minute.

"Because I wanted to," she finally said. "Goodbye Joel."

Iris walked up Galatea's spiraling street to Governor Buckley's house without looking back. When she got back to her bedroom she undressed and went to sleep with a faint smile on her face. She thought she'd like to have sex again, and maybe even with someone she truly loved. She knew she hadn't met him or her yet, but nothing was impossible, because she owned her life now. No more of the atrocities she lived in childhood, no more hiding her past from everyone she met and no more living as an outsider. She could do anything she wanted to do and it was ambrosial.

Meanwhile, by the time Iris had arrived at Joel's house, Leon and Lilian were laying side by side in bed, covered in sweat. Leon reached for his jacket and pulled out his cigarette holder and opened it. He'd run out of Jeremai's cigarettes before they boarded Galatea but luckily he found a local herbalist and helped him around his shop in exchange for a free pack. He pulled one out and stuck one end in his mouth and offered one to Lilian. She plucked it from the case.

"Just don't tell my husband," she said jokingly.

"I think I can keep it a secret," he replied.

She took the cigarette case from him and gently ran her fingers along its etching. Leon reached in his coat pocket again and found the lighter Jeremai had given him on Sao. It felt like a year ago. Lilian rested her head on his shoulder, her large breasts pushed against his side, one naked leg draped over his crotch. He lit their cigarettes and casually tossed the lighter onto the floor next to the bed. They were silent for several minutes as they smoked and watched the trails coming off the lit ends of their cigarettes dance and twirl and mingle together as they rose.

"What's it like on Triton?" Lilian asked.

"Not so different. I mean it looks different. The main berg is flat, and it's bigger and busier. Underneath we got a rough neighborhood hanging by chains. Whole damn place is lousy with folks on the bum. But it's the same grind as over here – bunch of guys and gals trading and working for a bit of grub, occasionally need a shamus like me to straighten 'em out."

"Do you miss it?"

"Sure," he said. "I was born and raised in that city. I've ankled it off-titan before, but a fella can't help but get homesick. Why?"

"Lately William and Angúo have been getting into some tense arguments behind closed doors. I can't usually make out what they're saying but the tones in their voices get awfully heated and I hear a bit here and there. Angúo says he can't maintain order, that he's not up for the job, and William tells him he has to keep it up for the sake of when we're off Galatea."

"So William's planning on moving you to a different leviathan and setting Leung up for his replacement."

"I've never lived anywhere else," Lilian said.

"Ah, it ain't so bad, doll. Plenty of people migrate. Iris has lived everywhere; tomorrow you should bend her ear about it."

Lilian smiled at the mention of Iris, remembering her altercation with Alderman White several hours prior. She and

Leon finished their cigarettes. She took the end of Leon's cigarette from him and stood, opening the window a crack and throwing both butts out. He admired her body while she did so.

"Iris," Lilian said, getting back into bed. "She is a little firecracker though, isn't she?"

"I hope to tell ya," Leon said. "It's good odds she's loonier than a shithouse rat. Then again, she's also a good woman – a real green-label dame. Did she tell you we ended up riding Sao from The Big Apple to Miami? She stood her ground with all those batty lifetakers like it was nothing. If she hadn't been there to keep the peace, the whole lot of them would've –"

He stopped speaking and shot up in bed. Lilian looked up at him. "What? What is it?"

"That's it."

"What's it? I mean, that's what?"

"Son of a bitch *that's it!*"

He jumped up out of bed and started dressing himself. Lilian covered herself with the bedsheets and sat up. "Leon, what's wrong?"

He didn't answer. Leon opened his bedroom door and crossed it, closing it behind him. He knocked on Iris's door but she wasn't answering. He knocked harder, then banged on the door, but she still didn't answer.

She must still be out, he thought. *Shit! I need her with me on this.*

Lilian emerged from his bedroom, smoothing her crumpled dress over herself.

"Listen, if this is some elaborate excuse to kick me out of your bed –"

Leon walked quickly to her and held her by the shoulders. "I need you to listen very carefully to me," Leon said. "Tomorrow, Iris and I are heading down to the harbor to wrap this whole thing up; we should have our mastermind in bracelets by sundown. Don't leave this house until you get my say-so, clear?" He ran into his bedroom to write a note to Iris and slip it under her door.

"What?! Leon, you're not making any sense. And what makes you think I'm taking orders from you?"

"The less you know, the better, baby. But I need you to trust me on this one. Stay here and don't breathe a word of this to anybody – not William, not the aldermen, nobody."

Leon picked up his note and carried it back to the hallway, finally slipping it under Iris's door.

"Leon, what's down in the harbor?"

"A case of The Blues," he said with a laugh.

carapace

Iris awoke in the mid-morning and found the note slipped under her door. She dressed and followed the note's instructions to meet Leon at a café in Alderman White's district that protruded out from the main walkway. When she got there, she saw him sitting alone at a table for two. Other diners peppered the surrounding tables. Leon saw Iris and gestured for her to join him. A cold autumn wind blew through the theriopolis.

"Happy October!" he exclaimed.

"Is it the 1st already?" she asked.

"Yeah. We should be somewhere along the Colombia-Venezuela border, headed for Cayo de Agua."

A waiter arrived with plates of food for both of them.

"Feels like we haven't had a chance to talk alone," Iris said.

"I noticed that. They've been playing host a little too well. Makes me feel like they're trying to keep an eye on us."

"Look, before we talk about the case," Iris said, "I've been thinking about the Tlingit on Psamanthe. We promised them justice for the attack on Kiviaq and for the death of his father, but we failed to deliver on that promise."

"We said what we had to in order to get to Sao," Leon said. "I don't have time to worry about a years-old assault out of my jurisdiction when I've got fresh Triton bodies piled up – and neither do you. We're up to our eyeballs in the Mackey case and that should be our main concern right now."

"So we just lied to those people as a means to an end."

Leon didn't respond.

"Y'know, I've learned out here that I have to let that old, deceitful, Machiavellian part of myself go," Iris said. "I know I was dishonest with you in the past, and I'm sorry, but I want to do better – I want to *be* better."

"I understand what you're saying, but even if we had the time to help we couldn't. That crime was never dealt with by local law enforcement on Psamanthe –"

"I don't think they *have* law enforcement, Leon," Iris said.

"- And we have no proof of wrongdoing by any one individual."

"Kiviaq is minus an arm and a leg," Iris shot back.

"And which one of Sao's residents did it? Tell me. Who was it?"

"Well...I mean I don't know, but...what about Jeremai 1?"

"What about him?"

"He has a responsibility and duty to keep his citizens law-abiding and to punish the ones who don't, right? Isn't there some kind of culpability there?"

Leon knit his brow and thought for a minute. "I think the closest charge anyone could bring to him in that situation would be criminal negligence for the boy or maybe

288

constructive manslaughter for the father – but those are long shots."

"What are each of those?"

"Well, criminal negligence is when someone fails to do his or her job and it results in harm or death to another person. Let's say Galatea picks us up from Miami Beach and only one guy is working there. He puts us in quarantine and forgets about us so we starve to death. Criminal negligence. As you said, Jeremai 1 has a responsibility to keep his people safe – and to keep others safe from them. Clearly, whether intentionally or not, he allowed *someone* to abduct Kiviaq, dismember two of his limbs and sew him up before throwing him back to his parents. That type of thing seems damn hard not to notice, so I'm betting he saw it and didn't care or he knew it was coming so he tried to stay away from the scene to avoid accountability. That's called 'willful blindness.'"

"And what was the other one then?"

"Constructive manslaughter," Leon said. "That's when you perform one illegal act that accidentally leads to the death of someone seemingly unrelated. Whoever would be liable for Kiviaq's abduction – and let's just pretend we could link it to Jeremai 1 for a moment – caused his father to panic and go searching for him on the surface, contracting a fatal disease and sending him to an early grave."

"So how do we pin those on them?" Iris asked eagerly.

"I'm telling you, there's no way to at this point," Leon said. "But, maybe for future use, I have a present for you that may help."

He reached behind his chair and grabbed Iris's backpack and handed it to her.

"How did you –"

"I walked down to the harbor this morning and talked the guard into giving me our things back. I told him they'd been airing out long enough and that Alderman Leung ordered them returned."

"Won't Leung find out about that?"

"I'll get to that in a minute," Leon said. "First, about Jeremai and Kiviaq…" He pulled a piece of paper from his pocket and handed it to her. It was the sigil of The Order, with Jeremai's handwriting on the back.

"Now this *does* help the Tlingit," Leon said. "At the very least, when we get back to Triton, we show this to Mayor Davis and see what we can do about getting a warrant for Jeremai 1."

"On what charges?"

"Conspiracy, withholding evidence, obstructing justice – the more the better. He knew damn well who sent Jeremai 21 to Triton, and why, and he lied to our faces about it. This paper is the proof."

Iris was nodding, a real smile spreading on her face.

"Now, I know it may not be for the assault on Kiviaq or his father's death, but we put the squeeze on Davis and we can rally enough lawmen and volunteers from Triton and Psamanthe alone to take him in – nevermind whoever else may help out. We need backup, and we'll have it in spades."

"We're really going to arrest him," Iris said.

"It may be a few months, but we'll get him. We'll get him."

Leon put the paper back in his pocket. "Now I have something to ask you."

"Sure thing."

"The night we came up here…"

"I saw them too. The kids. There's always been an urban legend about –"

"That's not what I wanted to ask you about."

She paused. "I know."

"Help me out here. Why in the Hell did Galatea light up that sickly purple?"

"You have my word; I've never seen that before in my life. They've always lit up blue, just like me. And aside from when Sao approached us in New York, none of them have ever…" She looked down at her arms, rubbing them shyly. "I don't know what happened."

"Has it happened again?"

"Not that I've seen."

"Have you felt any different since we boarded?"

"No. I'm at a total loss on this."

Leon weighed her answer. "Okay. I believe you. But if anyone else saw it, this whole damn place could turn rogue on us real fast."

"I know. I've been thinking about it since we came up to the harbor."

"Alright. As long as you know."

"Now what's this about Alderman Leung?"

"I got something out of Lilian Buckley last night."

"I bet you did."

Leon's face flushed red.

"I…I don't care about that," Iris said. "Just keep going. What did she say?"

"Something's going on with Governor Buckley and Leung – something big. They're in cahoots on some plan; five gets you 10 it has to do with The Order."

"What makes you say that?"

"She said she overheard Leung saying he 'can't maintain order much longer.' Only I think he said he can't maintain *The* Order much longer."

"More cover-ups," Iris nodded.

"And what's more, Buckley said something about 'Once we're off Galatea.'"

"So the Buckleys are planning on ducking out before the shit hits the fan."

"You said it, sister," Leon said.

"So what's our play?"

"I gummed it up on Sao; why don't you tell me what you think we should do?"

Iris was surprised. "Do you think Ghadavi and White are in on this too?"

"I don't know," Leon said.

"It's probably best not to approach them until we know more."

"Right."

"Well, if Leung's our only lead for now, obviously we need to go down there and get answers. You ever hear of the 'good cop, bad cop' routine?"

"Yeah."

"Well, with the way things have gone for us this far, I'm thinking we do 'bad cop, worse cop' instead."

Leon laughed. "Alright. Keep your eyes and ears open and let's go gumshoeing."

Their bags and weapons in their possession once more, the detectives felt like themselves again. They descended Galatea to the harbor and asked the harbormaster for Leung's whereabouts. He directed them to Leung's office and they knocked on his door.

"It's open."

They opened the door and greeted him.

"Ah, detectives! Wonderful to see you. Are you enjoying your stay in our fair city?"

"Aces," Leon said. "Hell of a berg you got here, Alderman."

"We do our best to keep it that way," Leung said. "Please, sit."

They sat in chairs in front of his desk. He offered them drinks but they declined.

"So, how goes the investigation?" Leung asked.

"Slowly but surely," Iris said. "Of course it's hard to believe that a lovely seafaring vessel like Galatea could be home to the type of people we're chasing."

"Yes," Leung said. "It seems that no matter how much we thrive, the criminal element still seeps in somehow from time to time. Tell me, have you two uncovered any new leads or clues since arriving?"

"I'd say we've learned a thing or two," Iris said. "Say, we just had a wonderful breakfast up at this little café in Alderman White's district; do you know it?"

"The place that juts out over the edge of our main road?"

"That's the one."

"Excellent cuisine!" Leung said. "Galatea's best gardener, Donnie Suzuki, provides them with most of their vegetables. He lives down here in my district; he's got a green thumb like nobody I've ever met."

The detectives chuckled.

"Maybe we should ask him about the castor beans when we're done here?" Iris asked.

A heavy silence fell in the room.

"I'm sorry?"

"No you're not," Iris said. "The other night at dinner you asked about the nature of the clues that led us to Galatea, and I've got a good guess why. What do you know about ricin poisoning?"

"Surely the food wasn't that bad!" Leung joked. The detectives' faces remained blank. "Iris, is this some more of that sharp wit from last night's dinner party? If so, I'll admit it's gone over my head."

"Alderman Leung, please answer the question," Leon said.

"I'm afraid I have no idea what you're talking about."

"I think you might," Iris responded. "But let me start at the beginning and bring you up to speed. A few months ago a man came all the way to Triton to steal its supply of castor beans. Beautiful ornamental flowers, but…I mean, come on. Triton's horticulturist caught him breaking in, and he beat her to death in the streets."

"And he was caught, wasn't he?" Leung asked.

"Killed, actually, but not before he murdered Detective Adler's former partner," Iris asked.

"I'm sorry, Detective, I –"

"Here's what we couldn't understand," Iris said. "What makes a man desperate enough to travel from Sao – did I mention he was Sao-born, like myself?"

"I'm not sure you did, Iris," Leon responded playfully.

"What makes a man desperate enough to travel from Sao all the way to Triton to steal castor beans? I've seen dedicated gardeners, but nobody who would kill for inedible houseplants."

"Surely there must have been another reason for him to steal them," Leung said.

"Well, I did some research on them and it turns out they can be boiled down and used in a recipe for skin cream," Iris said. "But you take one look at this guy and you can tell he isn't exactly one to exfoliate," she added with a laugh. Leon followed suit, and Leung managed a nervous chuckle. She glared at him and he fell silent. Iris rose from her seat and walked slowly around the office.

"Other than that, poison is at the top of a short list – and he had taken so *many* of these castor beans, it was enough to poison a hundred people. And he had this…weird tattoo."

"T-Tattoo?"

"Damnedest thing," Iris said. "It was like a …well, here, I've got a mock-up of it on me." She produced the drawing of The Order's sigil from her pocket and opened it, dropping it on Leung's desk. Leung's heart sank. He grew quiet.

"So we go to Sao looking for answers and end up locked in a prison cell for a week for our troubles. As it turns out, Sao's king, Jeremai 1, Generation Four, was our killer's father – and he was *not* happy that his son had died on this errand. I say 'errand' because we gleaned from Jeremai that his son had been sent to Triton by a larger group – some kind of secret society, maybe, or perhaps just a gaggle of all-around ne'er-do-wells operating out of Galatea. They call themselves The Order of Terran Reclamation."

"Listen, I've got work to do, and this is obviously wild conjecture. Do you honestly believe that a group of that magnitude could thrive right under our very noses without us knowing about it?" Leung asked.

"No, they couldn't," Iris said. She stopped pacing in front of Leung's desk and placed both her gloved hands flat on it. "As you said, not without you knowing about it. Obviously they'd need to partner up with someone who had power, influence, authority…"

"If you're going to make a baseless accusation at me, you can get the Hell out of my office."

"Show us your arms, Alderman," Leon said.

"What? Why?"

"The tattoo on our killer's arm turned out to be the insignia of this group," Iris said. "Or at least it looked that way before Detective Adler put a bullet through his skull and sent him overboard in…Where was it, Detective? Zimbabwe?"

"Johannesburg," Leon replied.

"Well, wherever," Iris said. "It seems that the leader of this group, this 'Order,' has a bit of a complex when it comes to its members. He needs them branded for life. I'm assuming it's some kind of password, and my guess is, you roll up your shirtsleeves and we'll find that same symbol inked on *you*, Alderman Leung."

Leung stared at her. He breathed heavily through his nose. Several seconds passed.

"Alderman?" Leon asked.

Leung swept his arm along his desk and a flurry of papers washed over the detectives. He made for the open door but Iris caught him before he got out. She grabbed his right arm and wrenched it upwards behind his back and swung him around, violently slamming him onto his desk face down. It knocked the wind out of him. Leon had stood out of his seat and drawn his service pistol.

"You're under arrest," Leon said.

Leung gasped to get more air. "You can't stop them now; it's too late," he said. His nose was broken from the impact on the desk and had begun to bleed.

"The Order?"

"Who else?"

"Who are they?" Iris screamed. "What is The Order of Terran Reclamation?"

"Go to Hell."

She brought his arm up another couple inches and he screamed in pain. Leon could tell that as much as Leung was squirming, he couldn't get up. He holstered his pistol.

"Hey Iris," Leon said. "You forgot to tell Alderman Leung how you got our killer to talk."

"I'm not afraid of you or your little bitch."

Leon reached in Iris's bag and retrieved her new pair of pruning shears, slamming them on the desk next to Leung's face. When Leung's vision focused on them, his eyes widened.

"You might want to watch your mouth," Leon said, reaching in his pocket for his cigarette holder. "Snip snip."

Iris took the shears and opened them, gently placing Leung's restrained pinky finger between the blades.

"Detective, you have to stop this!" Leung exclaimed.

"Stop what?" Leon asked. He pulled a cigarette from the case and returned the case to his pocket.

"God dammit I'll have both your badges for this if you don't let me up. I'm going to count to five –"

"*I'm* going to count to three," Iris said. "One…"

"Detective, help me!"

Leon held his lighter in one hand, cupping the wind with the other, lighting his cigarette. "Can't. Busy."

"Two…"

"You know I can never get these damn things to light the first try."

"Three!"

"Okay! Okay; I'll talk," Leung said. Iris let him up. He checked his hand; all of his fingers were intact. "Just keep her away from me!"

"No promises," Leon said. He drew his gun, for warning.

"The Order," Iris said. "Now."

"They came to me a couple of years ago," Leung said. His hands were shaking, his nose still bled. "Back then they called themselves The Church of the Enkindled Hearth. There weren't more than a dozen of them. They seemed harmless enough, like some new religion worshipping the old life."

"Life on the surface," Leon suggested.

Leung nodded. "They said they just wanted to pray, hold services and memorials, remember the way things were, all that nonsense. And if you listened to them, it seemed – it *was* – really nice. 'Never forget the past; respect the earth from which we came' and so on. I helped them as much as I could, but as they grew they got more radical – protesting big trade deals with other colossi, trying to convince us to leave Galatea and return to the earth. One thing led to another and by the time I realized what they were doing, it was too late. They all but disappeared and I was too involved to bring them to justice without ending up behind bars myself. They renamed themselves The Order of Terran Reclamation and put that damned symbol on me to make sure I wouldn't turn on them."

"Are the other Aldermen involved? Buckley?"

Leung shook his head. "Buckley told me it's my job to shut them down. But they're too many; it's too much. No one besides him knows."

"Why are they doing all this?" Leon asked.

"They don't believe we were ever supposed to come up," Leung answered. "The Order believes we should've stayed on the surface. It's our home, from the primordial ooze to the Age of Information; humans are supposed to stay on the ground."

"But the fog…"

Leung shrugged. "How many natural disasters have we lived through? Volcanoes, earthquakes, tsunamis – even our manmade environmental hazards haven't stopped us. Oil spills, nuclear meltdowns – we've survived it all and we did it on firm terra. The Order believes that riding beasts until mankind peters out is embarrassing, unnatural."

"So the solution is to kill everyone by dumping ricin into the food supplies?"

"The food supplies?" Leung asked with genuine surprise. "Jesus, you two really don't know anything, do you?"

A shadow darkened the doorway; a Japanese man stood on the other side with his hands behind his back. Leung looked at him with puzzlement.

"Donnie…?"

Leon began walking towards the man to usher him away.

"I'm sorry sir; you can't –"

Donnie Suzuki's right arm reached forward. He had a gun in his hand and he shot Angúo Leung in the head before sprinting away. After the momentary shock, Iris drew her weapons and she and Leon left the Alderman and chased their suspect.

There's no maze of streets to lose us in this time, Iris thought. *No corners to turn. Nowhere to hide. Unless he runs to the top of the titan and jumps off, we've got him.*

…Unless he jumps off.

Just seconds after the chase began, Suzuki ducked into a house and closed the door behind him. Leon and Iris stopped themselves at the door and pushed. It was locked. Leon kicked the knob as hard as he could and the door began to collapse. After a second kick it broke inward. The house was small.

Donnie Suzuki was gone.

"What the Hell," Iris said.

"Check the…check the hiding spots," Leon said. There were sigils for The Order everywhere: in paint on the walls, as mobiles made of twigs and plastic hanging from ceilings. They searched under the bed, in the large armoire next to it, between the many rows of hanging gardens and in every corner and small space in the residence. Their search came up empty.

Leon was in the rear of the house when he heard a faint, faraway sound behind him. He spun around with his gun pointed at the source of the noise but saw only the rear wall of the house – the section of Galatea's pale shell into which the residence was constructed. He breathed a sigh of relief and disappointment and lowered his gun. Then just as he was about to turn away, something caught his eye. A six-foot line or seam ran vertically up and down the wall. He wasn't sure he'd really seen it until he blinked several times and stepped closer.

Is this a natural break in her shell? he thought.

Leon approached it and touched it with his free hand. He ran his fingertip up along the seam and came to a corner. Another line, just above his head, ran straight across for three feet before ending at *another* vertical line that ran down to the floor. He couldn't believe his eyes. It was a door.

"Iris, get over here."

Leon looked closer. The doorway was indeed made of Galatea's shell but its edges had been chiseled through to whatever awaited them inside. The entire façade made up a false wall. They had to get inside, even if it was just a closet-sized hiding space for Donnie Suzuki.

301

He felt around the door for a handle. He heard Iris step up behind him and she searched the nearby section of wall for other clues. Leon was just starting to lose his patience when he found it: an optical illusion, a small handhold at the top of the door. It was virtually invisible. The only reason he found it was that his fingertips depressed into a small groove.

"A secret passageway?" Iris asked. "Really?"

"Cover me."

Iris took Leon's pistol and he grabbed the handle with his right hand, bracing himself against the wall with the left. He pulled hard and the door came out of its frame and fell outwards towards the rest of the house, landing with a thud. It was thicker than they imagined. Iris aimed carefully at the opening but all that came from the other side was blackness. Leon took his pistol back and Iris drew her escrima sticks again and they peeked further into the secret room. Two spikes were driven into the floor with knots tied to them. Iris knelt and examined it.

"This is a rope ladder," she said. "The Order must have punched through Galatea's shell and set up shop inside its empty chambers."

Jesus, Leon thought. He felt the same uneasiness in his stomach and lightheadedness that had regularly plagued him since Sao. "We need light," he said.

He kept his pistol drawn on the dark room and Iris ran outside for a torch. She was back in a moment, much to Leon's relief. He had nearly 20 years on the job but this was alien to him. He'd seen fights, burglaries, murders, but nothing like the last two months. Her absence only reminded him how far from his home, from his world, he really was.

Iris handed him the torch and he lit it with his lighter. They entered the empty chamber and climbed down the rope one at a time. Leon held the torch high and his spirits sank once he saw what was illuminated. The Order flew its flags and banners around the chamber. Opposite the entrance, there were rows of arranged seats facing a pulpit, which was adorned with The Order's sigil and several unlit candles. On the wall to their right, which was formed by the end of the chamber in which they currently stood, a wooden display case housed several glass jars full of dirt scavenged from the surface. They were arranged ornately, likely in some arcane pattern unknown to the detectives. The opposite wall held various other trinkets from the surface and a high, wide curtain that was just barely rustling. The floor of the room was on a downward slope to the left, ending at the wall with the curtain.

"Over there," Leon said.

They crossed the room, their steps echoing in the hollow space, and pulled the curtain back. Another entryway had been bored into the wall behind the curtain, this leading to the next chamber, which was larger than the church. They entered it and found a compost heap of newly dead, flowering, leafy plants, most of which had been harvested.

"Don't touch anything!" Leon said.

"This is the castor bean plant," Iris said. "My God. Whatever they're doing, it looks like they're almost done."

"That's what I'm afraid of."

As they walked through this larger chamber, heading further downhill, they saw a workbench against one wall. The workbench had several beakers, conical flasks, separator funnels, heating mantles and condensers atop it. It appeared to have been used recently. There was an opened envelope on the desk, addressed in a sloppy hand to Donnie Suzuki. The handwritten postmark said it had come from Triton. A couple castor beans were still in the envelope.

Jeremai 21, Iris thought.

Leon spoke quietly to avoid blowing their cover but also to break the eerie silence that clung to them like summer heat.

"This must be where Suzuki's –"

In the distance, a large, empty piece of hard plastic hit the ground. Leon swung his pistol around at the source of the noise. His torch followed. The chamber was empty but they saw another curtain on the far wall.

"Go!"

They ran for the curtain. Iris realized they were still heading downhill, and were likely in as low a point of Galatea as anyone had ever been. They weren't far above the fog ceiling. She drew the curtain aside, charging into the next chamber to catch Donnie Suzuki. Neither Iris nor Leon were ready for what they saw.

The room into which they ran was the largest yet. Light streamed in through ventilated slits carved out of one wall. Three men stood in the center of the chamber, all of whom wore hazmat suits and rubber gloves. One man held onto a pipe, which had the girth of a man's arm and stood vertically from chest height to a hole punched into the floor. Another man held a funnel whose bottom rested in the top of the pipe, its mouth pointed at the ceiling. The third man was dumping a milk carton, full of some kind of liquid, into the

304

funnel. Midway down the pipe, a rubber accordion-like stopper separated the pipe into its halves.

The ricin, Leon thought.

An oil barrel half-full of the ricin was in the middle of the room, near the men. The hole itself was as big around as a coffee table.

"Freeze!" Leon shouted. The men looked up and stopped what they were doing.

"Put the equipment down and put your hands behind your head – slowly," he said.

The men looked to one another and complied. Iris sheathed her sticks and took Leon's handcuffs from his belt and approached the men, taking the opportunity to see what they were doing as she handcuffed two of the men together.

"What the Hell's on the other end of that pipe, Iris?"

"Galatea. I can see her moving; this pipe's stuck in her like…" Iris's toned darkened. "…an IV."

The ricin, Leon thought again. *The pipe, the bloodstream, the purple ichor.*

They're trying to kill her.

The scope of the conspiracy finally hit them both. The Order of Terran Reclamation had changed jobs from historians to some kind of death cult. Iris had figured they'd poison some food and call the theriopolises unsafe, hoping to garner favor with the locals. Leon imagined they planned to taint the water and demand ransom for the identity of whose water filters had been poisoned. It wasn't until they saw the makeshift access port and saline lock that they understood. The Order had harvested castor oil and made gallons upon gallons of ricin to sink Galatea and force her residents back to the surface to adapt or die.

Something in Leon began to break down. How could anyone contemplate killing these beautiful, eldritch creatures that had saved humanity from Red Lung? He shook his head gently and looked at the men in the hazmat suits. He lowered his gun, eyeing them pitiably, as Iris moved behind the third man, sidling between him and a low desk full of spare tools.

In a flash, Donnie Suzuki stood from behind the desk and shot one of the handcuffed men in the back of the head, sending him forward. As the man fell through the hole, dragging his screaming companion with him, Suzuki saw Leon's gun and reached for Iris from behind her, pulling her close to him to use as a human shield, his gun's muzzle buried in her temple. The third member of The Order cowered in fear; Leon raised his pistol and aimed it at the gunman. He didn't have a clean shot. Donnie Suzuki grinned. He backed towards the doorway to the next chamber with Iris as Leon kept his gun trained on him. When Suzuki and Iris got to the door, he took his gun off her and kicked her in the back, sending her reeling forward towards Leon. At the same time, he turned and ran.

Just as Leon charged the room to follow Suzuki, the third member of The Order snapped to and tackled Iris, who was still trying to regain her footing. The two of them tumbled towards the hole in the floor and went over the edge. The last things Leon saw were their legs and feet disappearing down the hole. He doubled back to the massive syringe, screaming her name. Leon's adrenaline surged. He dove towards where they'd fallen, landing on his chest on the floor, his head and shoulders peeking out over the hole.

Iris had caught a support beam with her right hand. Looking up at it, she realized the nails driven into the support beam had actually caught her thick glove. It wouldn't hold for more than a moment; she heard the tough fabric already beginning to tear. She swung her left hand up and grabbed the beam, which freed her right hand. She pulled it out of the glove and reaffirmed her grip on the cold steel, but something was wrong. Something was pulling her down. She looked at her feet. It was the member of The Order, still in his hazmat suit and gloves, frantically holding her by her left ankle. Her expression changed from shock to anger. Iris tried shaking him off but his hold was too strong. She heard Leon calling her name from just a few feet above but she barely registered it. She used every ounce of strength in her left leg to lift the cultist up, just far enough to kick him in the face with her right boot. She kicked once, twice, thrice and he lost his grip, falling through the fog and onto Galatea's soft, spinach-green body. Iris didn't see what happened next, but she heard it. His inertia bounced him off the leviathan like a rubber ball and he screamed, flailing his limbs desperately as he went out over her sloping abdomen and down over 1,000 feet to the surface.

Leon extended a hand downward and called her name. She eyed the situation. She could've made it back up through the hole alone, but she could tell by the look in his eyes that he wasn't leaving her until she took his hand. She did, and with her free hand she grabbed the lip of the hole and began pulling herself up. Once her arms and head were back in the room, she yelled at Leon to go catch Suzuki. He didn't want to leave her but something in her voice demanded obedience.

Leon ran after the killer, forgetting his torch. He entered the next chamber down, which was also lit by carved slits in the outer wall. There he saw dozens of people just rousing from their sleep in bunk beds.

The Order, Leon thought. *The whole damn lot of 'em.*

He jogged through this large chamber and ignored the verbal protests coming from the cultists, only stopping to draw his gun on those who approached him. They backed off towards the door he'd entered. At the far end of the sleeping quarters, he went through yet another entrance bored into Galatea's shell and into the fifth chamber so far, which wasn't lit. He cursed himself for forgetting his torch and tried to let his eyes adjust to the darkness. As he felt his way through the chamber, he tripped on something large and soft to his right. He braced himself with his hands and realized it was warm and not unlike a high curb coming up from the shell.

Sorry, girl, he thought. *Be outta your way in two shakes.*

Iris finished climbing back into the room and collapsed on the floor to catch her breath. She saw over a dozen identically-clad Order members emerging from the chamber Leon had just entered. When they saw her, they began speaking to one another without taking their eyes off her. Within moments, she could tell several of them were nodding and clenching their fists, raising them towards her. She laughed an exhausted laugh, removed her left glove and tossed it aside. She drew her escrima sticks with her bare hands then jumped up and down twice and shook herself out, the first of the cultists just starting to run towards her.

He was a middle-aged bald man and he threw a right hook. She blocked it with her left forearm and responded with a swing at his ribcage using her red right hand. She heard at least one rib crack and she reversed his momentum by shoving her upheld left hand out, sending him spinning. She kicked him square in his hindquarters and he crashed into a shelving unit against a wall. Arms came around from behind her and locked around her chest. Iris was restrained and a third attacker approached her quickly. This third attacker, an elderly Hispanic man, got a couple punches into her stomach and sides before she picked up her feet and kicked him in the solar plexus. The momentum sent her and the man restraining her backwards. He lost his footing and landed on his back, losing his grip on her. She rolled over and off of him – a squat, blonde man with ruddy skin – just in time for the Hispanic man to recover. He charged her again, more slowly this time, and she backhanded his face with one of her sticks as she held her stomach with the other hand. He only staggered for a minute, towards the oil barrel of ricin, but it gave her an idea. She ran up to him from behind and put him in a headlock, dragging him to the barrel and shoving him in face first by his waist. She stepped back quickly to avoid coming in contact with the poison. The barrel tipped over and fell over with his legs sticking out of it. He screamed and she heard the ricin enter his throat. He choked on it and gargled, sputtering it out, but they both knew there was nothing for it.

This turn of events changed something and three more of the Order members approached her at once – two women and a man. Their eyes said they were as afraid as they were determined. Iris dispatched the three of them so quickly in a flurry of swings that the rest of the cultists lost their nerve. She caught her breath, nodded and left her attackers on the ground, walking on to catch up with Leon. The remaining cult members parted for her as she approached.

As Leon recovered from falling on Galatea, he realized it must be the last room if her carapace were poking through. He kept his ears open as he awkwardly stepped through this chamber. Suzuki was in here somewhere but wasn't making a sound. Everything was silent; everything was dark. His eyes had just begun to adjust when he heard the hammer of a handgun click back. He turned to open fire but it was too late. The flash of the muzzle brightened the room for a fraction of a second and the roar of the gunfire echoed throughout the chamber. As Leon felt the bullet rip through his torso, he fired in the direction from which he thought he'd seen Suzuki's face behind the gun. He didn't stop until his clip was empty. Several bullets tore through the outside wall of Galatea's shell, taking fist-sized pieces of the shell with them. Light streamed into the chamber.

Leon couldn't see Donnie Suzuki. There was no noise. Then he heard a thump and the clang of a firearm on the floor. The killer was dead. Leon slumped back against the nearest wall and put his free hand over the bullet wound.

A shadow darkened the doorway to the sleeping chamber. Leon drew his pistol on the figure. It was Iris. She called his name and helped him stand up straight. She put his free hand around her shoulder and replaced it with hers, pressing against the gunshot wound in hopes of stopping the bleeding. They walked back to Donnie's house, through chamber after chamber. Along the way, the members of The

Order parted in front of them like the Red Sea. Leon saw the cultists bloodied and beaten on the floor. The pipe still stuck in Galatea's veins, but no more ricin was funneled through it. A team of doctors would have to be lowered to the point of injection to remove the pipe and help close the wound.

Iris helped Leon up the rope ladder, a trail of blood droplets leading back to Suzuki's body. "Jesus, Leon; this is really bad," Iris said.

"Yeah," he said.

They got back into Donnie's house and Leon told Iris to get the doctor, arguing that he couldn't keep walking. She agreed, sat him on Donnie's bed and ran out of the house.

"Good girl," he said. "Good cop."

Leon rested his head against the wall and let his eyelids fall shut. He knew this was where he was going to die. Blood leaked out of him and he was having trouble breathing. He thought of the good things. He chuckled as he thought of Lilian Buckley, although it hurt his lungs to do so. He remembered Sheila Gibbons had had twins the day of Allison's murder; they'd be over two months old by now. He thought of Carol Lee's moonshine and Iris coughing it up.

He thought of Iris.

Leon pulled his cigarette case from his pocket – its intricate Victorian etchings stained with blood – and removed a cigarette. His eyes slowly welled up with tears – not for himself, but for the chaos overtaking the theriopolises. He thought about all he'd seen since Bellamy's suicide. There were the senseless murders of Allison Mackey and Anthony Nash and the disfigurement of Kiviaq and the cannibalism and rape on Sao and The Order and the attempted Galatean genocide. Mankind was eating itself.

No more tents.

Iris ran back to Donnie Suzuki's house with Galatea's physician, Dr. Elias Tucker, who carried an emergency surgery kit with him. They reached the house and saw Leon still sitting up in bed next to the hidden door. Leon's cigarette was in his mouth, unlit, the lighter in his hand, his eyes open and unblinking.

epilogue

A knock sounded on Iris's door.

"Come in!"

Mayor Greg Davis entered and greeted her. She was just lacing up her boots, her hands finally free from the gloves she'd worn for 15 years. She stood and they left her house together, making small talk on their way to the celebration in the town square. The warm spring breeze was a welcome change from the frosty winter they'd endured and it showed in the spirit of the Triton residents. Iris greeted everyone she knew as they walked.

"Look, Iris, I wanted to thank you for coming out to this event today," Mayor Davis said.

"It's no problem Mayor Davis."

"I know it's been hard without Leon, but the residents say you and the other officers have been –"

"I'm…not staying on," Iris said.

"What?"

"The police force – I'm going to step down. There are half a dozen patrolmen who have a longer history with Triton than I do; it's really their torch to carry."

"What will you do?"

"I've got my eye on a few things," she said. "I still want to help, I just…"

"Alright, fair enough," he conceded. "Just do me a favor and –"

"Wait a little while before I give word?" she asked.

"Yeah."

They got to the center of the city and waded through the cheering crowds to the modest stage awaiting them. The other patrolmen and city officials were already seated. Iris took her place next to Patrolmen Chopra, smiling for the crowd of townsfolk. Mayor Davis stood at the front of the stage and raised a hand for silence.

"100 years ago today, our forefathers came up to the theriopolises from the surface of the Earth to begin life anew," he said. "The Ascension marked the triumph over the largest challenge humanity has ever faced. We lost billions to the fog, to the chaos, to the fighting, but we endured. Today we maintain the values, the ethics, the peace so long sought after by the human race…"

As Mayor Davis's speech continued, Iris's smile faded a bit. She looked off into the distance and thought about his utterances of peace and tranquility. After Leon's death, Iris rallied the Galatean government and its seldom-used volunteer law enforcement for a mass raid on the Order of Terran Reclamation compound inside Galatea's shell. They arrested dozens of their friends, neighbors and even family members for their involvement in an organized conspiracy that could've ended the human race. Galatea's injuries were patched up and her poisoned ichor was cautiously bled from

314

her by her medical team, although the physiology and biological facts of the leviathans remained largely unknown.

Iris dismounted Galatea in Miami Beach on October 24th at roughly 8:45pm Eastern Time. The harbormaster lowered Leon's body to her and she buried him properly. She stayed long enough to watch Galatea depart again. As the creature rose to leave, it flashed its ichor at Iris once more, a far healthier blue than it had been the month before. For her part, Iris wanted to keep her immunity a secret, so she had to find the nearest rooftop over 1,000 feet from which Triton, Proteus or Psamanthe could retrieve her. She found a wild horse and spent the next three days breaking it. Finally she rode it up the East Coast to New York, surviving on food and water she'd been given on Galatea.

It was well into November by the time she returned to Triton. Leon had never stipulated a will, and he had no more living family, so Iris was given his house on Triton. She hadn't yet decided whether to keep the house once she quit local law enforcement or give it to someone and move back to her trailer in Ghettobelly.

"Peace," Davis had said. The word stuck in her mind with an ill omen. In the months that had passed, Aldermen Leung's and even Governor Buckley's involvement in the Ichor Conspiracy – as it came to be called – rose suspicions on the other titans. Galatea became a name that harbored an unpleasant connotation as its entire leadership was called into question. The public opinion was that at the very least, Buckley was grossly incompetent and should be removed from office. "How could this have happened right under his nose?" people asked. Worse than that, most theriopolitans were struggling to believe that more Galateans weren't involved in The Order.

Justice for Kiviaq came at the slowest of paces. Iris took the lone evidence of Jeremai 1's involvement in the plot from Leon's pocket and gave it to Mayor Davis, who in turn forwarded copies of it to the other titans. Neso, a colossus that regularly traded with Sao, announced their skepticism of the evidence and Iris's testimony. They also declared their reticence to partake in a witch-hunt for Jeremai 1. Kiviaq's grandmother and her people were already frustrated with the politics and bureaucracy involved in avenging the boy's disfigurement and his father's death; Neso's doubts cemented their hostilities. Psamanthe responded to Neso's statements by requesting that the city councils of the other colossi in the Alliance of Skyward Republics intervene on their behalf.

To Neso, it was a slap in the face – either an attempt by the other cities to usurp Neso's independence and govern its trade partnerships or an implication of some associated guilt in the matter. Or both. In the end, Neso absolutely refused to help the upcoming raid on Sao, even hinting that they may further strengthen their relationship with Jeremai and his people.

Iris knew there would be no peace. The men ruling the colossi were becoming adversaries. War was coming to the theriopolises.

Additional Content

mjm: a *fogworld* radio drama

In August 2016, 2 Fat Guys Podcast collaborated with A Carrier of Fire to produce a podcast that takes place in the universe of *Fogworld*. Starting the week the colossi rise from the Mariana Trench and ending with a somber final episode nearly a year afterwards, MJM follows a trio of average East Coast men as they react to the changing world of the 13 titans, the poisonous fog that envelops the earth and mankind's plans to adapt and survive. They offer their personal stories, fears and several insights into *Fogworld* that aren't available anywhere else.

This short series is available to listen to for free at wanderingcityblues.com – please check the header of the page for a download link, which is a .zip file containing three mp3's. Your hosts are Mansa Herndon, jonny Lupsha and Matt Carroll. We here at A Carrier of Fire are very grateful to 2 Fat Guys for working on this with us; please enjoy their regular show at 2FatPodcast.libsyn.com and thank you for checking out this multimedia experience.

wandering city blues cocktail recipes

created by kevin bednarz.
videos available at youtube.com/user/kevinbednarz
please drink responsibly.

galatea

1.5 oz. Captain Morgan spiced rum
1.5 oz. Malibu coconut rum
2 oz. orange juice
2 oz. sour mix
splash of pineapple juice
dash of grenadine
¼ oz. Mount Gay dark rum
garnish: lime wedge, orange wedge, cherry

Fill a 14 oz. pint glass with ice. Pour Captain Morgan, Malibu, orange juice, sour mix, pineapple juice and grenadine over an iced shaker tin. Shake, strain and pour into the iced pint glass. Float Mount Gay on top of the drink and garnish with one cherry and wedges of lime and orange.

iris 13

1.5 oz. Absolut Citron
½ oz. Blue Curacao
½ oz. Peach Schnapps
½ oz. sour mix
splash of pineapple juice
splash of Sprite
4" blue glow stick

Fill iced shaker tin with Absolut Citron, Blue Curacao, Peach Schnapps, sour mix, pineapple juice and Sprite. Shake, strain into snifter glass, add glow stick.

leon's old-fashioned

2 cherries
orange slice
2 dashes bitters
splash of soda water
½ oz. simple syrup
3 oz. Bulleit bourbon
1 oz. blood orange liqueur

In a 16 oz. mixing glass, gently muddle one cherry, orange slice, bitters, soda water and simple syrup. Add ice, Bulleit bourbon and blood orange liqueur. Stir with a cocktail spoon, strain into a martini glass and garnish with other cherry.

red-orange fog

1 oz. Stoli Orange vodka
¼ oz. Grand Marnier
3 oz. orange juice
splash of Sprite
dash of grenadine
orange slice

Pour Stoli Orange, Grand Marnier, orange juice and Sprite into an iced shaker tin. Shake, strain and pour into a martini glass. Add grenadine (which should sink to bottom) and garnish with orange slice.

sao's jack and coke

3 oz. Coca-Cola
2 oz. (or 50 ml) bottle of Jack Daniels

Fill a 12 oz. glass with ice. Pour in Coke, open Jack Daniels
bottle and insert upside-down into glass.

recommended music playlists

As I wrote *Wandering City Blues,* I found myself listening to a very specific set of songs to get me into the proper head space to put it together. Eventually I compiled them all into separate folders in accordance with how they inspired certain sections of the novel and I'd like to share them with you.

Please do not regard this section as an "official soundtrack" for the novel. I have not contacted these musicians nor licensed their songs in any capacity whatsoever. I don't claim that they have endorsed or supported *Wandering City Blues* in any form, and they maintain the rights and copyright to their music – no infringement on those rights is intended here. These are just the tunes I listened to while writing – no more, no less.

Chapters 00 through 08, 11-13

AOS – "History Repeats Itself"
Peter Gabriel & Nusrat Fateh Ali Khan – "Taboo"
The Ocean – "Siderian"
The Protomen – "Intermission"
Radiohead – "Hunting Bears"
Atticus Ross – "Human"
Gustavo Santaolalla – "Home"
Saxon Shore – "May 26"
Tricky – "Ponderosa"

Chapter 09 and First Half of Chapter 10

Bounty Killer – "Likkle Dread Bwoy"
Burn the Priest – "Bloodletting"
Elephant Man – "Nuh Linga"
The Jesus Lizard – "Puss"
The Ocean – "Dead Serious and Highly Professional"
Screwball – "F.A.Y.B.A.N."
Sizzla – "Heard of Dem (Ante Up Remix)"
Tricky Ft. Bella Gotti – "Gangsta Chronicle"
Wu-Tang Clan – "Do You Really (Thang, Thang)"

Detective Leon Adler

Louis Armstrong – "Sweet Lorraine"
Miles Davis – "Blue in Green"

Ledisi – "The Man I Love"
Julie London – "Cry Me a River"
Terry Riley – "The Philosopher's Hand"
Yoko Kanno & The Seat Belts – "Cosmos"

Chases and Action Scenes

Nine Inch Nails – "The Perfect Drug (Meat Beat Manifesto
    Remix)"
The Prodigy – "The Big Gundown"
Trent Reznor and Atticus Ross – "Oraculum"
Yoko Kanno & The Seat Belts – "Piano Black"
Skinny Puppy – "Blue Serge"
Tricky – "Money Greedy"
Saul Williams – "Tr(n)igger"

Enjoy! Please support the artists and buy these songs.
They're terrific works of music and they more than deserve
your money.

colossi information

When I first started writing *Wandering City Blues,* aside from the creatures and poisonous fog I desperately wanted not to test your suspension of disbelief more than was absolutely necessary. I spent most of the four-month gap between finishing the prologue and starting "Timeshare" researching how feasible the world topside would be. Before I committed to a manuscript, I vowed to have real-world solutions for fresh air, clean water, food, medicine and other facets of human life in the theriopolis. Some of these problems took several weeks apiece to solve.

In this section I wanted to show some of my research on *Fogworld*. I'm doing this mostly for your own edification and to strengthen that suspension of disbelief. I didn't just pull the dates and times that the various colossi would arrive in Moscow, Paris, London, New York and Miami out of thin air; I built a global mass transit system by using fixed routes for each of the beasts. Here's info for the titans of *Wandering City Blues*.

Proteus

Proteus, who appears first in *Wandering City Blues,* is the second-largest colossus, after Triton. Proteus walks on all fours but his massive front legs are longer and slightly sturdier than his hind legs. His long black hair and the physiology of his limbs cause him to resemble a gorilla, though the structure of his face is closer to that of an owl. To compensate for the sloping descent of his back from his shoulders to hindquarters, The Founders constructed stilts on the foundations of the buildings on Proteus's back. As such, Proteus's original buildings stand perpendicular to the earth.

He began his journey on Year Zero, March 23rd, at 7 a.m. Pacific, from outside the Wilshire Grand in Los Angeles. Since his forelegs naturally encourage Proteus to keep his head up, Proteus has a curious nature regarding the tallest buildings he can find. He stops for one hour at each building before continuing on. This is a list of his stops and the distance (in miles) to reach each one from the previous destination.

1. Wilshire Grand, Los Angeles (Start / 5,487 from finish)
2. John Hancock Center, Chicago (1,746)
3. Willis Tower, Chicago (2)
4. One World Trade Center, New York City (713)
5. 432 Park Avenue, New York City (4)
6. Hermitage Towers, Paris (3,636)
7. Vostok Tower, Moscow (1,550)
8. OKO Towers, Moscow (0)
9. Makkah Royal Clock Tower Hotel, Mecca (2,371)
10. Al Hamra Tower, Kuwait City (747)
11. Burj Khalifa, Dubai (531)
12. Petronas Twin Towers, Kuala Lumpur (3,438)
13. Guangzhou Int'l Finance Center, Guangzhou (1,575)
14. CITIC Plaza, Guangzhou (0)
15. Kingkey 100, Shenzhen (70)
16. International Commerce Center, Hong Kong (20)
17. Two International Finance Center, Hong Kong (0)
18. Taipei 101, Taipei (501)
19. Jin Mao Tower, Shanghai (411)
20. Shanghai World Finance Center, Shanghai (0)
21. Shanghai Tower, Shanghai (1)
22. Greenland Center-Zifeng Tower, Nanjing (171)
23. Tokyo Skytree, Tokyo (1,229)

Proteus's global trip is 24,206 miles. At an average cruising speed of 15 mph, it takes him 68 days, 4 hours and 44 minutes to circle the planet. He completes this circuit 5.35212426 times per year.

Triton

Triton is the largest of the colossi. His physical structure is similar to a matamata turtle, though his body is slimmer and flatter and his legs stand taller and more vertically as opposed to the sideways manner of most turtles. The city of Triton is home to the largest number of humans and thus lends itself to more cultural diversity than the other leviathans.

Like Proteus, Triton left Los Angeles at 7 a.m. local time on March 23, heading east. However, his route takes him to 50 of the world's most populous cities (pre-Ascension), stopping for one hour in each. He also stops to rest in the final leg of his journey at Saipan and Honolulu on his way back to LA. His complete list of stops, with the distance from the previous destination listed in miles, is below.

1. Los Angeles (Start / 2,563 from Honolulu)
2. Chicago (1,746)
3. Toronto (435)
4. New York (344)
5. Philadelphia (81)
6. Miami (1,019)
7. Mexico City (1,285)
8. Bogota (1,973)
9. Lima (1,162)
10. Santiago (1,527)
11. Buenos Aires (709)

12. Sao Paolo (1,041)
13. Rio de Janeiro (220)
14. Johannesburg (4,437)
15. Kinshasa (1,728)
16. Lagos (1,105)
17. Madrid (2,377)
18. Milan (740)
19. Paris (400)
20. London (212)
21. Berlin (580)
22. St. Petersburg (823)
23. Moscow (394)
24. Istanbul (1,091)
25. Giza (769)
26. Baghdad (809)
27. Tehran (433)
28. Karachi (1,193)
29. Lahore (640)
30. New Delhi (266)
31. Mumbai (718)
32. Hyderabad (387)
33. Bangalore (308)
34. Chennai (182)
35. Kolkata (842)
36. Bangkok (1,002)
37. Ho Chi Minh City (460)
38. Kuala Lumpur (625)
39. Jakarta (733)
40. Manila (1,727)
41. Hong Kong (690)
42. Taipei (504)
43. Shanghai (411)

44. Tianjin (610)
45. Beijing (69)
46. Shenyang (391)
47. Seoul (347)
48. Osaka (517)
49. Nagoya (88)
50. Tokyo (164)
    (Saipan (1,459))
    (Honolulu (3,711))

Triton's global trip is 48,057 miles. At a cruising speed averaging 15 mph, stopping for one hour at each destination (including Saipan and Honolulu), it would take Triton 135 days, 15 hours and 22 minutes to complete his journey. Triton circles the planet 2.69083091 times per year.

Psamanthe

Psamanthe is one of the smallest titans, though she still measures several hundred feet from crown to tail. She resembles a raven and a dragon in nearly equal parts. Populated almost entirely by Tlingit and Haida Indians who strap onto her back, she flies from east to west.

Due to her bird-like nature, Psamanthe stops to perch on a dozen of the sturdiest skyscraper rooftops that still stand over the 1,000-foot fog ceiling, spending exactly four days on each. She has built nests for her residents on these rooftops, retrieving basic home furnishings from the surface to better accommodate them. Her maternal instinct also shines whenever she stops near the ocean. After her citizens disembark, she plummets to the sea and scoops up countless fish in her mouth, returning them to the rooftops to keep her people fed. Each of her stops, including the distance in miles from the previous destination, is listed below.

01. Wilshire Grand, Los Angeles (Start / 1,746 from Chicago)
02. Abenobashi Terminal Building, Osaka (5,724)
03. Kingkey 100, Shenzhen (1,539)
04. Shanghai Tower, Shanghai* (736)
05. World One, Mumbai (3,132)
06. Makkah Clock Royal Tower, Mecca** (2,146)
07. OKO Tower, Moscow (2,371)
08. Hermitage Towers, Paris (1,550)
09. The Shard, London (212)
10. 432 Park Avenue, New York City (3,471)
11. John Hancock Center, Chicago (713)

* Psamanthe perches here because the Shanghai World Financial Center's top broke under her weight pre-Ascension.
** Psamanthe accidentally broke the top of this structure off pre-Ascension.

Psamanthe's global circuit is 23,340 miles. Flying at 70 mph and stopping for exactly 96 hours per stop, she completes her journey every 51 days, 21 hours, 25 minutes and 43 seconds (6.30475016 times per year).

Sao

Sao's torso is the same shape as a flamingo's, though without its neck and head. He has large black eyes on the front of the torso with an equally large mouth. Sao has no arms but his long, thin legs have inverted knees like a chicken. In the century since The Great Ascension, Sao has been overrun with the inbred cannibals descended from the Ewell twins and has been adorned as such. Sao wears 30-foot speakers that face outwards in all directions; long-dried human blood paints him dark brown in indistinct patterns. Human skeletons, picked clean, hang from his crown by chains. Ropes pierce his ears and run to other features on his face (his lips, his eyebrows, etc.); skulls are threaded through them.

Sao's migration route is unknown.

Galatea

Galatea resembles a hermit crab living in a vertically-standing conical shell. From the bottom of her legs to the top of her shell, Galatea reaches over 1,400 feet tall. Since her shell spirals inwards and upwards to its apex, The Founders constructed Galatea's city around her outside, winding around her several times in one long staircase from the lowest point to the highest.

Galatea frequents a dozen of the North Atlantic's nicest beaches, spending 24 hours at each destination before swimming to the next. She travels in a counter-clockwise pattern; her destinations and the distance from the previous spot (in miles) are listed below.

01. Praia de Santa Maria – Santa Maria, Cape Verde (Start / 2,759 miles from Trunk Bay)
02. Playa de el Bollullo – Tenerife, Canary Islands (924)
03. Horseshoe Bay – Bermuda (2,886)
04. Miami Beach, Florida (1,027)
05. Clearwater Beach – Clearwater, Florida (223)
06. Playa Paraiso – Cayo Largo, Cuba (387)
07. West Bay Beach – West Bay, Honduras (470)

08. Playa Manuel Antonio – Manuel Antonio National Park, Costa Rica (505)
09. Cayo de Agua – Los Roques National Park, Venezuela (1,193)
10. Blue Beach – Vieques, Puerto Rico (449)
11. Barnes Bay – Anguilla (150)
12. Trunk Bay – St. John, Virgin Islands (107)

Galatea's journey is 11,080 miles. Traveling at 20 knots (23 mph), she completes one circuit of her trip every 32 days, 1 hour, 44 minutes and 21 seconds. She does 11.380479 laps per year.

proteus emerges

Concept Art by Nick Whitmire.

psamanthe

afterword

Wandering City Blues has been an incredible adventure for me. I haven't written fiction since the first (Bill) Clinton administration and I've never written sci-fi. The idea of giant monsters walking the earth first came to me in 2012 while driving to Ashland, Pennsylvania for my project *DisasterLand: Centralia.* The road was so foggy, the visibility so limited, that I suddenly got this overwhelming certainty that there were enormous monsters hiding just beyond the mist. Three years later I uploaded "100 Words about Walter Atherton" to my Facebook page and asked my friends if it seemed interesting. The response was overwhelming. I sat and researched 50 hours a week for three full months to see if the world was feasible. Then I wrote for nine months and the end product is in your hands.

If you liked *WCB*, please tell a friend and encourage them to support a small business and independent writer. Like A Carrier of Fire on Facebook for regular updates. Thank you for your support; it means more to me than you could ever imagine.

about the author

jonny Lupsha was born and raised outside Chicago. He obtained his BA in journalism, has written for IGN and was recently awarded a free menu and coupons from King Wok just off of Rte. 7. jonny lives in north Virginia with his wife and offspring; *Wandering City Blues* is his fourth book.